Lost Souls

First edition

ISBN: 978-1-3129-1473-5

This book is not yet rated. It does contain the following: Suspense and horror scenes, minor reference to recreational drugs, minor references to adult situations, and a few minor language usages. Parental guidance is recommended and this book is not intended for young children.

This book is dedicated to Stephen King.

To find out why this book is dedicated to such a great author, please read the whole book and then the blurb at the end.

Book: The Present

Chapter: Girl Gone

"*R*uth! Ruth!"

My feet carried me as qu. 'ly as they could over the uneven and rocky terrain. It was bad enough that I was on a slight incline of a hill and that it was full of small rocks, the same rocks that covered the mountains in this area, but the cast iron, the fallen and crumbled marble, the old barren trees and the desert scrub continued to hinder my progress. My legs were weak, my side hurt from running and my throat was sore from yelling her name over and over, yet I pushed on.

We had come to this dilapidated cemetery to look at some of the historical markers erected in honor of those that had died here in Virginia City. Now I had lost her. I had only turned my back for one moment to read the tombstone and she was gone. My daughter had disappeared.

John Smith, Mable Jones, Susie Weller, Dolores McKinney, Faye Samuel. All of these names were a blur as I passed them by. None of them even mattered any more. They were dead, long dead. There were strange symbols, dates of births and deaths, and elegies. It was no longer any of my concern. My concern was finding my daughter and getting the hell out of here. I had already been plagued by enough ghosts, wraiths, undead and nightmares since we arrived, all of them sending a chill down my spine. Now I was frightened beyond anything I had ever experienced. This was my worst nightmare. My thirteen year old daughter was missing.

I continued my run while calling out her name. There was no answer. There was hardly a sound. There were no birds, no animal life, and no response from any visitor that may have come to view the macabre scene that we had only recently chosen to view. Only the sound of my feet against the gravel rocks and my cries of her name echoed in my ears.

"Ruth?! Ruth?! Where are you?!"

The hot desert sun beat down upon my body and sweat poured onto my shirt. The branches of the dead trees slapped across my face, the desert brush tugged at my pants. A misplaced step twisted my ankle and I almost went down, yet I had to push on. My heart was racing with worry and concern as my mind was conjuring up thoughts that no parent should have. Was she simply sidetracked and found a grave that caught her sight and hadn't bothered to reply? Was she hiding and this was all a game to here? Had she wondered off into the desert and was now lost? Had she fallen and wasn't able to answer? Had a rattlesnake bitten her and her life was now hanging by a thread? Had a stranger taken her? Would I ever see her again?

"Damn it Ruth! Where are you?! This isn't funny anymore!"

My steps carried me through a set of stone pillars and to the top of the rise. Fortunately the cemetery wasn't that big. If I hadn't already driven from Lake Tahoe and hadn't already walked all around Virginia City and it wasn't so damn hot then perhaps I would have had more than enough energy to make the distance to the top of the hill. I was tired and thirsty, I had a cramp and was in pain, yet here I was, at the top of the hill. She had to be...

The cemetery only went a little further down the back side of the hill before it was gated off by the old, rusting metal fence. Beyond it the hillside dropped dramatically and the climb down, if I did go over the fence, was too steep and too treacherous. She wasn't here. I had looked all over the cemetery and she wasn't here.

My mind finally accepted what my eyes had seen but had refused to believe. At the bottom of the hill was another cemetery. The one that I had been looking through had been dedicated to the Masons that had lived in this area. My eyes scanned my surroundings. There was another plot dedicated to another group over to my right and it looked like another was dedicated to yet another group further on. This wasn't just some small area to explore in an hour as I had in this section, it was a massive layout of the dead that was several square miles that stretched for as far as I could see. One could get lost exploring this region. My heart sank. My daughter could be anywhere.

A cold chill ran down my spine, like someone had just stepped on my grave. I was getting tired of feeling those. I knew what they were now. It was the dead trying to talk to me again. They had haunted me for far too long on this trip and I was tired of it. I had no time to figure out what they were trying to say, or why they were here. I had to find my daughter.

A slight wind momentarily picked up, like a wraith coming to haunt me, and the cold chill returned. This time it carried the stench of open earth and rotting wood. It had the smell of death. I shook it off.

"Leave me alone!" I shouted. My cry only echoed off of the mountain cliffs that surrounded Virginia City.

A raven flew in and landed on the rusted iron fence before me. It gave me a look of understanding, perhaps even a pleading look. I picked up a rock and threw it at the beast in anger and frustration and almost hit the creature. It went flapping away, screaming its displeasure back at me. Its cries could be heard echoing off of the mountains, yet I didn't care. I couldn't be bothered.

There were only two things left to do. I could either return back to the car and get as much help as possible or I could continue my search, all day and all night if I had to. No, I shook my head. I already knew that there was only one decision and I had already made up my mind.

I couldn't turn back; I couldn't return to the car and call the police for help. That would be an admission that she was beyond my reach. That would be an admission that I, as her father, had failed her. But it was more than that. I would be returning to my wife without our daughter. I couldn't do that, I wouldn't do that. I couldn't look her in the eyes and tell her that our daughter was gone, missing. It would break her heart.

She had already been worried enough when we first discovered that our little girl was gone. Our first thoughts were that she had gone back to the car and my wife was going back there to find her while I looked through the rest of the cemetery. My wife's knees had been bothering her since her knee surgery and there was no way she could make the search with me over the uneven, rocky terrain. She had already traversed Virginia City with me and she was tired, overheated and in pain.

I had already scoured the majority of the cemetery, or at least this portion of it, when I had looked back toward the car. I could barely see my wife standing beside it. She was standing alone. With the exception of one other car, the black car that I had seen earlier, the one that made my skin crawl, ours was the only one there. My daughter wasn't in the parking lot, she hadn't returned to the car as we had hoped. Now my wife's hope of finding our daughter lay with me and I simply couldn't bear the thought of returning empty handed. I had to find Ruth.

Tears of frustration, anguish, anger, concern and worry fell upon my face. Was she at one of the other cemeteries? There had been an open gate back the way I had come from which had lead to a road descending down toward the massive burial ground below me. I hadn't known where that road had lead to when I had first seen it; I thought it was simply a service road or perhaps a private road leading to a few of the homes of the residents that lived here. I would have to backtrack, find the gate and continue my search. But, she wouldn't have just wandered off down this road without telling us, would she?

Before I headed down the road toward the other cemeteries and start up my search elsewhere in another plot, I had to ensure that she wasn't here. Had she fallen behind some tombstone that I had missed? Had she fallen over or had gone over part of the fence? Please don't tell me that she was lying in some ravine, unconscious. I had to exhaust this area before moving on and I had to do it quickly. I was sure that my wife was extremely worried about our daughter and I was sure that she was starting to get worried over me. I had left her sight some time ago. In her eyes she had two that were now missing.

I ran around the inner perimeter of the rusted metal fence that marked the barrier of this site. My eyes darted from the side of the cliff back to the cemetery. I kept hoping to find her, I kept hoping that she would jump out from behind a tombstone or a tree and surprise me. "Boo", she would say. "I scared you dad, didn't I?" I would be furious, but relieved. "Yes, yes you did," I would say. Only she didn't and my search continued.

My route turned back into the heart of this plot as I made my way toward the open gate. My pace increased as tears continued to flow. My cries out to my daughter were becoming weak as I was losing my voice. Panic was setting in, I had to …

My foot caught something. It was a branch, a root, a piece of warped, twisted and fallen piece of iron perhaps, I don't know. All I knew was that I fell. What seemed like slow motion the ground came up to met me. All I could think about was the gate that was in sight but was now falling out of reach. I was sure I would get back up again and …

I hit the ground harder than I thought. The blow knocked the wind from my lungs and I saw stars. Consciousness threatened to fade. I could feel the bruises start to form on my chest and thighs from hitting hard marble and stone pieces that had crumbled from their markers. I was going to have scrapes and cuts from sliding across the hard rocky terrain. It was only after the impact did I consider myself fortunate beyond all belief when I saw how close I had come to smacking my head upon the massive rock that was only inches from my face on one side and almost impaling myself upon an iron rod sticking up from the ground on my other.

If I hadn't known better I would have thought that the dead was trying to stop me from reaching my only child. I was beginning to think that the deceased had felt violated by my presence or perhaps that they had taken her and now they were doing everything they could to prevent me from retrieving her. They were trying to trip me up, they were trying to impale me or kill me. The ghosts had already haunted me enough on this trip and if they thought that they were going to take my child then they were wrong. I would fight every spawn from the deepest levels of hell to get her back and there was nothing in this world or any other that could…

I froze. I froze where I lay. It wasn't out of fear or pain. It wasn't out of panic or frustration. It wasn't out of sorrow. It was out of sheer terror at the sight that lay before me.

It was a joke, it had to be, and a very sick and morbid one at that. I shook my head. No, it was too elaborate to be a prank. It was a coincidence then. Yes, that was it. What I was seeing before me didn't pertain to me at all. At least that was what I kept trying to tell myself over and over again. I couldn't be seeing the vision that was before my eyes. After all, I had been seeing and hearing ghosts that no one else was seeing. It was stress; that was all.

But I knew deep within my heart that this was no vision. It was no joke. It was no coincidence. The tombstone standing at a slight angle before more, the one that marked the grave that I had fallen upon had the name of my child engraved upon it. There, chiseled in stone were the words:

In memory of Ruth

Died   1915

I could read no further. The rest of the words on the gravestone no longer mattered. There wasn't a last name or a birth date. Yet, I knew, I knew deep in my heart that my child, my daughter was dead and that she had died a hundred years ago. I don't know how I knew, I just did.

Tears of anguish came upon me like a flood gate bursting open as I screamed in a vocal cry of distress that would have woken the dead if that were possible. I was sure that my wife could hear me despite the distance between us. I was sure that my wail of brokenness would break her heart as well. She would know that I wasn't coming back with our daughter. Now, I didn't want to come back at all.

My hoarse throat continued to cry out in anguish. My heart felt as if it had stopped beating. The world seemed to stand still. Time meant nothing. The heat beating upon my back was nothing. The bruises and scrapes that had covered me were nothing. The only thing that mattered was the numbness in my chest that was spreading over my body. The grief had gripped my like a vise and shock was setting in. I couldn't move as I cried out again and again. My girl was gone. My world had ended.

No more would there be my daughter running into my arms to welcome me home. No more would there be the cutest smile in the world beaming back at me. No more would there be wiping away her tears over her first boyfriend problem. No more would there be late nights helping her with her homework. No more would there be playing catch with the baseball or hearing her play on the flute or the violin.

Her bedroom would be as empty as my heartfelt. The house would be empty as I felt. The world would be empty and cold and featureless and there would be less joy in it. The trophy that sat upon my shelf that read *"Number one dad"* no longer had meaning. My life felt as if it no longer had any meaning. I felt as dead as those around me and I had no other desire than to join them.

My only thought was, why did we come here in the first place? What in the world could have possibly lead us here? My mind could only rush back down the memories of the past few days that brought us to this graveyard and this nightmare.

Chapter: Packing

"*L*et's go on a vacation," my wife stated with excitement. "We can go down to some of the places I had visited before I moved to Washington. We can go to Lake Tahoe, go river rafting down the Truckee River, and perhaps go to Virginia City, maybe even Nevada City. I want to take you guys to Donner's Pass and around some of the highways I used to travel on. It would be a great family adventure. We can stop at my aunt's place and she can take us to the ranch."

She always wanted to emulate her mother who always took her family on trips and vacations and she had fond memories of family adventures and road trips. Now, she wanted the same for us. She was always good to our family like that. We had gone to Hawaii, and Cancun. We've been to Chichen Itza, and Tulum. We've gone to see Native American museums in Neah Bay and in Vancouver, Canada. We've traveled the Oregon coast, the Olympic Peninsula, been on Hurricane Ridge, have gone to Paradise and Lake Diablo. We've been on the Lewis and Clark Trail and that was just to name just a few of the great adventures we've been on.

The "ranch" that she was in reference to was just over the Oregon border in California. It was a large horse ranch sitting on over five thousand acres from Cottonwood Creek, an offshoot of the Klamath River, and continued to the west side of Interstate Highway 5 until it hit the Klamath National Forest. We had been there a few times and it would be nice to go again. The last time we were there, Ruth had won a horse competition and had the time of her life. Though, she really didn't "win". There were only two contestants and neither she nor the other rider were experienced enough to actually compete so they just sat on their horses while stable hands ran the steeds by their reins. Ruth had won because her stable hand was the quickest. But to her, it had been as if she had won some great event and she finds every opportunity to retell the story over and over again each time that we are in this area. I'm sure I'll hear it several more times before this trip was over.

The trip would be enjoyable and would be a warm welcome change to the Seattle climate of overcast skies and light drizzle that we have been having lately. It wasn't this way all of the time here in Seattle.

Our autumns are colorful with the deciduous trees turning bright red and orange, yellow and gold. At times it looks like some of the forests are on fire. We usually go down to the local pumpkin patches in Snohomish or up to Arlington. We would spend our time trying to find our way out of a corn maze, eat too much kettle corn, buy a few knick knacks, try the local produce, get muddy, and watch a pumpkin fling.

In the winter we sometimes have a light dusting of snow that only gives an excuse to snuggle close to each other near a fire in the fireplace or spend a cold winter's evening in the hot tub out on our deck. Then there would be neighborhoods with all of their festive lights and decorations and with it getting dark earlier, there would be more time to see and enjoy these lights than the longer lasting days of the summer.

Sometimes we would go over the pass to Leavenworth and experience the town that seemed like Christmas had exploded and threw up every possible light array, greeting card, and every display imaginable in the cute Bavarian town. There were far too many tourist trap shops, a fudge store, a hat shop, decoration shops, more food than we could possible experience, and plenty of snow. There was skiing, inter tube riding, and German musicians.

The spring brings tulips and the tulip festival up in Roozen Garden in Mount Vernon. We try our best to make our annual pilgrimage up there to see all the wonderful and beautiful array of colors and the various assortment and diversity of flowers. Sometimes we would even buy a bulb or two for our garden.

We also have lovely summers. It seems it hits right at July 5th and comes into full swing by the first weekend of August. All the boats come out into Lake Washington until there doesn't seem to be any water left and the sun feels so wonderful. But the summers are usually too short and a little more sunshine was always welcome, hence the vacation to sunny California and Nevada.

On top of that I had never been river rafting before and my wife said it was a lot of fun. She had always enjoyed it when she was younger and had fond memories of drifting down the Truckee.

Of course we had to make vacation plans from work, have someone come over and feed the cats, plan the itinerary, get the house ready, juggle the finances and finally pack. The preparation period was almost as time consuming and energy spending as the vacation would be.

The only real downside to going on vacation was the fact that my real work, the work I actually get paid to do, not my novel writing, wasn't going to get done while I was gone. The work would pile up on my desk and once I returned I would have a week's worth of work to get caught up on. I didn't have the privilege of a personal secretary or some magical work fairy that would make it all disappear.

My wife starting packing way too much as usual, at least that's my opinion. Being a guy I'm pretty much alright with just packing the essentials. I tossed in my usual, an extra pair of pants, my bathing suit, two shirts, enough socks for the trip and …. cat?

I had turned around and one of my cats was sitting in the middle of my suitcase, on top of my clean, packed, nicely folded clothing. It was the youngest one, still basically a kitten. I guess she simply liked the idea of sitting in the middle of everything that I was trying to do. She's there when I try to write my stories, try to read the paper, try to watch TV, or even trying to go to sleep.

Quickly I picked her up, tossed her on to the floor and went to continue my packing. When I turned around, she was there again. Two more times did she play this game with me before I picked her up, tossed her out of the room and closed the door. Game or not I still needed to pack.

When I turned around I was shocked to see my second cat sitting in my suitcase. Now that was a surprise. She's an older cat and rarely gets up on the bed and even rarer was the fact that she's in the middle of anything. This I didn't expect from her. What was up with these cats today?

But it was more than just her presence. She seemed to stare right at me as if she were looking deep into my soul. There was a slight guttural growl deep in her voice and the hair on her back started to stand on end. Something about her didn't seem right.

"Mitten? Are you ok?" I asked as I reached for her.

Her sudden hiss seemed to come out of nowhere. Before I could react, she launched both of her front paws at me, sunk her claws deep into my skin, and then bit down hard with all of her strength. I yelped in pain and before I could do anything, the cat ran off in absolute terror.

My wife helped bandage my hand and gave me the usual lecture about how I shouldn't play so roughly with the cats. Of course she would never believe me, and why should she? I didn't believe it myself.

I went to bed early, with my hand all bandaged, hoping to get a good night's sleep before our early departure the next morning. My mind went over the final packing that we would have to do first thing in the morning and I made sure that everything else was already set to go. When I was content, I closed my eyes and drifted off to...

The beach.

The sandy beach on Lake Tahoe was wonderful. I had spread out my beach towel and was laying on it face down with only my swimming trunks on. The sun was warm on my body and I couldn't think of anything better, well, perhaps one other thing, but this was close enough.

I opened my eyes and couldn't see my wife or daughter. Perhaps they had gone off back to the hotel. Oh well. I was just going to lay there and soak up the sun. I was, after all, on vacation.

A cold chill ran down my spine. My wife had told me that it gets cold up here, especially in the winter when there's a lot of skiing. It was just a cold wind blowing through.

Yet it didn't just chill my body, it chilled me to the core. It was as if something walked on my grave and touched my soul. It was a chill take took my breath away.

As I gasped from the icy blast that wracked me, I noticed that I was able to see my breath. My warm exhale mixed with the chill in the air. I hadn't realized that it was that cold.

Suddenly the ground erupted all around me. Arms reached through the sand and started to grab for me. They were dead arms. They were corpse like, rotting, decomposing arms. Flesh had peeled away, muscle had wasted, puss was seeping out and bone was exposed.

I screamed in horror and panic as I fought back the undead bodies that proceeded to pull themselves from the sand. I kicked and I hit and scrambled out of the way.

My eyes took in the beach as soon I was clear of the initial onslaught. The beach was littered with bodies coming up out of the sand. There were hundreds if not thousands of undead corpses trying to pull themselves to freedom and they were all coming toward me.

However, it wasn't just the dead bodies that had caught my attention. The lake had turned blood red. No, that wasn't right. It had simply turned to blood. I could smell it, almost taste it in the air. The sky had turned dull and ashen and it was as if all of the color of the world, except for the red lake, had disappeared. Death had come and it was coming for me. I had to get out of there, I had to...

I woke with a start. Sweat was pouring off of my body and my heart was racing as if it were trying to break through my chest. It had been a nightmare, probably just stress from packing or spending too much time reading my favorite horror story author or even spending too much time writing my series of books. Yes, that was it. I shouldn't stay up too late writing.

But I was still cold. Did the heater shut off? Did a chill come over the Pacific Northwest? Whatever it was, it chilled me to the bone and I felt as if I would never get warm again. It was then did I notice that I was able to see my breath, but only faintly as it disappeared. It was starting to warm up.

Something else caught my attention and my heart started to race for another reason. I smelled smoke. There was a fire somewhere. There was a fire in the house. I had to get everyone awake and get them out of here.

The smell drifted away as quickly as it came. It had been my imagination. There were no smoke alarms going off as there would have been. We have those very sensitive ones that go off when we open our oven door or sometimes light a fire in the fireplace or even start up the barbeque grill outside. All of the alarms would have gone off if there was a fire.

I started to relax, but I was still wide awake and my consciousness and curiosity needed to be sated. A quick look to my right told me that my wife was still sleeping soundly. Good, let her sleep, I would only wake her if necessary.

I rose and made my way down the hall to my daughter's room. A quick check told me that she was sound asleep and was fine. I gave her a quick kiss on forehead and tucked her in, making sure she stayed warm during the night. A smile came across my face. I don't know what I would do without her.

I did a quick look around downstairs and found nothing out of place. All the doors were still locked and there was no fire. It was all in my head, only a bad dream, a terrible nightmare. It was time to go back to bed and finish what little sleep I would get.

Chapter: Washington

*W*e got up early Saturday morning, before the sun even rose upon the horizon, to ensure that our trip would hit less traffic than we normally would have had later in the day. Usually the traffic was thick around Northgate, the U district, downtown Seattle, then again in Federal Way, Tacoma, Olympia and finally in Portland. If we could get a jump start on our trip we would be able to bypass the majority of the stop and go slough that was typical through these spots. It was easily a three hour trip just to Portland that could stretch to four or more depending on the traffic.

Of course Ruth had to be woken up first. She's not a morning person and it takes about a half an hour for her meds to kick in. Then there was my deepest suspicion that she hadn't packed like we had asked her to the night before. My suspicions had been confirmed when I found her empty suitcase at the other side of the bedroom.

I had made the morning coffee for both my wife and Ruth. My wife drinks hers with just enough creamer to make it turn a light tan. Ruth, on the other hand, takes her with about one quarter coffee and about three quarters creamer.

I doubled checked everything on my list and made sure we were packed after bringing in some last minute items and Ruth's suitcase that my wife had to pack for her. Just as when we had thought that we were ready to leave and was about to get into the van, Ruth ran back upstairs to the bathroom.

"Good thinking," I cried after her. "We have a long journey ahead of us. Make sure that you…."

"Daaaad!" She said in a sarcastic fashion. "Don't embarrass me. Besides, no, I don't have to go. I have to do my hair, makeup, and put in my earrings."

My jaw almost dropped. She had a habit of waiting until the last moment before doing something that she should have done a half an hour ago and it was usually her hair, makeup, and earrings. I wondered if this was a typical teenage girl behavior or if we were somehow privileged to be subjected to such a wonder.

Once we were finally loaded and Ruth had joined us in the van, we turned the radio on to some relaxing music. After all, it was early Saturday morning and it was still dark. It was time to ease ourselves into the long haul that we were about to face.

"Ewww….I don't like this song," came the protest from the back seat. "Can we PLEASE change the station?"

Of course Ruth's "please" had been drawn out in sarcasm as if it were the most difficult thing in the world for her to say and it was only out of protest that was she saying it.

"Of course sweetie." The response came from my right. My eyes only rolled. Ruth wasn't the one driving, why did she get to have the pick of music?

My wife went through a series of channels, each with the appropriate response from what I expected to hear.

"Oh no, not that song. Oh gross. That one's terrible. Can't we find a station playing anything good?"

We had gone from some smooth jazz, not something I usually listen to but then again I wasn't quite awake yet, to some hip hop, rap, country, a cool eighty's song, another hip hop station, classic rock, a few commercials, a radio talk show, a Christian rock station, something in Spanish, an all disco station (that none of us wanted to hear) and another rap station. Here the channel changing stopped. We were sure she liked this one, or at least we thought she did.

"Oh yuck, not this song."

"But I thought you liked this song."

"I USED to like this song mom, its soooo last year."

"Why don't you listen to your iPod, Ruth?" I asked, hoping that she would take the hint that I really didn't want to listen to her music at this time.

"Dad, it's NOT an iPod, it's a Sansa MP3 player."

Again my eyes rolled. It was times like this that I regretted not drinking coffee. Again the channels changed until the final, and relieving response had been pronounced.

"No wait. Stop. Go back one. Mom, you missed it."

It was another hip hop station playing a song I'm sure was on another station that had already been previously rejected. Well, maybe not, they all sounded the same to me. At least my daughter was happy. However, my desire of slowly waking up to this drive and starting us out with something that I could handle had been squashed. My only hope of having this end quickly was hurrying up my drive so we could get out of the radio frequency range. Once the static hit the radio station then my daughter would revert to her headphones and I would be able to pop in a CD that I brought along for the drive. With any luck I might actually be able to listen to it.

The Seattle overcast was quickly left behind and we made great time once we got through downtown Seattle. We watched as we passed the Space Needle and the large "R" on the old Rainier brewery. The Tacoma Dome and the Capital Building were also landmarks that came and went.

We had even watched as Mount Rainier had drawn closer. The mountain stood majestically against the background and seemed to reach toward heavens like a hand of god. Its grandiose form climbed from the ground and pierced the sky. Its snow and ice capped peak was obvious as the mountain rose above all others around it. Then the great, active volcano fell away behind us. The sky had cleared enough that we swore that we could see the individual glaciers on the mountain and we had joked that we would be able to see any climbers if there had been any that day.

But what really amazed me was, not the sights that I had seen countless times and would continue to see over again, it was the site that had only recently come into the Seattle area. This was the presence of large blue flags with the white number twelve upon them. Seattle was still in full swing over its football team winning their big game. It had been several months ago that they had won their victory, yet it seemed that the whole city was still behind them. The flag was being flown all over the place. It was on cars, houses, buildings, and just about everywhere we could see. Now, if only our baseball team could start winning more games.

The traffic was the lightest we had ever seen and after two bathroom stops, thanks to Ruth drinking a large bottle of sugar infused, glucose packed, and artificially flavored and colored drink, and after one driver switch, we made it to Portland in record time. By this time Ruth had put on her earphones, was listening to her favorite tunes on her player loud enough for us to almost hear, and was reading her latest Teen Magazine.

With only one confusing lane change, in a desperate attempt to get out of a left hand lane exit that would have taken us in the wrong direction and set us back at least another hour, we made it through the spaghetti like array of freeway lanes that seemed to crisscross each other and then go off into obscure locations beyond the like of which we desired to explore. Portland was then added to the list of cities that came and went.

Chapter: Eugene

"*W*e need gas."

The comment to my left had caught me off guard. I had almost completely dozed off to catch up on some much needed sleep while my wife was driving. But it wasn't the sound of her voice waking me from my snooze that had startled me, it was her words. I was sure that we could have gone further on a full tank of gas.

"Did you fill up the tank before we left?" I asked as I yawned and turned to her.

"No, I thought you did."

It was amazing. I quickly went through the list in my head and was sure that we had packed and thought of everything else, yet neither of us had remembered to fill up the van before we left.

The next exit of Eugene had an advertisement for gas at Costco and since we had a membership, it was worth pulling off here and getting the best price that we could. As my wife took the exit, I started pulling through the tons of notes she had written down all over her notebook.

"No, it's on the next page. No, not that next page, I mean the next one."

She was trying to give me directions on where to find the information she had on the various cities along the way just in case we needed them. She is extremely organized but since I didn't share her line of thinking I had no idea where anything was.

The exit wound around back over the freeway and through a residential area before I was able to find the address I was looking for.

"Now go up this road."

"Are you sure?" She asked.

"Yes, the numbers are going in the right direction. See?"

"It's still a long ways away from the exit. We've already gone too far. Are you sure we're heading in the right direction?"

"Yes, I'm sure." No, I wasn't but it seemed right. "Take a left at this stop light. Way up there, I think I see it."

Fortunately my guess had been accurate despite the distance we had traveled. I was beginning to wonder myself rather or not we were even still in Eugene. What we thought would have been right off the freeway had taken us quite a bit out of our way.

As I got out of my car to fill up my tank, I heard the attendant call out to me.

"No, no. You, sir. Please get back in the car."

I looked at him strangely.

"I can't allow you to pump your gas."

Again I looked at him strangely. What did I do wrong?

"I have to pump the gas for you. It's the rules, go ahead and get back into your car and I'll pump it for you."

I nodded. I had forgotten that Oregon has a law about the attendants pumping gas instead of the driver.

As I got back in I asked him, "Which way to I-5?"

He simply pointed. "Just a little ways down that road."

This was the road we came in on to get our gas and from here I could now see the entrance sign. Getting back on the freeway would be a breeze. The assumption had been correct; the gas station was just off the freeway, just not the exit we had gotten off.

Just before we got on the freeway I heard the words from the backseat that almost made me cringe.

"I have to go to the bathroom."

I had no idea why she didn't think of using the restroom two minutes ago while we were pumping gas.

With a sigh, we turned back around to find the nearest rest stop before getting back on I-5.

"Wasn't that the exit we got off?" My wife asked as we drove further south on the freeway.

Sure enough, she was right. We had driven so far north that we had backtracked two full exits and here we were right back where we started. We had spent at least an hour going around in a circle. It felt like we were in a "Twilight Zone" episode, the one where the woman keeps driving past the same exit because she had died in a car wreck some time ago.

"Remind me next time to never pull off into Eugene again," I said as we finally drove past our initial off ramp and finally started back on our journey.

Chapter: Rural Oregon

*T*he scenery had changed. What had been an eyeful of city and landscapes, of hills and mountains, of trees and buildings was now replaced by nothing but flat rural land. There seemed to be nothing out here, not even an exit. The exits we did find seemed to go off into somewhere between Nowheresville and Timbuktu with roads that disappeared somewhere beyond the horizon. This was the most boring part of the drive. If anything were to happen out here, there wouldn't be anywhere to go. This was the place that we didn't want to hear "I have to use the restroom", or "We're out of gas", or anything out of the ordinary like...

Thump.

The sound brought me out of my daydream, which I shouldn't have been having in the first place since I was the one driving. The lack of scenery had put me in to a lull that had now been suddenly interrupted.

The splatter pattern on the window told me what had created the noise. Whatever the insect was, it used to be big. Now, it was dead.

"We grow them large and suicidal," I recalled one gas attendant saying the last time we were here in Oregon.

He was in reference to the several splatter patterns that were plastered across my windshield that he was trying to clean off at the time, with little success. I didn't want to see what my grill looked like.

Recalling the attendant's lack of success, even while putting in as much elbow grease as he could, I doubted that I would do any better while driving. However, my vision was now slightly impaired and I had to do something. I attempted to use the windshield wiper fluid and the wipers to try to knock the bug ichor off of the window but it had only smeared the creature and left a larger mess than what I had started with.

"Ewww!" The protest came from the back. "That's gross."

"Don't worry," I replied to Ruth's comment. "It's only one bug, I'm pretty sure that we won't hit too many…"

Thump.

The sound brought my attention back to the windshield to see the second splatter pattern. I could only shake my head. As long as we didn't run into too many of these things then we should be alright. There was no telling where the nearest gas station was where I could pull over and clean my windshield.

"What's that cloud?"

The question came from my right and had a bit of worry and concern in her tone. I had come to recognize the various tones from my wife and this one was to be taken very seriously. This one had a slight tone of panic and concern.

My eyes drifted off of the road for just one moment to catch a glimpse of where she was pointing. Sure enough there was a large cloud that was filling our view from horizon to horizon. At first I thought it was some storm that was rolling in. I didn't recall any storm warnings for any portion of our trip. We were pretty much ensured blue skies all the way through, that's why we planned this trip for this time of year. Then, I realized to my horror what it really was.

Thump, thump, thump, thump, thump.

The swarm of insects hit our car hard. It was like hail but worse. Hail would have slid off and allowed us to see. Hail would have let us use our windshield wipers. This, however, let us do neither. Each strike of the swarm left smear marks and within moments it was getting difficult to see. Pieces of bug chitin and were flying all over the place and only added to the smeared mess that was obscuring our view.

I did my best to try to stay on the road, but my visibility was being cut by each passing moment. I had no clue if there was a car next to me anymore or not. If I recalled correctly there hadn't been and I hoped that this was still the case.

But my visibility wasn't just cut by the splatter patterns of each insect hitting the windshield; it was also cut by the swarm itself. The enormity and vastness of this plague was like a dark, thick cloud of oppressive hatred and depression that had enveloped us. Even if we weren't getting plastered by the plaguing swarm, the sun had been blocked. I simply could no longer see.

Cries of protests out of complete horror were coming from behind me and from my right. Screams of panic had erupted. Between the cries of terror and the pounding of insect bodies upon the car, it was hard to hear myself think.

The ground was becoming slick. The squashed insects had gotten on to the wheels and their ichor had smeared all over the tires. I could also hear a crunching sound as I was running over hundreds of these things by each passing moment.

Crunch, crunch, crunch.

Thump, thump, thump.

Crunch, crunch, crunch.

I finally lost control of the van and we slid to our left. I tried my best to steer back onto the freeway but only managed to overcompensate making the van slide to our right before it spun and slid back across the freeway. I felt the hard pavement of I-5 give way, followed by the give of the soft rural earth that we had come to drive on. We only traveled a short distance due to our momentum before we came to an abrupt and sudden stop.

Thump, thump, thump.

We sat there, off to the side of the road in the soft terrain, and listened as the insects continued to pound our van. We were being assaulted by their bodies as if they were trying to throw themselves as hard as they could to break through our car. Despite how unlikely that may have sounded, I was actually starting to believe that they would. Then I remembered the windows. The impossibility was becoming very possible and highly probably. Once they broke through...I simply didn't want to think about it.

Thump, thump, thump.

Hysterical cries of panic were being issued from behind me. My daughter was now completely out of control. Her screams of terror was piercing and had cut above the thunderous noise of the bombardment we were having.

Thump, thump, thump.

I unbuckled and climbed toward the back. My arms held her body tight and my words tried to give her comfort, yet she couldn't hear me. Her mind was frightened beyond anything she had ever been through, even more frightened than the time when we first went through a carwash when she was a lot younger and she had nearly pulled herself out of her car seat carrier in an attempt to run for her life.

Thump, thump, thump.

As I held my daughter, I could feel her body tremble and shake. She was in complete flight mode and there was nowhere to run.

Thump, thump, thump.

She was sobbing and crying as loudly as she could. She was in shock. I doubted that she even knew that I was there.

Thump, thump, thump.

I felt another set of arms wrap around me and I knew that it was my wife trying to find the comfort that I was trying to give to our daughter. She buried her face into my side as if trying to hide herself from the onslaught. She was as scared as Ruth was. My only regret was that I couldn't console either one of them, they were too far emotionally gone and their panic was overwhelming. The best that we could do was sit there and hold each other and hope that this nightmare would quickly end.

The van suddenly swayed.

This had startled me more than anything else had. I was ready to face the onslaught of the bugs, the torment of the swarm, but whatever had happened had moved our entire van. That wasn't something small, it was something big and something fast.

The van swayed again.

I opened my eyes and looked out the side window to try to get a view of what horror was plaguing us now.

What I saw wasn't what I had expected to see. I had expected to see the window plastered with ichor and chitin. I expected to see a dark, ominous cloud, a harbinger of death surrounding us. I expected to see some large creature attacking us.

The window was completely clear and clean, it couldn't have been more pristine if I had run it through a carwash and then personally hand washed the window. The visibility was completely perfect and spotless. There was no ichor, no chitin, not even a speck of dirt or grime. The window was crystal clear. The cloud that had surrounded us was also gone. I could see as far as the end of the horizon.

The onslaught wasn't just over; it was as if it had never happened. There wasn't a trace of any insect anywhere. There was none on my windows, windshield, the hood, or even on the road. Nothing. They had simply vanished as if they were never there in the first place.

The sudden swaying of the van brought me out of my bewilderment.

A large semi-truck, with a long massive trailer and many wheels had just passed us by while doing seventy miles an hour. The wind gust displacement by the passing beast of a vehicle had shaken our van. Traffic was flowing and there was nothing, completely nothing, out of the ordinary, except for our lonely van off to the side of the freeway.

With a sigh of relief and some time to gather our wits, we pulled back into traffic and continued south toward our destination.

Chapter: Roseburg

*B*y the time we came upon Roseburg the evergreen trees had fallen behind us, the farmlands were gone and the landscape had dramatically changed yet again. We had now come upon rolling hills filled with brown grass, rocky terrain, and it was dotted with periodic trees of brown, red and yellow leaves.

"Roseburg is coming up. Why don't we pull over? We can switch drivers, find a rest area, and stop at the South Umpqua River. There's a nice place called the Riverfront Park I would like to see. We still have plenty of time to make it to Yreka before it gets dark."

My wife's voice had cut the silence of the last several miles since the "swarm of bugs" incident that had left everyone speechless and in shock. I took a glance in her direction for a brief moment before returning my attention to the road. The moment's glance told me everything that I needed to know.

She had put up a good front since the horrible scare of the swarm and was still trying to get over the shock of the incident and its disappearing act as if it never really happened. Her face was slightly pale and her body was still shaking a little.

A quick look in my rearview mirror told me that Ruth was in a similar state. I could still see the tracks of her tears. Her eyes were wide and she was as pale as her mother. She hadn't bothered putting her earphones back on.

I quickly agreed to pull over. This had nothing to do with a rest stop and everything to do with calming our nerves. We needed a break.

We followed the exit and continued until we came to the Riverfront Park. It was a bit further out of our way than I had expected but once we got there I realized that it was well worth it. Instead of the rocky and dead grass terrain that we had been experiencing, the park was luscious green. There were plenty of trees and a huge open field of grass. It was one of those picture perfect scenes that I thought never really existed.

Once we got out, my wife had said that she had seen a place to get ice cream and that she would be right back. As she drove away I was sure that it had nothing to do with ice cream and everything to do with the desire to let herself cry outside of mine and Ruth's vision. I completely understood. She didn't want her daughter, and now her husband, to think that she didn't have the strength to face the horror that had happened; it might actually scare Ruth more. I probably would have done the same except that I didn't seem to be as shaken up as my wife had been. I wondered how Ruth was holding up.

"Oh, look, a playground. Can I go and play, dad?" She gave me that look, the one that no dad could resist and with the tone in her voice she was sure that she had me wrapped around her finger. She already knew the answer before I gave it.

The plus side to Ruth's medical condition was that she processes emotions a lot quicker than everyone else. Her emotions may run higher and stronger, but they play out very quickly and before we know it, she's moved on.

"Ok," I said and before I could get the rest of my sentence finished, she had shot off.

"But don't go far," I yelled after her, hoping that she hadn't tuned me out like she usually does when she gets sidetracked.

I looked over toward the river and realized that I needed to do some brooding of my own. The others had already found a way to deal with their stress; it was time to deal with mine. Perhaps the incident had affected me and left me more shaken than I had initially thought.

The river was wider than I thought it would be. It was crystal clear with a hint of light blue, a reflection of the perfect sky above. The water didn't seem to flow very fast nor did it seem very deep, yet I knew better. There were undercurrents that could easily catch an unwary swimmer and it was deep enough to drown in. Yet, despite my knowledge of the dangers below, the scene was very serene and calm.

A smile finally came across my face. The tall evergreens, lush grass, clear sky, and the sound of the running river lapping against the river banks was tranquil enough to wash away my stress. This was what I needed.

I was able to enjoy a light, puffy, single cotton ball of a cloud as it floated by. I was able to savor the sounds of the birds and the children playing and giggling in the background. I was able to appreciate the calm river and the ... dead fish?

My eyes caught the sight of a dead rainbow trout floating down the river. It was a pretty decent size and if I had caught it while it was still alive while I was fishing it would have been good enough to keep for dinner. I thought nothing of it until I saw another and then another.

I blinked my eyes. Never before had I seen any dead fish floating down a river, let alone several. I needed to make sure and confirm what I was seeing. When I opened my eyes the sight before me made my blood run cold and a chill ran down my spine.

The crystal clear river with the reflection of the light blue sky had turned blood red. But it wasn't just the color of blood; it had the consistency and the putrid smell of blood. It stank of sweetness and iron, and had turned thick, making the river flow slower, almost like molasses. And it was worse than that. Above the sweetness smell, there was an odor of rot and decay, of decomposition. This smelled like the time a raccoon had crawled under my house and died. This smelled like the time a large rat had crawled under my refrigerator and died. This river stank of death.

The dead fish had been replaced. Instead of the aquatic inhabitants that should have been there, in their place were bodies and body parts of dead people. Dead, bloated, rotting corpses filled with pus and ooze floated down the putrid river. This was no longer a life giving and sustaining flow of crystal clear and refreshing water. This was the River Styx; this was the river of death.

I turned from the horrific sight. My mind raced to my little girl. It was bad enough that she had faced one nightmare and now she was about to face another. If she witnessed this scene it would give her nightmares for life. I had to find her and get her out of here.

As I turned toward the playground that was off in the distance behind me, I froze. The sight before me sent greater chills down my spine then the river of blood and bloated bodies that was now behind me.

There, not more than a few feet away, was a little girl. She was perhaps only a few years old, perhaps four. Her dress seemed something that an individual might wear to a costume period fair. If I were to guess, it looked something like a "Little House on the Prairie" outfit. However, instead of a flowing and nice looking dress, the outfit seemed charred, burned, and singed. It was as if she had been in a fire, yet her body hadn't been marked by the flames.

It wasn't just her attire that caught my attention, it was her eyes. They had a cold, blank stare about them. Then I realized why. Her eyes were black. They weren't black as coal or black as ebony; they were black as if they were soulless. They were black as if they were lifeless.

The little girl pointed in my direction. At first I thought she was pointing at me, and then I realized that she was pointing behind me, at the river, the river of blood, the river of death, the River Styx. Somehow I knew that she wasn't shocked by the sight, she just wanted to show me something. Yes, I knew that the river had turned a horrible nightmare of blood and bodies. Yes, I knew that death was behind me. Yes, I knew...

I turned to make sure she wasn't pointing at anything else and saw...

The river.

The crystal clear water with the reflection of the light blue sky had returned. There was no blood and no bodies. There was no odor or stench. There was only the river as it always had been.

I spun back around to try to get any indication of what else she might have been pointing toward. I should have known. She was gone. She had simply vanished as quickly as the river of blood and the swarm of insects.

I had to chalk it up as not getting enough sleep the night before from my nightmare and perhaps from shook from the swarm that we had encountered. I had to chalk it up as simple hallucinations rather than losing my mind. I thought I was stronger and that these things hadn't bothered me, but apparently they had. I was having a nervous breakdown; that was all. There hadn't been a river of blood with dead bodies filled with death.

There hadn't been a "Little House on the Prairie" ghost girl with soulless eyes and charred, burned clothing. It was all just my imagination.

Before I was able to fully recover from my horrible and terrifying experience, my eyes caught our van driving up. Apparently my wife had found a soft serve ice cream place and had bought three, one for each of us. However, I could tell that my assumption had been accurate. She had been crying. Her eyes were all puffy and red and I could still see the tracks of her tears. I didn't say anything. She had needed her privacy and I wasn't going to intrude.

We had called Ruth back from the playground and we slowly had our treat. It was good to see the both of them happier than they had been when we had first arrived and I was in no position to destroy the happiness on their faces by talking about the vision that I had just seen. It was better to not mention it. Once we finished the ice cream, with Ruth letting it drip all over her hands and having to make a trip to restroom to wash them, it was time to head out and to continue our trip, putting our nightmares behind us, hopefully for good.

Chapter: Siskiyou

As we made our way up one incline after another we noticed that the big rigs were going slower and slower. They crept along like some beasts of burden under protest. Their engines whined in a desperate attempt to conform to the driver's demands. It was only a matter of time before I started having to pass them one by one on this stretch of the two lane freeway.

My first passing was easy enough; all the trucks were going in the slow right-hand lane. But as I was passing the second, a car came barreling up behind me going twenty miles over the speed limit. It was one of those red, supercharged, high horsepower, performance, "look at me I'm better and richer than you can ever dream of", convertible sports cars that you only see in car shows. The driver was a young male, off to prove that his testosterone was at a higher peak than everyone else's. I was quite sure that he was overcompensating for something.

Before I was able to pull back over to the slower right hand lane, the driver slammed on his breaks just before hitting me and laid in on his horn. It was only after I rejoined the slow lane did he zip past me. His engine whined in almost a glee as he shifted from one gear to another. He did slow down for just one moment before giving me the dirtiest look and presenting the one finger salute in my honor of slowing down his certain and impending death that would be composed of crushed metal and broken bones. I secretly hoped that we would find him again, just around the bend, getting a ticket for speeding and reckless driving as I smiled and waved him on. Of course no such luck occurred and we never saw him again.

At the final incline, we came to the top of Siskiyou Summit. Its elevation was 4,310 feet, the highest point on I-5. It was all downhill from here.

This summit was known for treacherous weather of snow and ice during the winter, bad enough to close the pass and stop any travel between Oregon and California. Fortunately we had taken our trip during the warmer season. Instead of snow and ice, we had a clear view of rocks, boulders, and gravel.

At the top of the summit we passed by many large trucks off to the side of the road like some dead animal that had attempted to surmount some great feat only to die in the process. They sat there, lifeless and unmoving, a graveyard of large trucks. Perhaps some of the drivers were giving their trucks a break from the momentous climb and were letting their engines cool before attempting the long descent before them. Perhaps some had pushed their rigs beyond their limit and had to stop and change a blown gasket or some other overused and malfunctioned part. Either way; the trucks lined the side of the road and we were in the clear to continue in the slower lane allowing the suicidal drivers to pass us by with insane and reckless speeds.

The sign had me confused. We had been over this mountain pass several times and I had never seen it. Perhaps it was because it was during the night the last time we were here or maybe it was because I had been paying attention to the road while driving. This time I had seen it despite it being there for many years.

"Jefferson?" I asked aloud. "Oh, this is the county of Jefferson." I thought that it might be some county in one state or another.

My wife shook her head. "No, this is the State of Jefferson."

I only gave her a confused look. We should either still be in Oregon or we should have crossed the state line into northern California. As far as I remembered, there wasn't a State of Jefferson nor was there a state between Oregon and California, unless I had crossed into The Twilight Zone again. Please tell me that I wasn't losing my mind.

She read my confusion correctly and answered back.

"Northern California doesn't want to be part of the same state as Southern California. There's been a movement for a long time now to have the split and they have named it Jefferson."

I had heard about potential splits in California before but I didn't know that it was taken this seriously. I guess the State of "Jefferson" wasn't too bad for a name; after all I just came from another state that was also named after a president, Washington. However I just couldn't imagine too many other states named for presidents. I could see Lincoln perhaps, but not Ford, Bush, Bush Jr., Obama or perhaps even Nixon. It wasn't just their legacies as presidents, I'm sure each one had their own positive and negative contributions to our great country, I was just thinking about the names. No, I simply couldn't imagine a sign that stated "Welcome to the State of Ford...Obama...Bush Jr." I wondered if the State of Nixon would have the state slogan of "I'm still not a crook." I wondered if the State of Clinton would have a state icon of a cigar. I didn't want to go there.

Our journey continued downhill through dizzying heights and fantastic views of the Siskiyou Mountain Range until we saw our exit sign. With a sigh of relief that the first leg of our adventure was just about over, we turned off the exit to Yreka.

Chapter: Yreka

"*W*elcome, welcome. Make yourself at home."

My wife's aunt came out to greet us as we pulled up to her driveway. She was always accommodating. She would always let us stay at her place in Yreka whenever we were in the area. She gave us the use of a couple of rooms where we could sleep and stay while we were there.

Her place was the halfway marker between home and any further destination in California, and it wasn't really in Yreka. We had pulled off the freeway at the Yreka exit, which was in the middle of nowhere, and then drove further out into the middle of nowhere. The small town that she actually did live in had a train track and a couple of small business buildings surrounding it as its "downtown" section, a section so small I could see its entire two block area before I drove up to it and turned down some unnamed road leading deeper into the Northern California desert.

"And remember not to mind the dogs."

She had two dogs. The first was old, half blind, and slobbered all of the time. Periodically he would get the notion that he was a lap dog. Of course he as a big as a couch and despite every attempt to push him off, he still continued to clumsily climb upon anyone's lap as if it were his privilege and right to do so, despite the laws of physics that stated that such a mass couldn't possibly fit on such a small area. Perhaps it was his way of saying "hello" and being friendly but a little less friendly would have been just fine by me.

The other one was younger, but not very sociable. He would bark very loudly and consistently at just about anyone and then run and hide under the porch. Apparently he didn't like company, although he wasn't a mean dog. It wouldn't snarl, snap or bite; it would just continually bark and then go run and hide.

It was good to stretch my legs out after all of that driving. A nap was a definite must and my body confirmed my thoughts with a yawn, but the nap would have to wait until after a brief walk through the back yard to further my stretching and getting the blood starting to flow properly again and then unpacking the van of the items that we would need for the next day or so. The sun was out and there was fresh air to be had. A few minutes around the yard while it was still daylight would do me some good.

After unpacking I went back out the back door and admired the view, postponing the desire of a nap and figuring that it was too late for one anyway. Of course, I had to ignore the younger dog barking at me and after a while it simply went and hid under the house and ignored my presence.

The view was fantastic and bleak simultaneously. The flat rocky desert stretched as far as I could see, right up to the Klamath National Forest. The rocks were various hues of red and brown, copper and rust, tan and ochre. It was definitely something I was not used to. I was used to the various colors of green such as pine, kelly, moss and forest. The only green there was out here were a few trees and bushes the color of olive and a drab yellow-tan.

I had a great view of Goosenest Mountain, which I was told was volcanic. I don't know if it still is, but something had been. There was plenty of volcanic rock all about me. I picked up one such rock, studied it for a short bit. It was volcanic red with lots of pocketed holes. It felt coarse like sandpaper. When I was done, I tossed it randomly toward the middle of the landscape. There was nothing out there.

There were a few trees scattered about the area, I could have probably counted them on one hand, on two if I really tried. Mostly there were patches of brown, dried grass which blended into the rocks. This place was in desperate need of rain. I would have given them some of ours from the Seattle area if I could have brought it with me, but this vacation was about getting out of the drizzle, so this area that was lack of rain was just fine by me.

I had been told that this summer was one of the worst droughts that they have had for the longest time. There was even a water-rationing being enforced. There would be no watering the yard and our showers would have to be short. We would be drinking bottled water bought from the grocery store back in Yreka.

This was what I needed, a desperate change of scenery. Yes, Washington was green and wet, but sometimes I just needed a shock to my system to remind me of the great big world that I lived in. After a few days of this, I would miss the luscious trees and greenery back home. Until then, this was paradise.

The sun had started to set and the sky was turning vibrant hues of red and orange that reflected off of Goosenest Mountain which finally gave me the image I needed to imagine the peak to be the volcano that it was. The volcanic rock reflected the fiery colors in the sky and the whole ground seemed to be a flowing sea of lava that stretched as far as I could see. It was as if fire had swept through the area, through the sky and across the ground, as the colors danced with a life of their own. This was not a scene that I would have the privilege of having back in Washington, well, perhaps in Eastern Washington, but since I lived on the Western side I had nothing like this to dazzle my senses.

The scene had only a moment of playing out before my eyes until it faded to purple, then dark blue, and then black. The sun had set and it had sprayed its array of colors in a fantastic and wondrous view leaving me breathless at the spectacular display that I had been given.

With the setting sun, the stars had come out. Oh, how I had missed them. I had always wanted to be an astronomer astronaut when I grew up. I suppose most kids do at one time in their life. I knew all of the planets (before Pluto had been reduced to a minor one), all of their aspects, all of their known satellites at that time and various other fun facts that no child in their right mind would want to sit down and study let alone memorize from the set of encyclopedias that we had in our house, long before the internet. I knew the closest stars and how far away they were. I knew the major nebula clusters, the different life phases of stars, and much more. I would always lay in my backyard and watch the stars when I could and point out the ones that I knew and all of the constellations. I would watch falling stars and be able to point out the differences between a star, what kind of star, a planet, and a galaxy although they all seemed to look the same to everyone else from this distance. I still can, to some degree, although I'm a bit rusty.

Back in Washington it was difficult to watch the stars. We often had overcast nights, although not as much rain as people might think, there were still enough clouds to block my view. On top of that, the city lights were always too bright. My stargazing time in Washington was often limited to when I could get out of the city and find a clear night sky and even then it would be at some campsite filled with massive trees that continued to block my view.

Now, now I was able to enjoy what I had missed. The stars were like diamonds on a velvet backdrop. They came out in mass with spectacular arrays of color. I could see white and red and blue stars. I could see pulsars that twinkled between colors. I tried to make out the stars that I remembered in the sea of amazing dazzling of lights and did my best to remember those that I had long forgotten. There were just so many that I almost felt lost under their beauty.

I heard the sliding door open bringing me out of my reverie. I knew who it was without even turning around. I had come to be familiar with her footsteps after seventeen years of marriage. I knew the scent of her perfume. Without stating a word my wife sat beside me on the porch. I heard her open her bottle of beer, another indulgence that I didn't partake in. After she took a sip I could hear a sigh of relief.

She was trying to put the whole insect swarm behind her. I didn't want to tell her about the river, or the nightmare, or the cat or the ghost girl. She needed this vacation as much as I did, and she didn't need to spend it worrying about odd and unexplainable situations of ghosts and possible bouts of insanity.

After a few moments she shifted her position and straddled herself on my lap, facing me. Her eyes looked deep into mine. I knew that look and knew what she wanted. Perhaps, once everyone had gone to sleep, I could help her forget the nightmare we had on the freeway and help her enjoy this vacation and our time together.

That night, after some extracurricular activities, I rested well. The driving had made me tired and I couldn't wait to fall asleep in a comfortable bed. And this bed was...not so much. However, once exhaustion overcame me, I was out.

I didn't recall any dreams and I was glad for that. The last nightmare that I had dreamt the night before had shaken me to my core and I wasn't looking forward to having another one. All I wanted to do was sleep in. I was, after all, on vacation.

However, that was quickly dashed aside once I heard the dogs barking. I said something quickly under my breath while trying not to wake my wife. It was still the middle of the night, and everyone should still be sleeping, including me. I only hoped that the dogs wouldn't wake up my kid. Once she was awake, she would be cranky and moody for the first half hour and then bounce off of the walls for the rest of the day. I was in no mood to listen to either. It was time to go see why the dogs were barking. Hopefully it was some coyote or deer that had wandered too close to the fenced yard. With any luck I would be able to scare the creature away and go back to sleep.

I crept through the house, trying not to make any noise despite the fact that I ran into unfamiliarly placed and unseen furniture several times, enough times that I was sure that it would leave a bruise, and made my way to the back door. Outside was cooler than I had expected and had I known how cold it would have been, I would have put on my pajama shirt. As it was, the bottoms were the only thing keeping me warm. Had I taken the time to think about the situation further, I would have at least put on my sandals. This thought didn't cross my mind until I stepped outside onto the uncomfortable and rocky terrain. A few painful steps completely and abruptly woke me up.

I told the dogs to be quiet in as much of a hushed voice as I could so not to further run the risk of waking up my host, my family or the surrounding neighbors. My presence and my commands were ignored. Both dogs were facing the same direction, somewhere off in the distance toward Goosenest Mountain. I scanned the area. There was nothing that I could see. There wasn't an animal or person. There was nothing out there for the dogs to bark at.

I went to quiet them down again when suddenly both dogs whimpered, scared of something hidden beyond my sight. Then, both dogs ran off like a shot and hid under the house, frightened by some unseen presence in the night.

Quickly my eyes turned back toward the open field of gravel and rocks, of boulders and sage brush. I scanned the area over and over again. There was nothing, nothing at all. Yet, something gave me the shivers down my back and had the hairs sticking up on the back of my neck. I shook my head; it was just the cold, cold enough to see my breath. It was time to go back to sleep.

Chapter: Hornbrook

"*H*as anyone seen the two dogs?" My wife's aunt asked. She had a concerned tone in her voice.

"I thought I saw them go under the house", I said with a yawn as I tried to finish my breakfast.

She had been such a great host and had served us up some eggs and bacon. I found that bacon went well with everything, including more bacon. Both my wife and Ruth had their morning coffee with the appropriate amount of creamer. We had been told that we would need our energy if we were going to go out to the ranch and go horseback riding.

"Did something spook them?" She asked as she went outside.

"Not sure, I didn't see anything," I had replied as I stuffed another piece of bacon into my mouth.

I could hear her calling out to her dogs and only got whimpers of fear as a reply. I felt really bad for the mutts. Something really had them scared straight. Perhaps, after all that has already happened on this trip, I could relate.

"Well, we're off to the ranch. I hope that the dogs are alright," my wife said as we started gathering our supplies. This included hats, shades, and plenty of sunscreen. We all had the Washington tan, which was to say we were very pale and would easily burn, well, I would easily burn. Both my wife and Ruth would tan while I fried. If I didn't take care of myself, I would end up in a lot of pain from unwanted sunburn.

"Do you remember the back way?"

The back way was a series of roads through the hills that paralleled I-5 back North. It wasn't necessarily quicker; it just bypassed all the crazy truck drivers that wanted to go well over the speed limit, and bypassed all of the construction that brought the traffic down to a crawl. It was also more scenic.

I said I did remember it, it wasn't difficult to forget. There were only two roads leading out of town, the one we came in on and the one going the back way to the ranch. It would be extremely difficult to get lost.

Our dirt road turned into a pothole filled excuse of a roadway before we finally made our way on to something completely paved. Even then there weren't any sidewalks; the sides of the road had only disappeared off into the slight rocky terrain that enveloped our landscape.

We passed by the "downtown section" of our area, all six buildings, and headed out of town. The houses became further and further apart until they turned into ranches with acres and acres of land space. My wife's aunt had mentioned that these were cattle ranches and she always had a story about how she had helped drive cattle along these hills. We were to be on the lookout for any cattle herds along the road. We didn't see any and it was difficult to imagine trying to make a living by herding cattle in these parts with there being so little grass.

The landscape continued to evolve from fairly flat terrain to rolling hills of rocks and boulders. Waist high fences of barbed wire paralleled the road to prevent any cattle from straying into oncoming traffic. We still didn't see any cattle, but we did have to stop for some deer crossing which had my daughter very excited to see. She probably wouldn't stop talking about them until we made our way to our horseback riding adventure where she would immediately forget that they had ever existed.

We crossed back over the Klamath River and turned back into more populated area. Houses started to appear again and we even passed a car or two as we turned toward Hornbrook.

There were more trees here, being closer to the Klamath River and the subsidiary creeks, although they looked unhealthy. Many seemed parched and dry from the desert terrain. Their greenery had lost their luster and it seemed that their foliage had collected a thin layer of dust that helped them blend into their surroundings. The environment was choking the life out of these trees. My eyes had missed the true color of green back in Washington.

We passed by abandoned buildings with windows blown out or broken in and doors missing or simply hanging on their hinges. Roofs were a patchwork quilt of boards. Graffiti was on the more dilapidated buildings. Rusted out cars were sitting on the side of the road and it was doubtful that they had moved in a very long time. Broken fences attempted to guard un-mowed and neglected lawns of brown weeds.

We passed by an old building on a corner lot that looked as if had been a tavern, or perhaps it used to be some mini-mart type store. Actually, it was difficult to tell what it used to be. Now, it was abandoned.

We passed by another storage building that was missing its doors and windows. It had been overgrown with weeds that seem to be taking over the majority of this town. Like the rest of the buildings as far as we could see, this one had long been forgotten about.

It was difficult to imagine anyone living here and from the looks of things no one did. There weren't any children playing, people mowing their lawn, neighbors hanging over their fences gossiping about the latest news. There weren't any dogs or cats running about. There weren't any cars driving on the road or bicycles being ridden. The stop signs at intersections were nothing but a joke. There wasn't anything to stop for.

This was a modern day ghost town. The ranching had been bad, the weather had been harsh and the rains hadn't come. Most people had simply walked away and all that was left were these shells of houses as a poor reminder of how life used to be like here. It was time to move on and let the ghosts of the past rest in peace.

Chapter: The Ranch

*T*he ranch sat on more than five thousand acres of desert, mountainous scrub land between the Klamath River and the Klamath National Forest. It was known for its RV campsite near the Cottonwood Creek, an offshoot of the Klamath River. The ranch also boasted hunting, fishing, hiking, swimming, camping, and horseback riding.

Rock, boulders, alpine evergreens, chaparral, sage, mesquite, manzanita, gravel, dirt, and desert underbrush dominated this area. It was a great place to twist an ankle or get bitten by a hidden rattlesnake. The sun was hot and overbearing.

Yet, despite this, or because of it, the area had a pleasant, relaxing feel. The smell of sage filled my senses, the air was fresh, and the sky was clear.

We had pulled into the driveway for the horse riding and I followed Ruth to the stables. My wife decided not to go. Her knees were still bothering her from her surgery and she was afraid that she wouldn't do well on the horse. With her blessing, the two of us went to be introduced to the stable hands and trail guides that would be on the ride with us.

My step hit something slick and I slid for just a short distance. There was no need to look to see what I had stepped in, I already knew. My next few steps were more cautious.

"If you're concerned about stepping in it," a female voice said from further down the stable, "you're in the wrong place."

I wasn't too concerned about stepping in it, I had stepped in worse. My concern was about tracking it into the van and not only making a mess, but making a stench that would be complained about for the rest of our vacation.

The young woman introduced herself to Ruth and me and waited for the others to join before giving us our mounts to ride for the day. We were given boots to wear and a helmet. I felt ridiculous, but I guess it was better than winding up in the hospital with a concussion and feeling stupid.

We rode our horses in single file following our lead guide with another guide taking up the rear. The trail was rocky and wound between the manzanita and alpine evergreens and up and down several trails along the fairly steep incline of the mountains that we were in.

It was more difficult to ride a horse than I thought. It wasn't just the pleasure of sitting on some animal while it did all the work. We were instructed to lean forward while going uphill and backwards while going down. Then, with each movement the horse made, I had to readjust my center of balance. My thighs, hips, and stomach muscles were constantly making adjustments. With the constant light bouncing that I was doing on my backside and the workout that I was getting, I was sure that I was going to be sore for quite some time.

I had to remember a video that an old friend had shared on the internet. The question was, do you ride like a girl? In the video it showed several women riding very quickly and expertly around barrels, over jumps and making very sharp turns all the while making it look very easy. I was having the worst of time just sitting up straight. So my answer was, no, I don't ride like a girl, I simply didn't have the grace.

Despite the heat and the soreness that I was sure I was going to feel later, the view was wonderful. I was able to look back toward the ranch and then further down toward the Klamath River. The whole landscape opened up before me and the rugged, rough terrain seemed to go on forever reaching from one end of the horizon to the next. Patches of olive and drab green dotted the brown and dust colored mountains of this rocky area. Red and tan mixed with burnt umber and rust. There was ochre and amber, charcoal and slate. All of this blended together to give a patchwork quilt effect over the towering and jagged mountainous landscape. This was a slice of heaven.

I was starting to get used to the movements of my horse and was able to anticipate how I should react. There was a rhythm that I just needed to follow and when I did, it made riding easier.

We came down out of the mountains and were starting to make our way back toward the ranch. The terrain had flattened here and became more of a meadow of wild flowers and sage brush. I thought the hardest part of the ride was now over, but that's when my horse stopped. There had been no reason for my horse to stop.

We had been warned about small creatures that might spook a horse and how to react. It could have been anything from a squirrel to a snake. There was nothing that I could see that had caused the sudden stopping. Nothing had crossed our path and from the looks of things, there was nothing to the sides of us. I gave my horse a slight kick on the side of ribs to prod him along, but got nowhere.

My horse started to snort and whine a little. Something was definitely agitating my horse. He started to back up in a desperate attempt to get out of our current location. My eyes darted around for the closest guide but she had ridden too far ahead of me.

Suddenly the ground next to me erupted. My first thought was that it was some groundhog or mole or some other burrowing creature that had decided to poke its head up just as we were able to trot by, or perhaps some small unseen animal that was finally coming out of hiding behind some rock or bush. No, it wasn't that at all.

My eyes went wide with horror as soon as I saw it. The thing, the grotesque horrible thing, was a rotting, decomposing hand rising from the ground. It was trying to dig its way out of the ground to me, trying to free the rest of its putrid body that was buried just to my right.

My horse reacted as I did and panicked. He reared up on his back two legs while giving a whine of sheer terror. I threw myself forward, towards its neck in an attempt to keep my center of balance. If I fell backwards I would not only be on the ground with the undead hand that was trying to reach toward us, I would also run the risk of hitting my head on any number of the sharp rocks that populated this terrain and I also ran the risk of being kicked by the horse's hind legs when if finally decided to bolt in sheer terror. I had to hang on for dear life.

The horse stomped with its front two hooves toward the ground as if trying to push the rotting appendage back into the ground without any thought or consideration to the rider, namely myself, that was currently and dearly attempting to hang on. It reared again and again he attempt the shove its hooves toward the hand.

Suddenly my magnificent and terrified steed took off like a shot out of complete and utter terror. What I had thought was difficult before to keep my balance was mere child's play compared to the struggle I was having now. The horse moved too quickly and too powerfully for me to keep up let alone anticipate. I was thrown from side to side and each stride threatened to throw me from the horse. I was horrified. I didn't know what scared me more, the thought of falling or the thought of being closer to that thing in the ground.

Almost as quickly as the horse had started its panicked run, it had stopped. The sudden stoppage of movement had nearly completed my disembarkation from the saddle. Our lead guide had reached her hand over, just as we caught up to her, and took the reigns. I don't know how she did it, or if it was the fact that the horse was used to her and not me, but whatever she did, the horse had stopped being terrified and had returned to its normal, passive self.

I quickly turned back toward the thing that had clawed its way through the ground. It wasn't there. Nothing resembling any hand, or corpse, or any hole from its presence was noticeable. I turned toward my guide with pleading eyes. It was as if I was trying to say "honestly, there was something there."

She seemed to read my thoughts. "It was probably just a snake. Don't worry. There's hardly a time we come out here that at least one of the horses doesn't get spooked."

I shook my head. No, her attempt at trying to make me feel better had failed. I didn't see a snake, I saw a corpse hand and my horse saw it too. It was like when I saw the blood of death, the River Styx and the dead girl, and like the time I saw the insect swarm.

Or was I seeing these things? Was it my imagination about the insects and that it was my overactive driving that had scared both Ruth and my wife? Was it just a snake and only I saw the hand?

I hoped I wasn't coming down with another nervous breakdown. I had already spent a week in a hospital during my last encounter and I wasn't looking forward to doing it again. Perhaps I would call my doctor once I got back in the Seattle area and make arrangements to increase my meds. Until then, I was going to keep my mouth shut and do my best not to scare my family any further with any nonsense of Blood Rivers, bloated corpses, dead ghost girls, and undead appendages.

We made our way back to the stables without any further incidents and I had hoped that the entire encounter was going to be put behind me despite the fact that my heart was still beating wildly as if it were trying to escape from my chest. I was wrong.

"Mom! Mom! You can't believe what daddy did. His horse went all crazy like and it took off very fast and he was really great. Hey, daddy, can you do it again?" Ruth was talking very quickly like she usually does when she gets excited.

My wife gave me a curious look, one mixed with fear and concern. I put my hands up, palms toward her, in an attempt to placate her rising unsettlement.

"I'm sure it was just a snake," I said. "Nothing to be concerned about." With any luck the conversation would be dropped and wouldn't be brought up again on our way back to my in-law's house for one more night's stay.

Chapter: Shasta

We said our goodbyes to my wife's aunt as we finished packing the car the next morning. It was time to continue our adventure. I was looking forward to relaxing on the beach at Lake Tahoe or even river rafting along the Truckee River to help put the nightmares behind me.

After Ruth and my wife had their coffee fills with the appropriate amount of creamer and the last minute bathroom break for our daughter who needed to redo her hair, makeup and put in a different set of earrings, we were off on our next set of adventures. We made our way back to Yreka and were just about to hit the freeway when the voice behind me cut through the silence and sent a twinge of frustration through my entire body.

"I have to go to the bathroom."

"Why didn't you go when you had the opportunity?" I asked somewhat impatiently.

"Well, I didn't have to go then."

I rolled my eyes, bypassed the I-5 onramp and continued into Yreka in search of a public restroom.

Once we finally got onto I-5 we followed it south and followed the mountainous terrain. The environment had changed though. We were no longer in the desert but instead were now in the alpine forest full of evergreens. This could easily be back in Washington with the exception that the trees weren't as tall or majestic, nor were they as vibrant green. They still continued to have the sage green or dull-dust covered green that every other plant around these parts shared.

"Weed?" I asked as we passed by the sign.

I ask that each time we pass by it and each time it seems to draw a little giggle from my wife. To this day I still can't understand why anyone would want to name their town Weed. My only guess was that it was the same person who went into Oregon and named a town Drain. A little weed went down the drain. I started to giggle as well which only made my wife laugh a little louder. It was one of those times where we simply got the giggles and couldn't stop which only made the reference to weed that much funnier.

"What's so funny?" The question came from the back seat. Apparently Ruth could still hear us despite the music blasting out of her earphones.

"Nothing honey."

"Ah, come on mom. Tell me."

This only made the both of us laugh louder. I'm so glad that my daughter wasn't raised during the seventies. Needless to say we weren't going to tell her our inside joke.

Mount Shasta rose from the horizon and stood like some "Juggernaut" on our left. Its grandeur and spectacular form was breathtaking. It stood before us like a guardian monolith standing vigilance over the freeway. Its snow covered peak reached toward the heavens and it only reminded me of Mount Rainier.

However, I simply couldn't enjoy it as much as the mountain peak that dominated my landscape back home. Perhaps I was biased. Whatever the case was, no matter how grand this mountain was, it simply didn't have the same results as Mount Rainier.

"It doesn't have as much snow as it used to," the voice from my right announced with almost an air of disappointment. "There hasn't been enough precipitation to keep snow up there. It's kind of sad, really. There used to be so much snow, now it's lost its luster."

That was the reason right there. With less snow on the mountain, no matter how great it was, it just couldn't compare to the splendor of the ice capped and glacier riddled Rainier. Yes, Shasta was impressive, and still had a lot of snow, but it had lost its beauty somewhere along the way. It was now a large rock lacking some of its personality and was a mere shadow of its former self. This was not to put down the glorious mountain that stood before us, it still stood tall and proud and perhaps still one of the world's most beautiful mountains, at least one of the most beautiful that I would ever see. I just wondered what it looked like twenty years ago, or perhaps thirty.

The wondrous mountain came and went while my mind was still transfixed upon the water shortage of area. We had just left Yreka that was having water rationing and now left a mountain with the least amount of snow it had ever had the displeasure of having.

"Wow, great canyon," I said as we passed over a small bridge spanning a great ravine beneath us.

"No, that's not a canyon," my wife said as we drove over it. "That's a lake."

"What lake? I don't see a lake. If that's a lake, then where's the water?"

"This is Lake Shasta and we just passed over one of its arms. You'll be able see more of the lake around the bend. Just a second."

My wife pulled out her smart phone, which I wanted nothing to do with. There was just something unsettling about using an appliance that was smarter than I was. I'm sure my daughter would be able to figure one out faster than I would and would probably giggle at my inability to handle the fairly newly invented piece of technology. I'm sure I still shake my head when my mom tries to program her VCR, now my daughter does the same when I try to use the phone. I wonder what gadget will be out when she has a child that will leave her struggling while her thirteen year old reprograms it.

"Ah, here it is," my wife continued, disturbing my thoughts. "The fullest the lake can be is around 1067 feet above sea level. Currently it's about 960 feet above sea level."

I had to think about that. That was a drop of about 100 feet of water. But that wasn't just 100 feet from any one given area; it was 100 feet of water multiplied by the area of the whole lake. As we rounded the bend I was able to see more of this area and realized that this was a very large lake. In other words, this lake was missing a lot of water.

We could see where the waterline had changed. The banks of the new landscape were a light tan color, in deep contrast to the dark brown soil that was originally the lake's water level. Above the darker color was the tree line that would have sat almost at the water's edge. Now, it was almost a car's drive to the lake from the trees.

As I continued to look, I could see some of the docks sticking in the middle of the air Most of the docks, however had been moved down onto the newly established lakeshore. This also included the newly established roads that lead from the dock houses to the piers. The entire scene was just eerie and creepy and was only a driving point of how bad the drought was in this area.

Chapter: Highway Hell

*I*t was shortly after Lake Shasta where we turned off the major freeway of I-5 and headed east onto Highway 44. Our plan was to follow this to Highway 89, then to Highway 36, then back to Highway 89 and finally to Highway 267 where we would wind up at our destination of Kings Beach on the Northern tip of Lake Tahoe.

We entered the Plumas National Forest on a two lane highway. The evergreen trees were shorter than the gigantic evergreens we had in Washington. Of course I had to remember that we were in a higher altitude. The thinner air, harder soil, presence of more rock and less precipitation had stunted their growth.

We passed Greenville and Crescent Mills and decided to stop to get gas at Quincy and have lunch. It was the first major town that offered any amenities and was on the main highway. There were a few other towns that had offered more but by their locations on our map, they were completely out of our way. This would be the last major town before our destination and it was best to make our stop here.

The town reminded me a bit of Index or perhaps a better example was Leavenworth without all the Christmas decorations. There were mountainous peaks that surrounded the area, not as glorious as either Index or Leavenworth but I was sure that once winter struck the similarity would be greater. This was a little hideaway from the major hustle and bustle from the rest of the world.

We found an American/Mexican restaurant to stop to have lunch at the far end of town that tried to appeal to both cultures simultaneously and seemed to fail in both. The clientele was a couple of blue haired elderly patrons that seemed to have nothing better to do than to hang out here. A streamer of plastic flags representing many countries lined the inside of the dining room that inspired my daughter to try so hard to guess their appropriate nationalities.

Ruth ordered a hamburger without lettuce or tomato and with a side order of fries and a soda, there was no surprise there. The hamburger was larger than I expected and I was sure that it was beyond her ability to consume in one sitting. I should have known better. She devoured the meal as if it were the last meal she would ever have. My growing girl often had a ravenous appetite and a high body metabolism. She could eat all day and not gain a pound. My metabolism used to be the same, until I hit thirty. Now I had to watch what I ate and go to the gym three times a week just to hope that I hadn't gained anything.

After lunch my wife and Ruth dropped into a small country store to pick up some snacks for the road while I went to go look for gas. I had been told by the cashier from our exceptional restaurant that there was a gas station just around the corner. Where this had proven to be accurate, she had neglected to mention the fact that it was no longer in business and by the looks of things that it had been for quite some time. The gas pumps weren't even on the premises anymore and weeds were growing through the cracks of their driveway. I was glad she didn't tell me where the bathrooms were, who knew where that would have taken me and what state of affairs they would be in.

Since this was the end of town and no further gas station would be found until we reached Kings Beach, I had to turn around and find a gas station that we had passed earlier upon our entry. My investigation for gas brought me all the way back to the beginning of town where I found the cheapest fuel available, and that wasn't saying much. The remote location of this town had driven up the price and I figured that it cost more in fuel to get the gas tankers up here to deliver the fuel in the first place. Eggs might be cheaper in the country, but gas sure wasn't.

The station wouldn't accept my card. Of all the places to not have my card be accepted, this was it. With a sigh of frustration I continued my search, found the second lowest price, filled up, and went back to the other side of town where I had dropped off my family.

I was sure that they would be waiting for me after all of my sidetracked adventures but Ruth had to return back to the restaurant for another bathroom break before returning to the store. Even then, it took twice as long to pick up snacks for the road with Ruth in tow since she automatically vetoed anything she didn't want without a constructive criticism about what she did want. I was starting to wonder if I had the better end of the deal getting gas then the task of getting snacks.

We continued to pass by small towns and even passed by one that I'm sure only had a population of only twenty and as we drove passed the small shed-like structure that could have been some country store, I was sure that the entire population was sitting outside. It was straight out of one of those horror movies where the family goes on vacation and is harassed by a small town until they disappear into the woods and are never seen again. I've watched too many horror movies and read too many books by my favorite horror author. I vowed to cut back on these once I returned home as I drove on deeper into the very woods that I was still sure that I would never come back from or be heard from ever again.

After Quincy I realized that we were now entering an area that was mostly devoid of civilization. Any accidents or incidents or blown tires or being out of gas out here would have to wait for quite some time before any help would arrive. I wasn't even sure if we had coverage on our cell phones out here. It would be a long hike back to any form of help, and I sure didn't want to stop at that last small town of twenty people. I also didn't want to stop at the "helpful" woman at the register that had told me about the gas station. I was sure that she would only direct me to yet another derelict and out of business building. No, it would be better to not have any accidents.

I let my mind settle back into the rhythm of the scenery. The trees were all the same shape and size and color and were neatly lined parallel to the highway as if someone had planted them just so. The forest was thick and nearly impossible to see into and quite honestly, it was boring. The scenery didn't change. The side roads promised great sights of waterfalls and dazzling views from high cliff view points. However, neither of these was on our route.

The road rose and fell on small hills that continued to rise in altitude. Our road was basically deserted and we had the entire trip to ourselves. All I had to do was set the van on cruise control and this set of roads would basically take us to where we wanted to go. That was until I came over the next rise.

The large logging truck took up the majority of the lane and the view ahead of us. The driver's load was full of thick de-branched tree trunks that seemed to be a larger load than the metal frames that were trying to keep it all in place, the kind of logging truck I was familiar with in the back roads along the northern portion of the Olympic National Forest. A big red flag was attached to the back of one of the logs signaling their presence from drivers who had problems in depth perception. Actually it was for drivers who were looking directly at the extended load who might have problems determining how far it was ahead of them.

It seemed to me that the trucker was out having a Sunday drive. He was easily going ten miles an hour under the speed limit out here. At first I thought that he was having an "end of world syndrome". This was a condition that my wife and I made up for drivers who slowed down to an almost crawl simply because their visibility wasn't as great as it was when they were driving on a straight flat road. This could either be for a bend around a corner or going up a slight incline. We understood that cars and trucks would, and should, slow down a little bit, but what we referred to were those that almost stopped. This was that guy.

However, once I realized that there weren't any hills or curves on this stretch of the road, I understood that he was simply enjoying himself at the expense of others, namely us. I was also sure that once the driver saw me in his side view mirror he decided to slow down even further.

"Just go around him."

The voice came from my right. My wife was vocalizing the very thought in the back of my mind. Neither of us wanted to view the back side of this oversized rig for the rest of the voyage.

I turned on my signal, checked my mirrors and blind spots and went to pull into the oncoming lane to pass the truck. My foot went down on the pedal and I could hear the roar of my v6 engine revved up.

As I went into the other lane to pass the truck, the truck swerved over and cut me off. I had to quickly turn back into my own lane just to avoid him as his trailer and his load flew just in front of our van.

"That jerk," My wife stated. Her tone was full of anger and stress, of fear and anxiety.

Actually she didn't say that. What she really did say was a few choice words, or colorful metaphors as it were, few of which I would have taken the liberty of enunciating myself if it wasn't for the presence of my daughter in the back. She had already demonstrated that she could hear quite well even with the headphones on and had also demonstrated a talent of repeating said choice words.

"Mom! I heard that!" The exclamation from the back of the car had only validated my suspicions that my daughter was fully capable of hearing anything and everything we said.

I fell back into the slow pace behind the tail end of the truck so we could all collect our emotions. All three of us were a little nerve wracked and frustrated. I wondered how long help would come if the truck did run us off the road.

Once I had calmed down, I made sure I was clear again and was just about to move over when we went into a turn. The single dashed line had become a solid line with a dash and our visibility around the corner had been greatly diminished. I eagerly awaited the next opportunity then went to go around him again.

Another curve came upon us and we weren't able to pass in time. Again I fell back behind the truck. This had happened a couple more times with a couple of hills, a few more curves and then a few missed opportunities as cars were coming in the opposite direction. It seemed that I was destined to be cursed behind the backside of this logging truck until some time that it decided to take a side road or worse yet, until we reached our destination of Kings Beach. All I could think about was the saying "the view from the second elephant never changes."

Then I saw my luck change. The road up ahead was flat and there would be no curves or hills for a long time. There weren't any oncoming traffic and I was ready to make my move. This time, I was going to outsmart the driver ahead of us. Two can play these kind of games, and although his rig was much bigger than mine, I was sure that I was a lot smarter than he was.

If my plan was to work, I had to do a series of events in quick succession and I had to do what he expected least. That is exactly what I did. I slowed down.

As expected, his rig pulled way up ahead of us before he even noticed that I had fallen behind. Once he did notice, and I can only assume that it was a man driving, he slowed down as well. As a matter of fact he slowed down so much that we immediately caught up to him.

I pulled the wheel to my right, toward the shoulder and started to speed up. This caught the rig off guard and immediately he swerved to his right. The sudden turn of his wheel had flung the overloaded weight dangerously close to going over the shoulder and into the rocky terrain full of short evergreens. One wrong move and his truck would tip.

"What are you doing?!" The protest came from my right. "You can't pass on the right! You shouldn't be driving on the shoulder!"

"Daddy!" Another protest was issued forth, this time from the back.

I did my best to ignore the panicked protests from my side passenger and back seat passenger drivers. I had a plan, darn it, and I was going to utilize it. This was only half of my idea and it was based on the hope that the driver in front of me was good enough to keep his rig on the road. If he went over then our car, doing the speed that it was at such a close distance, would find it and us impaled upon his load of trees.

My assumption had proved to be accurate. His tires squealed, his truck slightly tipped, and rocks shot up from behind him spattering our windshield, but he didn't lose control. Now was the time to make my next move.

I immediately turned the wheel to my left, slipped into the oncoming traffic lane and gunned my engine. My foot went straight to ground. My van's powerful v6 was starting to work in overdrive as the engine started to whine. We had slowed down to about thirty miles an hour before my little diversion. Now I was watching as the speedometer was climbing. The needle was going higher and higher. We were doing forty, fifty, sixty, seventy, and then seventy five.

I could feel the van start to waver. At this speed, with this much mass, the slightest movement on the wheel was causing our van to over steer. I had to keep control of our vehicle at this speed or the resulting accident would be fatal.

The rig pulled back onto the road just as we were about to pass. We could hear him blow his horn out of protest as his truck started to accelerate. He was bound and determined to not let us pass. Yet, despite his desire, and despite the power of his engine, his truck was not responding as our van was. His huge truck and large payload was slowing his truck down. We had faster acceleration. All it would take was a few more seconds and I would be able to get back into our lane.

The rig moved faster and faster, making it harder for us to pass him. My acceleration continued to climb. It moved to eighty then eighty five. We were going to make it.

The oncoming car brought me out of my focus. We were going too fast and there was nothing we could do. I couldn't swerve back into my lane with the big truck in my way and I couldn't slow down enough to let the truck pass so I could get over. There just wasn't enough time. There was only one option left.

I continued to gun the engine and prayed for the best. My speedometer continued to climb as I blew passed the logging truck. With one quick movement of the wheel I maneuvered our van back into our lane, cutting off the logging truck and just missing the oncoming car.

Both the truck and the car blew their horns in protest at the near collision.

My heart was racing and I'm sure so was my wife's and Ruth's. No one said a word. Everyone was completely scared stiff. Ruth had even taken off her headphones and I could tell she was terrified and on the verge of crying. A quick look to my right confirmed the same from my wife.

I looked into the rearview mirror and watched as the truck fell back from view. He had slowed down to his usual pace and our momentum carried us further and further away from the prideful, arrogant, road raged, road terrorist that tried to run us off the highway.

My foot came off the pedal as soon as I was sure that I had put ample distance between us and the terror truck from hell. The last thing I wanted was for the rig to slowly creep up on us during our trip and deciding to finish his task of prematurely ending our vacation. With any luck, he would take a side road and this would be the last I ever saw of him.

We settled back into a routine again, trying to put the nightmare behind us, not just physically, but emotionally as well. No words were said, none had to be. It would be a smooth drive from here to…

The little girl came out of nowhere.

There wasn't a town, a city, or a walkway. There wasn't a sidewalk, a house, a school or anything out here that would constitute the presence of a little girl.

Yet, there she was, standing in the middle of my lane. She wasn't just in the middle of the road where traffic would be able to miss her; she was standing in the middle of my lane, directly in my path. My course, with the mass of our van and the speed that is was going; we would plow down anyone and anything. The little girl would be dead before her body hit the ground.

However, this wasn't just any little girl. This was the same little girl I saw back in Oregon along the Umpqua Blood River Styx. What was she doing here? Was she just a figment of my imagination? Did I transpose the girl's image onto someone who was actually there? Was there anyone there at all?

I turned the wheel frantically to my left, into the opposing oncoming traffic lane. If I had turned to my right I would have gone off the road and into the very solid and unforgiving trees that paralleled the highway. I would have endangered my entire family.

My quick reflexes were able to maneuver our van away from the pending disaster. The little girl was missed, but only just barely. She hadn't moved, hadn't run and hadn't reacted and I'm glad she didn't. If she had decided to turn to her right, that was my left, then she would have run into wrong side of the street. My desperate attempt at missing her would have been in vain. I would have done the unthinkable and would still have plowed her down.

My over steering to my left sent the van into a tail spin. I had lost control and we started to veer too much to the left. We were heading straight for the trees on the other side of the highway at a dangerous and fatal speed.

I cranked the wheel to my right as soon as I thought I had cleared the girl and did my best to get back into my lane, away from the forest barrier and away from any possible oncoming cars. I ended up over steering again out of my panic. The van started to spin out of control in the opposite direction. The wheels squealed as we slid sideways across the road. Our tail end of the van spun completely around, leaving us backwards, facing the direction we had just come from. Our course left skid marks in an arched semi-circle from one side of the road to another. Our sideways and backwards skid brought the van going back toward the forest I initially wanted to avoid.

Frantically I tried to correct my steering while traveling backwards while trying to apply the brake. If I slapped the brakes on too hard then our momentum would continue our flight sideways and we would tip over.

We came to a sudden stop, just over the shoulder of the road. The back of our van had hit a small tree and had snapped it in half, knocking it over. The softer dirt of the shoulder had done what I didn't want my brakes to do. The stop was too quick. Our weight shifted and the top of our van continued to move while the base of our van was at a dead stop. We were tipping over sideways.

There were several screams echoing in the van as panic turned to sheer terror. I could feel the weight of our luggage shift; I could feel our body weight sift. We were going to go over.

Suddenly the van shifted back the other way, wobbled and came to a stop. We sat there for a moment as if trying to capture the reality of what just had happened. Then I started to hear crying. My daughter had just had enough and her tears started to flow.

However, my mind wasn't on my daughter, who was shaken but not physically hurt. Her comfort could wait a moment or be taken care by my wife. My mind had shifted to the only individual that could have been hurt.

My sight took in the scene of the road ahead of us, the road we had just come from. My eyes darted from one side of the highway to another. I had expected to see the girl still standing there. I had expected to see the girl huddled on the ground crying in fear and horror. I had expected to see her dead body lying motionless. I had expected to see her blood pooling on the highway.

She was gone.

She wasn't just dead. She simply was no longer standing where she had been. The "Little House on the Prairie" girl from Oregon, the little girl I had almost hit, was nowhere to be found. She had vanished into thin air.

I got out of my van and slowly walked toward where the girl had been. Had my van hit her and thrown her body into the forest? Was she dead? Was she wounded? I continued to scan the area for any sign of her with mixed emotions. A part of me wanted to find her, wanted to ensure that I hadn't dreamt her up, imagined her. The other part of me was scared of what I would find. I did not want to find a dead girl with her skull bashed in and her body crumbled, shattered by the force of my van.

I couldn't find her and I didn't know what to think about that. There was no body, no blood, and no form of evidence of any kind that she had been there in the first place.

There was a scent of fire in the air. At first I thought that it was just the burned rubber left behind by my wheels. I would probably need a whole new set of tires after this vacation. However, there wasn't a burnt rubber smell; it was more a forest fire, though not the same. There was something familiar about this and it was associated with the little girl.

My eyes went back to my van. I could see my daughter huddling close to her mom, being comforted from our nightmare. They were both scared. My wife had given me the look as if asking "Was everything alright? Did we hit her? Can you find her?" I only answered with a shrug of confusion.

The logging truck came over the ridge behind me without notice and came barreling toward me as I stood in the middle of the road. I didn't hear it coming. The ridge had hidden its form. Nothing had given it evidence of its presence except the wide eyed panicked look from my family. It's engines revved up as it got a fix on me and the rig directed its trajectory to ensure that it would run me over and do to me what I had thought I had done to the little girl.

I dove frantically toward the forest, trying to get myself off of the road as quickly as I could. The same logging truck, the same maniac driver from earlier down the highway, was now trying to run me over. My nightmare wasn't over with this rig.

My body hit a tree, bounced off and slid into the brown grassy underbrush. My ribs felt bruised and it hurt to breathe. I was sure that my shoulder hit a large rock and I would be lucky if it wasn't dislocated. But my thoughts didn't go to my banged up and bruised body. It wasn't concerned about the pain that was coursing through my ribs and shoulder. My thoughts, my fears and my terror went out to my family. I was safe on the inside of the tree line and as the truck passed me, I knew that there was no way that it could turn to try to run me down again, it was too far ahead and couldn't make such a sharp turn. However, my family couldn't say the same. The vindictive driver was making a beeline straight for my van, my vehicle that currently had my family huddled together in horror and fear.

I could only watch in terror as it sped up, even faster toward my wife and daughter. Rocks and dust kick into my eyes as I looked on. My screams, my pleas went unanswered and unheard over the roar of the beast that was passing me by to find some other, easier prey. I prayed that they would get out in time but knew that they couldn't.

With the knowledge set in my heart and mind that there was nothing else I could do, I looked for the side mirror. I needed to look into the face of the man, the beast, the horrible being that would run down my family as they were trapped and helpless. I would etch his facial features into my mind; I would remember him and hunt him down for the rest of my life. I wouldn't rest until I found him. And I would find him and I would hurt him over and over again and again until he begged for death. Then, and only then, would I leave his body to rot, or perhaps I would leave it to be eaten alive by whatever predator was out here. Perhaps a pack of wolves, a few birds of prey, or perhaps even a bear would eat whatever was left of him while he was still alive.

I expected to see some crazed redneck. I expected to see some backwater, half scarred, half insane poor excuse of a human being. I expected a dirty faced, buck toothed, cross eyed, inbreed with a red bandana, a ripped t-top that stated "I eat my road kill", and a dead squirrel hanging from his rearview mirror. What I got was something worse, far worse.

There was no one in the driver seat. There was no one in the cab at all. For one moment, for one clear and perfect moment when his side view mirror lined unobstructed with my vision and I could see the entirety of the cab, including the steering wheel, I could tell that no one was driving the rig.

The truck continued its deadly course straight on. My heart stopped. My breathing stopped. I wish I could turn away from the horrible scene that was about to play out before me, but I couldn't. I screamed out one more time.

The truck blew past my vehicle, past my family with only inches to spare. The van swayed from the displaced force of the truck as it blew its horn out of contempt for those of us who had dared to pass it on the road.

Chapter: Gold Lake Highway

"*L*et's take this Gold Lake Highway turn off."

My wife's unsteady and weary voice had cut through the silence like a hot knife through butter. Nothing had been said since the truck incident. There had been a few sobs from the back seat, but no one had said a word. I hadn't even mentioned that there wasn't even a driver. Both my wife and Ruth were still in too much shock and I doubted that they would have believed me anyway.

"It's a side highway," she continued. "We'll be able to get off of this road, avoid any more crazy drivers and shorten our route."

My wife was more than eager to get to Lake Tahoe as quickly as possible and I couldn't blame her. I was all for this decision. The quicker we got off this highway of hell, of ghosts, the better. I looked for the junction of Gold Lake Highway, which proved to be closer than I had thought, and turned to go down our alternate route.

The scenery slightly changed. There was more evidence of mountainous terrain here. We were no longer skirting around the mountain peaks, we were cutting through the middle of them. The tree line often gave way to cliff faces. Large boulders periodically replaced trees.

This was a great idea. There were more curves in the road here. Unless any logging truck was making a direct stop along this route, there wouldn't be a need to travel on it. The highway we were just on made a better straight shot. That highway allowed trucks and cars to travel at incredible speeds, here, that would be impossible. We were in for a slower drive and that was just fine by me.

We moved with the contours of the road. The change in scenery was a welcome sight. Each turn, each bend, was a new sight unlike the mesmerizing, fairly straight highway we just came off of. Our nerves were starting to calm and I would be able to drive like this all the way until it matched back up with our initial highway. That was until I rounded the next corner.

Brake lights caught my attention and I slowed down to a stop. The car ahead of me was stopped in back of the car ahead of him and likewise for the next several cars. All of their lights were off, their engines were no longer running and the one ahead of me just started to shut off his car. This wasn't a traffic jam, it was a long wait and from the looks of things the people held up had already been delayed for quite some time and it was probably going to be an even longer wait until they got moving again.

I shut off my car and gave my wife one of those looks that I should have known better than to give. After all, it was her idea to take this road. I instantly regretted it.

"Don't give me that look," she said with a slight snappish tone. "I had no idea that we would be stopping on this road."

I wanted to comment on her "smart phone" and how it probably would have helped to tell us that there was construction or a roadblock or a landslide or an accident or whatever it was that was holding us up. However, despite my bad habit of just blurting out the first thing that came to mind, I wisely decided against it.

Her tone calmed down a bit "Consider it part of the adventure. Why don't you get out and see what the holdup is all about?"

Tempers were threatening to run high and she had a point. The long trip and the stress of the near accidents were wearing thin on all of us. It was best to take a walk and take a breath of fresh air.

The air was, in fact fresh. I hadn't realized how stuffy the van had been until I stepped outside. There was a hint of sweetness on the light gentle wind that blew through the area, as if a patch of nearby flowers was in bloom. The air was crisp and clear and reminded me of one of those picture-perfect spring days after being cooped up in the house all winter.

There were other drivers and passengers who had gotten out of their cars as well and were walking about. Some had stayed with their families; others were talking to various drivers while a few had made their way toward the front of the line.

As I continued my walk along the side of the highway, passing stopped cars and drivers in conversations, I was able to see what the holdup was about. Apparently this stretch of highway was having its annual road repair.

My wife had frequently reminded me during this trip about how this area is often filled with snow and that Lake Tahoe and the surrounding area was known for its ski resorts during the winter season when the snow drifts can be quite large. It was difficult to image at this point in time the amount of snow and ice she had referred had to, and yet here was the proof. The harsh winters were tearing up the asphalt, destroying the road and it was time to repair them.

Up ahead I saw a construction crew laying down new street material on the highway. One large orange odd looking truck was spewing black tar gunk on the roadway while construction workers were smoothing it out. A steam roller was closer to me, flattening areas that the workers had already smoothed out. Another large orange construction truck was tearing up the road further ahead, at least what was left of it after the potholes from the harsh winter weather had claimed it.

From here the scent had changed. Hot tar and asphalt filled the air while dust and dirt was being kicked up. The smell of diesel and hot grease also filled the air; so much for my picture perfect spring day.

The whole scene reminded me of when I had those Tonka Trucks when I was a young kid. I'm sure every young boy my age had them. They were a set of construction trucks that were nearly indestructible and were a great part of my imaginary fun growing up. Now, I was able to watch them full size and it wasn't fun at all. My mind shifted to when I was young and I would push the trucks over small cliffs. A smile came across my mind as I could imagine being big enough that my massive paw could easily push these trucks over to allow access to our final destination.

The work had taken up one lane and the oncoming traffic was taking up the other. Several working crew and flaggers dressed in orange vests were directing the flow of traffic on the only one way lane. We were going to have to wait until the backed up traffic on the other side of the road repair had passed and then the coordination between the workers to move the trucks had transpired before we were able to make any progress.

The thought of turning my van around and heading back toward our initial highway was quickly dashed aside. There was already a line behind my vehicle and there was no room to back up to turn around. On top of that, the oncoming traffic was thick due to the line of cars that had formed on the other side of the road repair. Even if I could back up and turn around, the wait to get into the traffic wouldn't be worth it.

I felt tension start to rise again. No, I couldn't let it get to me. We were on vacation; this was supposed to be stress free, a time to relax. I let myself start to get lost in the warmth of the sun, the sound of the birds and the scent of the fresh air, despite the sound of the large trucks and the smell of freshly laid road and the carbon dioxide exhaust from the massive trucks.

"Alright everyone, back in your cars. The road is just about clear."

The announcement broke my reverie and finally brought the sigh of relief I was desperately attempting to find. The walk back to my car brought a smile from my wife as she understood that we would finally be on our way.

I got back into my car and waited for my turn to turn on my engine. I could see the various cars ahead of us start to turn on theirs and there was no need to do so until we were ready. As I waited, I watched one of the female flaggers start making her way down the line of cars making sure they were well instructed on how to follow the car in front of them. Actually I'm sure she was bored to death, standing out here in the middle of nowhere holding a flag all day long and she was looking for something more important to do or at least give her the impression that she was doing something more important. We all knew how to follow the car in front us and really didn't need instructions for that.

I started my car on cue, rolled down my window and turned to face the woman to listen to the instructions that she had given everyone else before me. I promised myself to nod my head while I half listened. After being married for seventeen years I've had ample practice at this and I was sure that I would execute my usual academy award winning performance.

I nearly screamed in terror. In place of the fairly attractive woman that was leaning into my car through my rolled down window, I now came face to face with a horror beyond which my sanity could handle. The horrible monster of undead and putrid mass was no more than a rotting corpse. Its face was half falling off, barely held together by its exposed sinew and half disintegrated muscle. Bone could be seen under the morbid and hideous features. Flesh was blackened by a horrific fire that must have destroyed its original form. One of its eyes was missing and the other seemed puss swollen and soulless. Its hair had been fallen out in patches; and what was left of it was wisps of ashen yellow.

"Honey? What's wrong"

The sound to my right snapped me out of my panic and reminded me that there were others in the van with me. I jerked my head to my right to say something, but only got a blank look of confusion back at me. Didn't she see the creature that was right there, just inches from me? I turned back, remembering that the creature could have taken my head off.

"Anything wrong sir?"

The horrid creature was gone. Before me was the construction worker I had seen earlier. Stress from earlier today had placed the terrible nightmare on top of a regular person. I was seeing things. There was a definite need to get to Lake Tahoe, post haste and relax.

"No, nothing," I lied. Of course I lied. How could I tell her "I'm pretty sure that you were some undead zombie come to eat my brains and suck out my soul?"

"Looks like the roads are clear," she stated pointing toward the line of cars ahead of me that were already being flagged forward. "Just follow them and you'll be fine."

'No I won't,' I thought to myself. 'I won't be fine. It's out there, the thing that's making me see ghosts and undead, the thing that is coming closer each day is out there.'

I took several deep breaths. If I wasn't careful I would have a panic attack. Please let there be no more ghosts haunting me, no more death following me, no more blood rivers with their putrid and disgusting sights and smells, no more zombies to come eat my brains and suck out my soul, and no more empty trucks driving on their own trying to run me and my family off the road. It was time for peace and relaxation on the beach. I pulled my van behind the line of cars and followed them.

We followed this stretch of road until it got us back onto the highway. From there we continued to pass small towns such as Clio, and Sierraville and others so small that they weren't even on our map. Usually the only evidence that these towns existed was a sign pointing off to some side road that disappeared further into the dense mountainous forest and off into parts unknown. It was to my relief that Ruth didn't have to use the bathroom as we passed by these signs. I had enough of this highway and I was sure that everyone else did as well. The quicker we got to Kings Beach the better.

Chapter: Kings Beach

"*W*elcome to Kings Beach"

The sign was a welcome sight for sore eyes and promptly changed the nagging questions of "Are we there yet?" and "How much further?" that we had to endure for the last few miles from the back seat, to the cheerful, ear piercing, glass shattering cry of glee that would keep my ears ringing for the next several days. Of course Ruth had another set of questions that rattled off like a barrage of machine gun fire.

"Can we hurry up? I've got to use the bathroom."

"What does our cabin look like?"

"What color is our cabin? Do they have pink? Can we ask for a pink one? No, wait, make it purple."

"Do they have a pool?"

"Do you think there will be any kids?"

"Will there be any puppies?"

"Do they have anyplace good to eat here? I'm hungry."

Again Ruth was talking fast like she usually does when she gets excited. I'm not sure if she truly expected an answer to any of her questions since they all seemed to run together and there was no way of answering any of them fast enough. I was planning on ignoring them since I was sure that she would quickly forget that she had even asked them. However, one comment caught my attention and for two different reasons.

'Anyplace good to eat' from Ruth meant a drive through fast food place that would serve a hamburger without lettuce or tomato and a side order of fries and, if she could pull it off, a small Oreo flavored shake. It was one of those places that we were doing our best to avoid. There were enough of those places where we lived, we were on vacation and we were here to experience new and exciting things. The second reason that her comment caught my attention was her desire to eat.

'Hungry?' I asked myself. 'I thought we brought a bag of ...'

"Why don't you have a snack?" My wife asked Ruth as if half reading my mind. "We still have to find our hotel, check in and unpack. It's going to be a little while until dinner."

I would have closed my eyes in frustration knowing the comment that was coming next except that I was driving and didn't dare do so. Ruth's announcement confirmed my suspicions.

"I ate them already."

"WHAT?!" My wife had turned to our teenage daughter with surprise. "All of it? You ate all of the snacks? That was supposed to last us until ..." She simply couldn't finish her sentence.

My wife turned back around and muttered a few things under her breath. Fortunately Ruth took the hint and didn't say another word knowing full well that she had pushed her mom to near the breaking point.

Kings Beach sat on the intersection of Highway 267 and Highway 28 and seemed to me that it was only a couple of blocks wide. The back side of the town, where we came from, butted up against the rocky terrain of the mountains while the front of the town faced Lake Tahoe. However, what the town lacked in width it made up in length. The town snaked around the north end of Lake Tahoe from Tahoe Vista to Crystal Bay. There was no place for this town to grow.

We took a right and my wife navigated us through the town as she brought forth one of her maps and the motel reservations. I was glad she was keeping an eye out for our place of stay since I was keeping an eye on the road. It seemed that the Gold Lake Highway wasn't the only stretch of road under its annual road repair. There were orange cones everywhere redirecting traffic around various potholes and repaving projects. My eyes were darting from one lane change to another. Then there were the people. Construction crew were cutting in front of us constantly while pedestrians were looking for places to cross since their sidewalks were dug up and their crosswalks were blocked. Other cars were just as confused as we were and I had to keep an eye out for merging traffic.

"It should be around the next bend," my wife said. "No wait, the next bend. No, wait, there it is."

Of course once I saw where she was pointing, I had already driven past it. In my defense, the hotel didn't make their sign visible enough and there were too many distractions. Never the less I had to find a place to turn around, slog through traffic and construction again and then wait for a break in the oncoming vehicles before crossing the highway and driving to our motel.

Our hotel was on the north side of the highway, across the road from the lake. We wouldn't be having a lakeside view, but I suspect that those motels that did were twice as expensive as the one we were getting. However, what our motel did have was an old rustic feel. It was surrounded by the alpine pines on either side of it with the mountains behind it. The rooms were all on one story and were connected a few to each building with several buildings. This gave the feeling of having a rustic duplex condo with a log cabin atmosphere instead of a motel room.

To complete the rustic cabin feel, there was a sign that stated "Do not feed the bears." At first I thought that it was kind of funny and played along well with the staging of the motel. That was until I saw the dumpster. It was specially designed to only be opened if one pushed on a certain lever to unlock it, a technique used to keep out bears that aren't capable of such a feat. The sign was serious.

"Wouldn't it be cool if we saw a bear? Bear cubs are so cute. Can we see a bear cub?" The questions came from my daughter as she caught sight of the sign.

No, no it wouldn't be cool. I've already experienced what it was like to stand between people and their morning coffee; I definitely didn't want to stand between a bear and its desire to get to food. On top of that, any mother bear would be very protective of any cubs it might have. As far as I was concerned, any bears in this area could just stay away.

Upon registration we were told that the pool was too cold to swim in, but we had access to their bikes if we wanted to cruise up and down the bike lane to travel to the various towns along this part of Lake Tahoe, the very bike lane that was being torn up by the construction workers and heavy machinery. We were also told that we could use their kayak and take it out on the lake if we wanted to. This was very appealing.

Our room had two queen size beds and a kitchenette with fridge and stove. It really did feel more like our own condo than any motel or even luxury hotel that I've ever been in. This was going to be nice.

I started to unpack as my wife started to organize our gear in the room. I hauled in food; she put it away in the fridge. I brought in our bags; she put them in the drawers. I brought in the camera, laptop, and then went to look around for help with rest and realized that Ruth had only carried her in her IPod or whatever device she had connected to the headphones that she had yet to take off and had promptly made her way to relax on one of the beds immediately tuning everyone else out. For a girl that was hungry, she had made no attempt to speed up the process that would allow us to get to our food faster.

After unpacking we went in search of a nice restaurant. This wasn't as easy as we first thought. There were small cafes that we immediately discarded, pizza places that were in abundance similar to those in the Seattle area, fast food places that we were avoiding, a couple of Mexican places that only duplicated what we had for lunch and then a few very expensive restaurants that were clearly out of our budget and we had nothing appropriate to wear even if we were to splurge.

"Let try that seafood restaurant," my wife proclaimed as she found something on the opposite side of the street. As with the motel, I had passed the place she had pointed to.

It took some time to find a place to turn around and come back to the restaurant only to find that the 'what little parking' was available due to the construction in the area, had already been taken by others who were also desperately trying to find a place to park. Perhaps those bikes back at the motel were a good idea after all. I ended up circling around again before finding a place to park two blocks away.

However, this proved to be more advantageous than I initially thought. The air was warm from the summer day and the evening offered a slight breeze that kept it cool. We could hear the water softly lap against the shore. The air was fresh and clear. The moon was coming up and its reflection could be seen upon the serene view of the lake.

I turned my attention to my wife and gave a smile. This was the vacation that we were looking for. I slipped my hand into hers as we strolled along the walkway.

Upon our arrival at the restaurant my wife went toward the front door and stopped to look at the menu that was posted. Suddenly she frowned and shook her head.

"It's far too expensive," she said with a bit of stress in her voice.

I could tell that she was being pushed beyond her ability to tolerate. She had planned this vacation out for us and everything was starting to fall apart. I gave her a comforting embrace. We turned to leave when suddenly she spotted it.

"Let's try there."

My wife had found a sandwich board on the other side of the driveway. It had been hidden by the shadows of the evening and would have gone unnoticed even during the day with the amount of cars parked in the lot. The sign advertised a barbeque restaurant that had just recently opened. The place had taken over the lower part of another building and was facing the lake so the general public would have passed it by without a second thought.

"But this isn't where I want to eat. I want…"

My daughter's complaint was suddenly and immediately cut off by a sharp, stern look from my wife. Ruth knew that she was in hot water already and now was not the time to push her own agenda. My daughter gave a solemn, sulking look of disapproval but followed us to the restaurant. At this point I really didn't care if she ordered anything or not. She could sit in the restaurant with her headphones on and be pouty all she wanted but this was where we were going to eat.

The restaurant was perfect. It was within our budgeted price range, served wonderful food and offered a great atmosphere. The view over the lake was divine. The lights from the city on the other side of the water and from the boats that were bobbing in the waves and the reflection from the stars in the sky sparkled like diamonds on the water.

I had ordered ribs which were to die for. The meat practically fell off the bones. Ruth actually ended up enjoying her meal and waited patiently until my wife and I couldn't finish ours before asking to complete those as well.

We went for an evening stroll along the shore in front of the restaurant after our meal much to my daughter's disappointment and embarrassment. She merely hung back and put on her headphones while my wife and I walked hand in hand along the beach. Despite everything that had happened, the most important thing was that we were seeing this through together. This was our vacation and we were going to enjoy it.

Back at the motel, my wife wanted to watch a little TV while Ruth enjoyed her music. Neither had appealed to me so I started a casual walk around the motel grounds, being mindful of bears. The layout still felt more like a state park and the brisk walk would give me inspiration for my next novel.

"Hello."

The voice broke my reverie and almost startled me. It was a female's voice that came from behind me and from the sound of it I could tell that it wasn't just a simple greeting. She had a calm, cool, sexy voice with an almost "come hither" tone.

I had to remember where I was. I wasn't too far from Nevada where "companions" were legal. It wouldn't take much for that business to travel over here into California, especially since this was a large tourist attraction. I turned to respectfully turn her down and tell her that I wasn't interested.

"Look, miss…"

"Madam."

'Madam?' I thought. Now I was sure that my suspicions were correct. My eyes took in her form. It was difficult to make out her exact features but she had long dark hair pulled back tight giving her an almost stern look and was dressed in some early 1900 black dress. It was one of those full length ones that covered her from neck to wrist to the ground. It wasn't very attractive or flattering. There was either one of those conventions in town where everyone dresses up in certain types of clothing or this was her choice of "attire". Whatever turned her on I guess.

"Madam Julia Bulette," she stated as she extended her hand.

"I'm happily married. No thank you." There was neither a stutter nor hint of desire in my voice. Perhaps if she were prettier or even dressed nicer I might have had a stutter, though my answer would have still been the same, it still would have been "No thank you". I was, in fact, a happily married man devoted to a happily married woman.

"She could join us," she said as she reached for my hand.

I pulled away and went to make a step backward. Suddenly she moved quicker than I thought possible. Her hand grabbed a hold of mine with a vice-like grip.

"You need to come with me now!" She said demandingly. This wasn't in a sexy voice or a dominatrix voice. Instead it was in an almost pleading but definite urgent and life threatening tone.

Now it was getting awkward. Now I was going to have to be firm but not yet rude, and I was going to be, except something caught my attention. It was something odd and beyond my understanding.

She was cold, ice cold. And it wasn't just the touch of her hand as if she had been out in snow or some other frigid environment for far too long, it was as if my soul had been chilled to its core being. Something had stepped on my grave or something had died and was reaching for my soul. Whatever it was, this wasn't right. It wasn't just her coldness that caught my attention; it was a numbing sensation that was overwhelming me, paralyzing me, gripping me in fear. I could barely move and I couldn't speak. I couldn't resist the deathly sensation washing over me. My soul was being consumed, or eaten, or something.

Her features started to change. She immediately started to age. Her body went from youthful to old and decrepit. Her face had wrinkles and her skin became paper thin. Her hair started to fall out in patches as it went from dark to light ashen. Muscle withered away and yet her grip remained as strong as ever. The hue of her face went from pinkish in color to blue as if she had been strangled and left for dead.

There was that smell again. It was the smell of a fire, something burning, like a forest fire but slightly different. I could just about smell and taste the smoke, and I could swear I could hear people screaming for help. The heat was starting to build up all around me despite the cold chill running through my body.

I quickly turned my attention toward my surroundings. A part of me was panicking and I simply didn't know what to do. I would have screamed, pushed, fought, or done something, but I couldn't. If only I could get the attention of someone nearby.

There was no one. There would be no one to save me. I could go missing for hours before someone discovered my dead body. I was going to die and there was nothing I could do about it.

I turned back toward the succubus, the hag, the witch, the nightmare, the "whatever" she was, in order to try to plead with her, beg with her. I didn't want to die. I didn't want to leave my wife and child without husband or father.

She wasn't there. She was gone. She had simply vanished as if she had never been there at all.

This was all too much for me. It was time to head back to my room, to my family and make sure that they were alright and then call it quits for the evening.

Chapter: Nightmares

I snuggled closer to my wife as I pulled the sheets over the both of to get cozy. Even if the woman that I had met had been real, had been good looking and hadn't attacked me and hadn't tried to steal or eat my soul, I still wouldn't have gone with her. I was, in fact, happily married and there wasn't anyone or anything that could separate me from my wife.

Actually, although it was still warm from the summer day's sunlight, I was chilled from the touch of the woman that I had run into. It was slowly leaving my system but it still had me freaked out. I hoped that a good night's sleep would be able cure me of such heaviness and I would be my normal self in the morning.

My eyes grew heavy and I fell asleep faster than I had expected. The encounter and the stress had worn me out worse than I had realized.

I woke up and found myself laying face down on my beach towel on the sand. The warmth of the day felt good and it took the chill from the evening before away. I just wanted to lay here and relax, listening to the lap of the water against the shore.

The sudden realization of my location brought me out of my relaxed state and sent me straight in to a panic. I didn't remember how I got here. I looked around.

This was so familiar. At first I couldn't place it but I could have sworn I had been here before. Then it hit me. This was where the undead came after me, this very beach. It was the same dock on my right, the same crystal clear water in front of me, the same bright blue sky and the same mountains in the background. There were even the same boats bobbing up and down slowly to the waves of the lake.

Panic was starting to set in. I knew what was going to happen, I had seen it before and now I was going to see it again. I was trapped in my own nightmare.

The sandy beach around me exploded from the projecting forms that had been waiting just beneath its surface. The creatures were horrid, disgusting figures of rotting and decomposing bodies. Their clothing hung like rags, tattered, burned and torn and barely hanging on to their form. The puss filled beings of flesh and bone, of moldy tissue and exposed muscle and sinew came upon me like a plague from a horrible nightmare, the very nightmare that I was sure that I was cursed and condemned to relive over and over again.

But it wasn't just the presence of these undead that had horrified me. My entire environment had changed. The sky had turned crimson blood red and the water of the lake had reflected the sky. The lake had turned to blood like the River Styx back in Oregon. There was a chill in the air that pierced through my body and attacked my soul with the smell of fire that was carried on the wind.

I screamed, or at least tried to but I was too panicked to have anything come out of my mouth. The horrible, terrible scene before me had me paralyzed. Fear and terror had gripped me beyond my wildest imagination. I had to get out of there.

I found my strength and bolted for my life. The undead, the ghouls, the ghasts, the zombies, the horrible lifeless corpses, the "whatever" they were, were after me. I could feel their horrid, deathly breath upon my body; I could smell their stench of death and decay that filled the air.

My feet beat against the sand as quickly as my legs could carry me. I had to get out of there. I had to find my way back to my family and make sure that they were safe.

My route carried me past the hotel that was sitting on the beach on this side of the highway and onto the stretch of road that separated my family from me that I was sure was back at the motel on the other side. I had figured that if I could keep the undead behind me and keep myself moving, then I would be able to keep ahead of them. I was wrong.

More of these undead forms, these grossly deformed and rotting corpses rounded the corner of the building from my right and others came from down the road on my left. There was an army of these decomposing entities coming at me from all sides.

My eyes tried not to focus on them. I poured on my speed in a desperate attempt to reach safety. Yet, despite my attempt to just focus upon my motel across the street, I could see even more of these festering bodies coming down the highway, filling the full width from one side of the street to the other and from both sides of me. I had to reach my destination, I just had to, or else these undead bloated bodies would eat my soul and drag me to the hell that they came from.

My bare feet slapped against the hard, cold asphalt street. My arms pumped as hard as they could. My heart beat as though it would break through my chest. Sweat was pouring down my forehead and was stinging my eyes. My muscles ached, yet I pushed on, at least I tried to until I heard the sound that froze me dead in my tracks.

The horn blast from my right echoed off of the mountains that lay ahead of me and off of the lake that I had left behind. It had echoed off of the buildings and stores that lined the highway. It echoed through my ears and resonated deep in my soul. I knew this horn blast. It had scared me more than these undead corpses ever had and it scared me now.

My eyes turned to my right to see what I had been afraid might be there. I had to confirm my nightmare. There it was; the logging truck from our trip. It was here barreling down upon me like some horrid predator coming to destroy me.

The truck plowed through the corpse bodies like I had plowed through the swarm of insects back in Oregon. I could hear the crunching of bones as the truck rolled over each one, splintering their mass into goo.

Their entrails splattered across the roadside and all along the truck's tires and along its frame. The road was becoming slick from the morbid scene.

Thump, thump, thump.

Crunch, crunch, crunch.

I was able to look into the cab yet again to confirm what I had seen when I first caught glimpse of the driver. My initial glance had been accurate, there wasn't a driver. The cab was empty; it was without a driver as these corpses were without souls.

Thump, thump, thump.

Crunch, crunch, crunch.

'Move! Move!'

My inner voice was screaming at me. The undead was going to catch me. The truck was going to run me over. I was caught like a deer in the headlights and all I could do was watch as the truck came closer and closer, crushing every corpse in its path. I was going to be next if I didn't…

"Move!"

I jumped to one side just as the truck came screaming past me. I could feel the air disturbance of the truck as it passed me by. Rocks and dirt from the road flew up at me as well as putrid entrails, bone, sinew and flesh from the bodies it had run over. Its horn blew in protest over the fact that it had missed me and I knew that, given a chance, it would turn around and make another pass. It wouldn't miss again. I had to ensure that it couldn't catch me.

The truck had given the corpses a momentary reprieve. Those that had been close to me had been splattered across the road leaving a violent smear of blood and ichor and those that were further behind had to wait until the truck had rolled out of their way. However, now that it was gone, they were able to start up their macabre scene of animated death again.

I laid there on the ground for a moment. There were several new bruises on my body. I wasn't looking forward to finding the massive black and blue areas that they would leave behind, nor was I looking forward to feeling of the aches and pains that would come later. There were also many road rashes that had scraped off skin and embedded rock and gravel deep in my tissue. I wanted to lay there and catch my breath, the very breath that was knocked out of me upon my impact. My head was swimming. Dizziness and nauseous was overcoming me. Yet, none of this could matter right now. I had to keep moving.

'Move.'

'Move.'

"Move!"

Quickly I got back up and ran. My dive had put me closer to the motel and I could see my room from here.

All I had to do was get to my family that I was sure was inside and get them to safety. My body responded to my pleas and got to me to the door. Without hesitation I opened, threw myself inside and…

This wasn't my room. I had no idea where I was, but this wasn't my room. There were no beds, dresser, or kitchenette. There was no family. Instead I was inside a wooden structure. It was a large building that much I could tell. Plaster was on the walls, but a good majority of it had fallen by the wayside. A few of the remaining patches of plaster even had thick wall paper that was peeling and faded from the lapse of time. Cobwebs hung in the corners like peeling flesh and dust seemed to settle on everything that was in my view. The floorboards were exposed and there were small gaps that led to darkness beyond my desire to imagine.

From where I was, there was a long hall in front of me that extended beyond my sight with several doors on each side that led to other rooms. Immediately to my left was a wooden staircase heading up into sights unknown. Its steps and railing looked frail and fragile and threatened to break away at the first sign of any pressure or weight upon them.

The air was stale and musty as if the whole building needed ventilating from a long time ago. I could smell mold and mildew, I could smell the decomposing plaster and the rotting wood, and I could smell cigarette and cigar smoke as well as some other smoke that stirred in the back of my head. Then it struck me, it smelled as if a fire had swept through here. It was the smell of burned wood, ash and of cinder. But it also smelled of humans that had been burned alive. It was disgustingly sweet and morbidly nauseating.

What little light there was had come from the windows of the adjoining rooms. The sunlight cut through the darkness, but with only streams of illumination, just enough to show the dust in the air and was done at angles to cast eerie shadows upon the walls that danced and moved ever so slightly as to look as if some specter or wraith was beyond my sight or just out of the corner of my eye. The darkness beyond these well lit areas only looked that much more ominous and foreboding.

My steps carried me through the hallway, despite the fact that I wanted to run and get out of there. Yet my feet continued one right after another as if they had a mind of their own. I wanted to scream at them.

'No! No! What are you doing?'

I couldn't stop. At least I was here, on this floor, and not on the floor above. There wasn't any way that I was going up those stairs. There was something up there, I knew it. I don't know how I knew it, I just did. I knew that it was something awful and dreadful. I knew that it was worse than the logging truck driver that wasn't there. I knew that it was worse than the "Little House on the Prairie" ghost girl with the burnt dress and soulless eyes. I knew that it was worse than the undead, zombie, puss filled, macabre scene of undead. I knew that it was worse than the river of blood and death, the River Styx. I knew that if I could just stay down here then it wouldn't get me, it couldn't get me. I was safe. Wasn't I?

My bare feet felt the rough grain of the wood and the dust that had gathered. The floor creaked with each step and the sound echoed off of exposed walls and unoccupied chambers. Dust scattered with each step and only danced briefly in the sunbeams before resettling upon the floor once more.

My cries out to my family only echoed back from the darkness and were unanswered. The only sounds were my own voice and creaking of the wooden floor under my feet. Nothing else stirred.

Something moved out of the corner of my eye. It was a shadow, a specter, or just the light playing against the darkness once again, or perhaps it was just my imagination. My imagination could easily run wild in a place like this and I didn't like where it was taking me. My heart started to skip a beat as I stopped in place, scanning my environment wondering what it was that was just beyond my sight. Time came to a standstill. I felt a prickling across my skin. A chill ran down my spine. The only thing I could hear now was the beating of my heart through my ears. It was pounding through my chest as if it wanted to escape and flee from this place.

Something moved again. This time I was sure that that something was there. Something was trying to steal my soul. Something was trying to stalk me and take me to my early grave. Something was trying to kill me.

I ran.

I sprinted as quickly as I could down the hall and toward one of the rooms. If I could find where the door was or even a window then I could get out of this haunted death trap. I burst through one door after another, entering a series of rooms and hallways than only seemed to twist and turn back on each other. I turned again and again, down another hall, into another room, through another chamber and back into another hall I just passed. Fear was overwhelming me. Horror had gripped me. My heart was beating, my mind was racing, sweat was pouring onto my body, and I was in panic mode. Terror had overcome me. The thing was coming for me. I could hear it. I could sense it. It was right behind me. It was...

The stairs leading down appeared before me and I stopped again. These were the stairs that had led up and here I was looking down, down to where I had started. I was staring down at the place where I said I wouldn't go up. Somehow I had gone upstairs. Somehow I had come upon the level where this creature was. It was going to get me.

Fire. I could smell fire again but this time it wasn't residual. This was real fire. This was current fire. The building was on fire. Smoke started to fill the hall. I could feel the heat start to build. I could hear wood start to crackle in a couple of the rooms as the fire was consuming them. I could see the shadows dance from the flames that were in the next chamber. I was caught in a raging inferno. I was going to be burned alive. The thing, the thing was going to burn me alive. It had condemned me to a raging hell of fire and brimstone.

My first thought was to run downstairs again, there would be a door down there. But then I saw it. I saw the thing. The shadowy figure of a man at the bottom of the stairs was looking up at me, staring at me. His deep piercing eyes shot straight in to my soul as if condemning me. I could feel his hatred as if I were the one that had killed him and now he was here, in this hell, and he was going to drag me down with him.

He seemed to be about my height, yet he was long in the torso and thin over all. He reminded me of a scarecrow or of an old time preacher man that stood at pulpits and condemned everyone in their pews with threats of fire and brimstone. I could see that he was holding a leather-bound book in one hand which only helped solidify my later assumption. But the worst features were his haunting and soulless eyes.

I was trapped. The fire behind me was now a raging inferno. I could feel the heat start to suck the oxygen out of the hall. The smoke was starting to fill my lungs. I started to cough and gasp for air, I can't breathe. All of the smoke and heat was rising from downstairs; it would be safer down there. Yet I couldn't go forward, not with him standing at the bottom of the stairs, standing there, daring me to come down and confront him.

I ran to my right toward a room that was off to my side. It had already caught fire and was filling with smoke fast, yet it was my best, and I felt the only, choice I had. I could see a window beyond the flames and from what I could tell, I was only one story above ground.

My body went through the fire that had blocked my way and I could feel the heart beat against me, the flames licking against me, threatening to burn me alive. My arms went in front of my face to protect my eyes but had further blocked my vision since it was already blocked by the fire and smoke. My only hope was to keep on course to the widow that I had put to memory. I braced for an impact hoping it would be the window and not the wall.

The glass and window frame broke all around me. Tiny shards of glass and wood pierced my already sensitive skin from the heat of the flames. Wood beat against my body to add more bruises to my already beaten body. The sudden rush of air fueled the fire behind me and I could feel the rush of flames hit my back.

I fell in a freefall as my body hurled through the air toward the hard ground below. Glass, wood, smoke and fire followed my form though the air. I had twisted in the middle of my flight in hopes of softening the blow of the impact. The scene was almost surreal as I watched everything spewing out of the window in slow motion. Yet, despite the cascading glass and wood, despite the billowing fire and smoke, there was something else that caught my attention. I almost gasped from the sight that I saw.

Silhouetted in' the frame of what was left of the window was the man from the bottom of the stairs. How he got up the stairs that would have failed to support his weight so fast and how he could stand in the middle of the burning, blazing, inferno of a room was beyond me. His body was untouched by the flames that had surrounded him. He was unaffected by the smoke that had encompassed him. He stood there like some vulture looking over its prey that had just gotten away. His eyes continued to flare hated in my direction.

The impact on the ground was harder than I had expected. It knocked the wind out of me and brought me back to my situation at hand. There would be a few more bruises to add to my already beaten body. I rolled the best that I could and came up in a ...cemetery?

The old tombstones and grave sites stood before. Old rusted wrought iron bars twisted from weather and time marked one site from another. Marble and granite markers were likewise subjected to the exposure of the elements, most of which had pieces missing or fallen off. The words upon the stones were faded.

The ground was desert sand and rock with a few underbrush of sage and a couple of old leafless trees in much need of much rain. A few weeds here and there gave a splash of color, but mostly they too needed water and had turned tan and dry.

There were no buildings around me. I couldn't tell where I had fallen from and the burning building was nowhere to be seen.

I moved like a wraith between the graves, doing my best not to disturb the dead. I've already had enough of the undead haunting me, I didn't need more especially in a graveyard.

As much as I thought that I would have felt a sense of dread and foreboding, that wasn't the case. Something here wasn't right and it wasn't the fact that I kept jumping from one place to another. I had a sense that these people, these poor souls that were at this grave site, weren't supposed to be here. I don't know how I knew that only that I did. It didn't make sense at all.

It was then that I noticed it again. There was that scent in the air, like a fire. Something was burning in the distance, beyond my sight, I just didn't know what. The scent carried smoke and cinder. Then the smell of burning people came again. I was going to get sick right then and there and it no longer mattered to me if I disturbed the dead or not.

I could hear wood burning and splintering. I could hear the crackling of the fire. Then there came the screams. They were inhuman screams of agony and terror, of pain and panic, of despair. They were crying out and it was my fault. They blamed me, I was killing them.

I couldn't take it anymore. Guilt was overwhelming me, guilt over something that I had no idea what I may have done. My feet started to move again as quickly as they could carry me. My arms pumped hard. My side started to hurt, my throat was parched, but I ran for my life. I ran hard between the tombstones and around the sickened trees; I banged into the iron bars and slammed against the sagebrush. I tried so hard to run faster, to get away, I simply had to …

I tripped and started to fall. My world spun as the ground came up to met me. As I fell down, the earth opened up in a rectangle shape, the shape of a grave, just as wide and long and six feet deep. My body fell into my own grave. Darkness took me. I died. I …

I woke up.

My body was shaking and trembling out of fear and terror. Sweat was pouring off my body. I had aches and pains from where I had bruised myself and cut myself in my dream, my nightmare. But where was I now? My eyes took in my scene.

I was back at my motel, lying in my bed with my wife fast asleep at my side. My daughter was fast asleep in her bed on the other side of the room. Morning had yet to happen and all was as it should have been, except for the bruises, scrapes, and cuts that now covered my body.

I took several deep breaths. It had been a dream, a bad nightmare. Or had it been? Perhaps the bruises came from thrashing about the bed in my nightmarish fit, but then what about the abrasions and the cuts? Perhaps they were psychosomatic. Perhaps I should think about this in the morning after a good night's rest, if that were even possible. I hoped it was. I was exhausted from all of the running that I had done in my nightmare. I was about to close my eyes again when I saw her.

It was the girl. It was the "Little House on the Prairie" girl that I had seen near the blood river of death, the same little girl with the burnt dress that I had almost hit on the road. She was standing between my bed and my daughter's. Her soulless eyes stared deep into my being. Slowly she raised her delicate hand and pointed at me. She was trying to tell me something.

Then the smell came again. There was fire somewhere. Something was burning. The motel was on fire. That's why I had been smelling fire all this time. I had to get everyone up and out and fast, despite the fact that the girl was standing there. She didn't matter anymore, nothing mattered except getting my family to safety. I jumped up out of bed and went to see if I could see the fire, if I could tell where we had to run to. I went to wake Ruth, I went to…

The thing from under my bed grabbed my ankle as soon as my foot hit floor. The decomposing hand shot out from under my bed and had gotten a hold of me. It was clawing at me. Its strength was inescapable.

I kicked back at it over and over again to no avail. I flipped over, and clawed at the floor in a desperate attempt to grab something anything. The beast, the creature, the thing that had me, it was too strong. It started to pull me toward it, under the bed, to disappear with it. I would die there and they would find me dead under the bed with no explanation of how I got there or what had happened. I screamed out of desperation.

"Honey? Darling? Are you alright?"

"Dad?"

The voices from my family came as the lights were turned on. I could hear the concern in their tone, their worry. I wanted to yell at them to get out, they were danger. I wanted to tell them about the ghost girl that had invaded our life and the horrible thing that was under my bed that had me and was going to drag me to my death and about the fire that was somewhere threatening to consume us all. I wanted to tell them…

Gone. It was all gone. The little ghost girl was gone and the thing that had been under my bed had only been my pants that I had left on the floor that had tangled around my ankle and had tripped me up. There were no monsters. There was nothing under the bed. There were no ghosts. But what about the fire?

The smell of fire was gone. There was no fire like there was no little girl like there was no monster under my bed. Everything had been a bad dream.

Or had it been?

Chapter: Lake Tahoe

I was glad to wake up the next morning after all I had been through the night before. All of these haunting encounters, or at least the imagining of the haunting encounters on top of the nightmares were starting to get to me and I was wondering if I was going to make it through the night. I was still a bit shaken from last night's episodes but I didn't want to alarm anyone. I was going to do my best to pretend like nothing had happened. My bruises still ached, my muscles were still sore, I still had a road rash or two and I felt like hell. I didn't get much sleep, but I wasn't going to spoil everyone's vacation. Until I figured out what was going on and what to do about it, I was going to act like nothing was wrong.

"What do we have planned for today?" I asked as I yawned and stretched, trying to get my muscles to wake up.

Since my wife had planned this vacation she had every day booked up. She had promised a time that I would never forget and I had no problem rolling with any plan that might come up. I just needed to know if there was anything that would push my body any further.

"We don't have anything planned," my wife yawned back. "But I was thinking about heading down to the beach and spending the day at the lake."

That sounded like a perfect idea. There wouldn't be any maniac drivers trying to run us off the road, any undead road construction worker trying to reach through my car window, or any undead prostitute trying to drag my soul to hell. There wouldn't be anything under my bed, grabbing at my ankles, or burning buildings, or condemning preachers. There wouldn't be graveyards and hopefully there wouldn't be any ghost girls. Yes, spending time at the lake with my family was the perfect idea. I would be able to relax and maybe catch up on some much needed rest.

"But mom," Ruth objected with her whiny voice from across the room from her bed. "I don't want to go to the beach. That's boring. There's nothing to do there. Isn't there something else we could do? Isn't there somewhere else we can go? Don't they have a shopping mall here, or a video game store, or an anime store? Can I just stay here and listen to my music? Do I really have to go?"

It was the same objection we heard everywhere we went. Yet, despite her initial reactions, she always found something to do and always ended up having a great and wonderful time. I was sure that by the end of this vacation she was going to ask when we could come back and do this all over again. She would talk about this vacation for months to come, but only after we were subjected to those initial rejections.

After our morning routines, and of course the coffee with the proper and ample amount of creamer for both my wife and Ruth, we made our way across the busy highway to the beach. We had taken up the offer from the motel office to borrow their kayak; after all, when was I going to be able to get an opportunity to kayak Lake Tahoe again? I'm sure we looked strange to anyone passing us by as my wife had her arms full with two of our folding chairs and the towels while I carried the last folding chair on one arm while carrying half of the kayak with my other hand. Ruth had the other half of the kayak. The paddles were precariously balanced on our aquatic vehicle and threatened to drop in the middle of the highway as we did our best to hurry across. I was fairly certain that we looked like a line of ducks trying to cross the road in a desperate attempt to make it to the other side.

As we rounded the corner of the hotel that sat on the beach on the southern part of the highway, my heart stopped. I stopped. I couldn't take another step. I wanted to scream. I wanted to run. There, before me was a scene that I had come to dread. There, before me was my nightmare come true. This was the beach that I had been dreaming about.

The dock to my right reached out into the lake like some wooden arm in a desperate attempt to touch the other side. Its structure was waterlogged and weather beaten, yet still very functional. This was the same dock in my nightmares.

The sky was bright blue with only a couple of wisps of clouds hanging in the air. It wasn't too hot with the perfect amount of a cool breeze that blew in from the mountains behind us. The air was clear and we could see for miles and beyond. This was the same scene as in my nightmares.

The water of the lake was pristine and clear. I was able to see the bottom of the lake and everything in it. It held the perfect reflect of the sky above, like a mirror. This was the same lake.

The sand was golden tan and it reminded me of Waikiki Beach or even the beaches in Cancun. It wasn't too hot when the grains of sand got into my sandals or too coarse like some beaches have been. This was the same sand.

There were a few boats gently and lazily bobbing in the water by the waves created by the soft and gentle breeze. These were anchored further out and only accessible by swimming or taking a smaller boat to them. It seemed obvious that these boats were more for spring breakers or for those that waited until the summer was in full swing when the lake would be filled with power boats and water skiers. However, at this time the lake was calm and peaceful. These were the exact same boats in the exact same places bobbing in the exact same way.

Across the lake was part of the Sierra-Nevada Mountain range, the same range that we were currently stationed from this side of the lake. The mountains surrounded the entire lake and gave a view of snow covered peaks from every angle.

But despite the peaceful and serene scene before us, I was shaking deep in my core. Everything was the same, the identical items in the identical places, as they were in my nightmares. I wondered how I could have dreamed of a place where I had never visited.

I expected undead to burst through the sand. I expected the sky to turn red. I expected the water to turn to blood. I expected the little ghost girl to come back. My eyes darted across the beach in desperation, looking for any sign of what I was sure was going to happen.

Nothing happened. The birds sang, the wind blew, the water lapped against the shore, the boats bobbed, but there weren't any ghosts, ghouls, zombies, or any undead. There was no little ghost girl. There was no blood lake. This was a regular beach with regular water and a regular sky.

"Honey? What's wrong?"

My wife's question had brought me out of my reverie. Apparently I had stopped mid-stride while carrying the canoe. I often stop mid-stride when my mind was focused on something else or was distracted.

"I was just admiring the view," I said with a forced smile. "It's wonderful here."

Ok, I lied, and I wasn't sure that she bought it. Hell, I didn't even buy it. But how could I tell her "I've been having nightmares about this place and I'm afraid that we're all going to die by a zombie invasion. I want to go home. Can we go home now? Please?"? After all, this was our vacation and my wife had worked so hard to get us here and now that we were here, it was wonderful. I couldn't turn my family around and head them home now over a maniac driver and a few nightmares.

"Come on daddy," Ruth said trying to rush me along. "I want to be first in the kayak."

My suspicions had been correct. My daughter had forgotten all about shopping malls and anime stores and playing video games and listening to her music. She was ready to have fun. She always did love to go canoeing, or kayaking or boating. It was one of her favorite activities while at her Campfire campouts. Now, she didn't have to wait for a counselor's approval.

"Just don't go out too far," I instructed her as she climbed into the kayak and I pushed her out into the lake. "Only as far as those buoys."

"Ok daddy," she answered back, but only half heartedly. Her mind was all set and focused and she was off before I knew it.

I watched as my daughter paddled the kayak like a pro as I unfolded my beach chair and got comfortable in it. She was fearless out on the lake. She went out as far as the buoys, as she had promised and started to navigate between them. She was having the time of her life and I could see the huge smile on her face all the way from here. She had learned how to navigate the kayak quite well while she was at camp and she swam like a fish so I had no worries.

I sat back and relaxed. The sun felt great upon my body and the sound of the waves that softly beat upon the shore started to lull me to sleep. I could stay here forever. I was about to fall asleep when my daughter's voice broke my reverie.

"Alright dad," Ruth said as she pulled the kayak to shore. "It's your turn."

"No, that's ok," said sleepily with a half yawn. I knew that I wanted to go out on the lake at one time, but now. I was fully relaxed; I thought that I might just pass.

"Why don't you go ahead darling," my wife said. "When are you going to get another opportunity to say that you've kayaked on Lake Tahoe?"

She had a point, she always did. That's one of the reasons why I loved her so. She always challenged me to live my life to the fullest and now was an opportunity to do just that. I've gone swimming in underwater tunnels, stood in the middle of an ancient Mayan ball court, snorkeled the reefs off of Hawaii, camped on two active volcanoes, have been on the most northwest tip of America, have been in the world's only non-tropical rain forest, and much more all because of her. It was time to add kayaking Lake Tahoe to that list.

The kayak was easy enough to handle once I got the hang of it and in a short amount of time I was paddling out as far as Ruth had been. It was pleasant and peaceful out on the lake, gliding across the water, but within a few minutes I realized that I wasn't eighteen anymore.

My arms were getting sore. I was sure that Ruth had less than half of my weight to push around and twice the energy to utilize. It was time to head back in. It may not have been a long adventure, but at least I could say that I had done it.

A quick turn to my left brought the kayak facing the correct direction toward shore, but that was as far as I went. I was sure that I had hit a sandbar. That didn't make sense though. I had seen a few of those closer to shore, but I was too far out. The water was too deep. There was something else that …

My kayak flipped over. It wasn't that I had run aground; it was as if something had hit my kayak from underneath and sent it sailing over to one side. As it turned upside down, I did as well. I plunged underwater.

I was trapped. My feet were deep inside the kayak and I couldn't get out. I only had moments of air in my lungs before I would drown. I had to think and fast.

The first thing I did was relax; there would be no clear-headed thinking if I was in panic mode. There was time, I just needed to think and then act. I didn't know how to use my paddle to right myself; I had to think of another way. I quickly gathered my thoughts. Once I collected myself I was able to push off with my hands against the sides of the kayak and twist my body to let my feet come out. With a rapid push off I swam around the overturned kayak and broke through the surface of the water with a gasp for air. A few more breaths to clear my head and I would be able to …

The overwhelmingly strong grip caught my ankle and pulled. Memories of the thing under my bed came rushing back. My body dropped beneath the surface of the water and I went under. My arms flailed in a desperate and fruitless attempt to stay afloat. Water filled my mouth and my nose as I submerged.

I could feel the creature, the being that had a hold on me, drag me further down toward the bottom of the lake. It wasn't too deep here, but the strength of the hold would keep me from coming up for air, depth wasn't the issue, lack of air was.

My free foot kicked out time and again out of desperation and missed more than struck at the thing that had a hold of me. I looked down to get a better idea of where I was kicking. The sight before me almost took my breath, what little I had left, away.

The "creature" was a man, a thin wiry form of a man that I vaguely remembered. Then it dawned on me. This was the preacher that was in the fiery inferno of my nightmare. This was the preacher that was trying to condemn my soul and send me to a fate of a burning hell. But then something else struck me. A memory came flooding back, a memory that had been too horrible to remember. This was also the thing that was under my bed. This was the creature that had a hold of my ankle then and it was the creature that had hold of my ankle now.

I looked deep into the soulless eyes of this unholy thing, focused and kicked one more time. The kick was no longer full of desperation, no longer filled with panic; it was filled with hatred and anger. I was filled with strength of rage. If this man, or creature, or restless soul or spirit or ghost or whatever it was, was going to declare a personal war upon me, then so be it. I was going to let him have it. My blow connected hard and nailed him perfectly in the face. I felt bone give way and I was sure that I broke its nose. He immediately let me go.

I swam for air and broke through the surface of the water giving a gasp of relief. As soon as my lungs were full of air, my attention went back toward the man that was trying to drown me, that had tried to burn me in my nightmare, and that had tried to drag me under my bed in my motel. He was gone and so was any evidence that he had been there in the first place.

A quick look back to shore had only told me that my daughter and wife had both thought that it was funny that I fell out of the kayak. I smiled and waved to show them that I was alright which only brought a few more giggles from the both of them. I was going to let them think that all was alright while I secretly harbored a war that I was going to wage against this restless soul that was now haunting me. I had no idea what I was going to do, but this spirit had endangered me and my family and now has found the wrong person to cross. I recalled how my kick had broken his nose and realized that I could do a whole lot more damage given the proper opportunity, an opportunity that I would keep my eyes open for.

Chapter: Truckee River

*T*he next night's rest offered only a peaceful night with no haunting encounters and no nightmares. However, I was sure that the restless spirits weren't finished with me; I was going to keep my eye out for any return.

The day's adventure included a whitewater river rafting down the Truckee River. Actually it wasn't really a "whitewater" adventure as there would be very few rapids. It would be more like a lazily float. We would start at a certain point, drift for quite some time and then get picked up further downriver. There we would catch a bus provided by the rafting company to take us back to where we started.

Our trip took us around the California side of Lake Tahoe. The towns ran together and it was hard to tell one town from another with the exception of the sign that stating we were entering it. We passed Tahoe Vista, Carnelian Bay, Dollar Point, and finally went through Tahoe City before we hit the Truckee River.

There were many companies that offered the rafting experience and my wife had found one online that offered what we were looking at the price that was affordable. Parking was chaotic since the road that was under construction miles back in Kings Beach was still under construction all the way here. Apparently everyone did construction on their roads at the same time. We had to pass the rafting company and turn back around before we found a place to park.

Ruth was very excited and couldn't wait. She was practically running toward the kiosk to help my wife pay for the trip as if her presence would help make the financial transaction any faster. Even afterward, she had to be the first one down to the dock to help pick out the raft that we were going to take, even though all of the rafts were the same.

We unpacked our supplies including the camera and a cooler of food and drinks. The trip would be a couple of hours long depending on how fast we paddled and as long as we kept our litter then there wasn't a problem about bringing food or drinks. Since we didn't have any other plans for the day, we were going to take our time, enjoy a great lunch and take lots of pictures.

We sprayed each other down with some of the spray-on sunscreen, which only brought Ruth to her typical complaints about how cold the spray was and how it was getting in her eyes and mouth and hair. However, the sunscreen really wasn't so much for her or my wife, it was mainly for me. I've been known to get extremely sunburned if I didn't watch myself. The two of them would probably tan while I fried.

After putting on our lifejackets, the dock assistant gave us a shove off while he took our picture. The picture was one of those extra fees that everyone ended paying for as a memento of their adventures and I was sure that my wife would buy ours as soon as she saw it up on the bulletin board when we returned to come back to our van.

Ruth took the point. She volunteered to help row, yet both my wife and I knew that she didn't have the strength to power the boat with the three of us in it and fight against currents and the few rapids we would come across. It was best to have Ruth sit up front so she couldn't see her mom do a majority of the rowing. My task, being in the rear, was twofold. I would counter stroke to my wife's paddling; that was I would paddle on the opposite side. Yet, I also knew that I would overpower her so I would have to change sides periodically to keep us going straight. The second task was to steer and act as rudder. This meant that I would drag my oar to help turn left or right depending on which side of the canoe I placed my oar.

Ruth had actually tried her best to row as much as she could, but in the end she sat back and enjoyed the ride. She had kicked off her shoes, sat on the very front edge of the raft and let her feet dangle over the edge and into the water. As a father I didn't know if I should commend her fearlessness or be afraid of it. However, since there was very little current for the most part, the water wasn't that deep, she was an expert swimmer, and she had a life vest on, I wasn't too worried, as long as she got back in the boat the moment we hit any rapids.

The rafting was pleasant. We were in no hurry to end our journey and we only paddled when we had to, when the water had become too still to carry us. For the most part, I simply applied my oar as a rudder and let the water gently take us downriver.

We were surrounded by towering rock formations with alpine trees that grew impossibly from them. I couldn't see any semblance of soil, yet these trees, this forested area, grew through the fissures of the rocks and boulders and continued to jaunt out from cliffs and ledges.

Ducks, and their ducklings, followed us for quite some time in hopes of us tossing out some piece of food that they would find edible and enjoyable. Nothing we had would have been healthy for them and they didn't seem to want the pieces of apple and cheese that Ruth tossed toward them. However I doubted that they would go hungry. By the looks of things it seemed that the ducks were very well fed and after not being satisfied from our contributions, or lack thereof, they swam back upstream toward the raft behind us to continue their begging.

We saw other rafting parties along the way with different degrees of skill levels. Some were doing their best just to move in a straight line and had ended up in the bushes along the river bank or simply turning in circles. Others were simply drifting a lot slower than we were and we passed them up with ease. Some were a lot more experienced than we were and shot past us by like we were standing still.

Some of the people were families with their kids, like us. Others were college age young adults having a blast while a few appeared to be serious river rafters with strong and coordinated paddling who seemed to be in a race against themselves.

Sometimes we would come to an area where a couple of the rafters had become stuck and started to create a jam. These we carefully navigated around, doing our best to stay away from the shallow parts of the river or places where the rocks would slow us down. A few times we came to a lull in the river where several rafts had stopped to have lunch. Mostly we rafted by ourselves with the view of a raft or two much further ahead.

We watched as we passed the scenery of tall mountains on either side of us and the thick alpine forests that dotted the area. Birds would fly overhead or chip off in the distance and periodically we would see a fish or two swim by.

Time had passed without notice or worry; there was no concept of such a thing. Nothing mattered. We had neither concern nor care.

That was until my shoulders started to hurt. Despite the fact that I look in the mirror every morning, I still seem to forget that I'm not eighteen any more. I had thought that I had reconfirmed that while out on Lake Tahoe, yet here I was pushing myself beyond what my age and fitness allowed. I was going to be sore in the morning. Yet, it would all be worth it. It was lovely, and peaceful, and…

My eyes caught sight of a dead fish floating not too far from my right. My first thought was when I first noticed a dead fish in the River Styx in Oregon. As long as there weren't any more, as long as no one noticed, everything would be fine. I was wrong.

The river behind me started to turn red. The transformation was creeping closer and closer to us, catching up with our raft. I looked further back to see if I could see any other rafts to come to our aid, or perhaps we could come to theirs. None were in sight.

I tried to paddle a little faster, yet my strokes were overpowering my wife's and we started to slightly turn. I had to switch more often to compensate. My biggest concern was hoping that neither my wife nor my daughter caught on and looked back. I didn't want to freak them out. If we could just reach another group of people or perhaps even the docks where we were going to end, then I could get help. Otherwise, all I would do is panic my wife and my daughter and we would go nowhere fast.

I noticed that the rapids were quickly approaching and I could feel the pull of our raft from its current. We were told that the rapids would be near the end. All I had to do was clear them and help would be just around the corner. The quickened current would keep my wife and daughter occupied and if I hurried then I could get them off of the river before death caught up with us.

I paddled harder and faster to fight the current. We were hit broadside by one boulder sending us sideways and then was hit by another. The current was so hard to fight. I dropped my oar behind me and pulled backwards so we would turn and just miss one of the rapids but another one that I didn't see caught the underside of our raft and started to lift us. With the speed that we were going and the mass that we had the impact thrust our side high into the air. Our ice-cooler slid to one side of the boat. Our body weight shifted. Water came in from one side. We were going over.

I thrust my oar hard into the river and gave it a quick thrust with all of my might. I didn't expect to move the whole raft, but it was just enough to pivot our weight. Our mass shifted again and sent us safely over this rapid and sent us straight into another.

A quick look behind me told me that the blood river was coming faster and descending upon us closer and closer. I hoped that the docks were just around the bend. All I had to do now was push off of the next set of rapids and we should be home free.

My oar became stuck. I wasn't sure if it got jammed in between a couple of rocks, got snagged by some underwater plant, or was caught in the current but my oar wouldn't come out of the water. If I didn't get it out we would crash headlong into the rocks ahead of us.

Another quick look revealed what I had hoped that I wouldn't see. Underneath the water I could see an undead body. It's putrid, charred body was right up next to our raft. I could see the remains of its burned husk as if some great, horrific inferno had engulfed its prior living body. Yet, despite its fragile looking body, it had a firm grip upon my paddle. But that wasn't what terrified me. What finally brought the fullest extent of my horror was watching the horrible creature reach up with its charred clawed hand and grab hold of the end of our raft. I was too late. We weren't going to make it.

It had dawned on me, and why at that particular moment I will never know, that every dead body that I had seen, every ghost and ghoul and zombie and whatever they were, were all charred and burned. This had gone with the fire odor that I constantly smelled when they were around. Even the little ghost girl had burned clothing. Only two hadn't been the woman prostitute and the preacher. I wondered what all the connections were. I wondered that if this burned dead body were to pull me into the river, right here, right now, that I would find out. I wondered if I really wanted to find out. All this had gone through my head in a matter of a fraction of a moment.

All of the chaos, all of the peril, all of the sensory input had cleared my mind. Suddenly I was sharp and clear and focused. I saw every action that I needed to do and how to do it.

As the horrid, burnt, undead creature made one pull with its arm on to the raft, its weight shifted off of the oar. Quickly I jerked the oar out of the water and slammed it back down, this time into the creature's face. Its skull burst open and what was left of its liquefied brains poured out into the river. Whatever energy or will had held the creature together died with that blow and the undead crumbled before my sight.

In one swift move I brought my oar back up and shoved it straight out to my right and slightly forward. It caught the boulders and gave us a slight push yet with our front still not stabilized by a counter thrust, our back end started to drift to our left. The river's current had caught us and was spinning us around as we came upon the bend.

I brought my oar back and slammed it back into the river, ignoring the water being splashed at us from all angles. I ignored the rocks all around us. Instead I brought my oar backward with all of my strength. I was enough to stop our forward momentum on our right side letting us miss the rest of the rocks but left or left side to the fate of the current. We continued our spin as we rounded the corner.

Just as we rounded, the dock became visible to our right. I continued my dragging of my oar and with the current continuing its push we came alongside the dock in a backwards parallel park.

My eyes went to the dock hands that had come to help us out of our raft and then shifted my eyes back toward the red river of death that had followed us, threatening to overtake us. I was hoping that they would see the River Styx and get us out of the raft and off the river as soon as possible. Yet, I should have known better. Neither the blood river nor any undead had followed us through the rapids or around the bend. Only I had seen these things. I was beginning to wonder why only I was so privileged.

The dock hands did their best to help us out of the raft and on to the dock, but with the river still pounding us, the wet slick raft with the several inches of water in it, and the soaking wet wooden dock, the best we ended up doing was being dropped unceremoniously onto the dock.

"Again! Again! Let's do that again!"

Ruth's overly enthusiastic exclamation had told my wife that it was all worth it. These were the memories that would last a lifetime. I simply couldn't bring myself to let them know that we were being haunted, not after seeing this much joy from my daughter. Until I figured out if I was just going out of my mind or if this was real, until I figured out exactly what I was going to do about it, I wasn't going to say a word.

We heard Ruth's rendition of our water soaked adventure several times on the bus ride back to the van. Her eyes were wide with excitement and her words ran together in one long stream without her taking a breath. As much as I was thrilled to hear that she had a great time, and secretly harbored the horrors that I had seen and so desperately never wanted to go back again, I was honestly tired and sore and didn't want to hear any more. I wanted to rest, and think. I was about to ask Ruth to calm down, just a bit but never had the chance.

Ruth gave a slight yawn, as if she had done all of the rowing herself and started to close her eyes. I could see that she wanted to stay awake, just a little bit longer to tell one more rendition, yet her body wouldn't let her. Her eyes grew heavy and she nodded off to sleep. I would wake her once we got back to our van.

As suspected, my wife purchased the picture that had been taken and had been displayed upon the bulletin board for the world to see. It was placed by itself as if it were on the wall of shame, as if saying "my owners didn't want to buy me, now I'll sit here alone and show the world who they were." I had a feeling that places like this had a way of displaying the pictures so those who were in them felt guilty if they didn't buy them. Anyway, I was sure that my wife didn't buy it because of the business's tactics; she bought because she wanted to remember our trip. This would remind us of the great rafting experience that we had. If only she knew.

I winced in pain as I tried to get back into our van. It wasn't from my shoulder hurting, as it actually was, from the paddling and stirring that I had done, it was coming from my legs. My glance down told me why. My legs were fried. They weren't just sunburned, they had turned beet red, as red as a lobster. I couldn't believe it. I was sure that I had sprayed my legs with the sunscreen, and that's when I saw it. There were a couple of white streaks where I had been too close to my legs. The sunscreen had worked, but between being too close and with the gentle wind that we had, the spray only focused on a few strips. Knowing my sensitivity to the sun, I would be in pain for the next week or so.

Chapter: Donner's Pass

I woke up the next morning in so much pain. My legs hurt so bad that I could barely move them. My thigh muscles spasmed uncontrollably. I did my best to hide the tears I wanted to shed and fought back the yelps of agony I wanted to scream. It was one of those pains that hurt so bad that it churned my stomach sick. It was difficult to stand and more difficult to get dressed.

The heat radiated down into my muscles and my legs continued to generate heat even through my jeans. My pants continued to rub against me and every step was a new sensation of pain. My muscles struggled to hold me and sitting made it worse. I felt nauseous. I did my best to smile as I turned to my wife.

"What do we have planned for today?" I secretly hoped that it was a day of rest.

"I was thinking about driving up to Donner's Pass. It's a beautiful drive and I want to take you two up there. There's this wonderful museum and several architectural sites are still standing. I had studied the Donner party when I was in school."

I smiled. Yes, I do remember her telling me about the studies she had where her class would follow the journey of a wagon train or some historical site. She had even done a study on the Lewis and Clark trail and had taken us to Fort Clatsop in Oregon to visit their end of their journey. I continued to smile and nod in my husbandly fashion that I've mastered after all of these years while she retold her informative study of Donner's Pass.

In 1846 The Donner family, along with a couple of other families, headed west to settle in California. Unfortunately the group had bought a map from a man named Hastings who had no idea what he was talking about. His shortcut would prove to be a horrible idea at best, but after several delays, the "best" had turned to worst. The group was driven 150 miles out of their way, had lost food and wagons and their delay brought their journey into the winter time. As the Donner party tried to cross the pass near Truckee, the strongest winter in the history of the area had hit. Starvation and exposure to the elements hit the group hard and out of the original 87 people that started the trek, only 48 survived and only after resorting to cannibalism. There were more details to this story, but that was jest of what I had gathered.

Our trek would be far different. Our route would be on a major highway paved with asphalt that flowed with the countryside instead of trying to cut over uneven, rocky and sometimes treacherous terrain. We had the warmth of our car if it got even the slightest bit chilly and we were out here during the summer where there wasn't even a hint of snow. The only cold air we would feel was if we decided to turn on the air conditioner. Finally, food was just a few minute's drive away; that was if Ruth ended eating all of our snacks again.

I had to keep all of this in mind and in perspective as we pulled up into the parking lot of the small building that served as the museum. It was difficult to imagine the snow at the level markers that were noted on a couple of the stone chimneys that still stood in the area. It was difficult to imagine the area without a road. It was difficult to imagine that there weren't any towns nearby despite the several that we had passed to get here. It was difficult to imagine that help was hard to come by as I watched cars come and go and as I looked upon the tourists that had made their pilgrimage here to pay homage to those that had faced their terrible hardship.

Contrary to the horror story of treacherous and difficult terrain, and contrary to the nightmare blizzard that had been infused into my mind, this area was very pleasant and peaceful. The alpine forest of pine continued to grow all around us and continued to grow out of mountainous peaks that surrounded us. The open fields that also populated this section were full of flowers. Birds could be heard all around us. The air was fresh with a sweet smell of the flowering flora and the sky was a clear light blue. In all regards this was no different than a state park in Washington or perhaps similar to Skykomish or Index.

We bought three tickets for the museum and made our way from one display to another. There were articles and artifacts. There were journals and letters and news clippings. There were maps showing the route that everyone else had taken and maps showing the routes that the ill-fated group had taken. There were accounts of how the party had met one disaster after another and it was hard to believe that this group had even survived just to get to this spot just to face their worst catastrophe yet.

I did my best not to show how much pain I was in while walking through the museum. My legs threatened to buckle with each step. I had to make several stops and feigned interest in the displays while I limped along. I was sure that I would be able to look back at this experience and appreciate it, but at the moment all I wanted to do was lie down and moan in pain and agony. This wasn't just sunburn any more; it felt like my thighs were bruised from an incredible beating.

We made our way back outside where my wife and daughter wanted to check out some of the plaques that had been dedicated to the events that unfortunately had transpired here. I had decided to pass despite my wife's insistence. I simply couldn't walk another step. I just wanted to sit here, on this bench, and enjoy the view while trying to ignore the pain that was wracking my body.

I closed my eyes and tried to get lost in my surroundings. I listened to the birds and the small animals. I smelled the sweet perfume of the flowers and enjoyed the fresh air. I enjoyed the warm sun upon my face.

A cold chill ran down my spine and I dismissed it as a gentle breeze that came off of the mountains catching the colder air at this altitude. The chill became worse and despite the heat that was still radiating off of my legs, I was now cold. I rubbed my arms to try to warm up, but it was to no avail. The temperature continued to plummet. This was no longer a chilly breeze, it was freezing cold. My body was shivering and my teeth were chattering. If it hadn't come on so fast, I would have gotten up and went back inside the museum, but now I was so cold that I could barely move let alone barely think. Even if I could, my legs were still so sore that they protested at every movement. Numbness and shock started to take over my body. I could no longer feel my toes or fingers. My core body temperature was dropping fast. Every breath I took was a frigid blast to my lungs that only reminded me of the time when I had pneumonia. I was freezing to death.

Suddenly I became hungry. I initially thought that it was lunch time or perhaps it was my body telling me that it had spent too much energy repairing itself from the awful sunburn and now from the shivering in the desperate attempt to keep myself warm. Then it got worse. My hunger turned into ravishing pain as starvation started to settle in. Dizziness started to overcome me and I was sure that I was going to pass out and didn't know if I was going to freeze to death or starve to death before my family came back.

Something else came upon me to add to my desperate situation. I smelled smoke. There was fire somewhere. It smelled of burning wood and I was sure that there was a forest fire nearby. No, that wasn't right; it didn't smell of burning pine or fir, it smelled like the same fire that I've smelled during this entire vacation.

I opened my eyes to gather my bearings. I hoped that there would be someone nearby that I could ask for help. I nearly screamed in horror. There, before me, was the little ghost girl in the "Little House on the Prairie" outfit with her soulless eyes. This was the girl that I had almost run over on the highway. This was the girl that was in my motel room. This was the girl that had been haunting me.

It was then that I realized that I wasn't just being haunted by the psycho preacher man; I was also being haunted by this little girl. My next question was if either one of them was responsible for the logging truck incident.

Despite the fact that I was shivering, freezing cold and I was ravishingly hungry, I looked at her more out of curiosity once the initial shock had set in. I was in so much pain and misery that I just wanted her to end it right then and there, but she didn't. Unlike the preacher who was angry and aggressive, the little girl was neither. On the contrary, she gave me a curious, pleading look. It was as if she was the one in need of help, not me. She raised her hand and pointed in my direction. No, she was pointing beyond me.

I turned my head and looked back. My wife and daughter were returning on the trail that they had ventured on. The girl's directional guidance was pointing at them. My heart finally skipped a beat. I broke out in a cold sweat.

'No!' I thought. 'Not them. Take me instead, but leave them alone.'

I would have yelled this, screamed this if only I could. I was in misery and agony and couldn't speak if my life depended on it. I turned back toward the girl to give her a pleading look, anything to keep my family safe.

The girl was gone. She had vanished as if she had never been there. There wasn't a trace of her existence and if she had been physically real then there was no place that she could have run off to. The parking lot was practically empty; she couldn't have run away without me seeing her.

With her disappearance the cold and the hunger also left. The ghosts of this area were gone and they left me with more questions than I could imagine I would find myself asking. I wouldn't freeze or starve to death, and I would live, but now I was more frightful of what might happen to my family.

Chapter: Drive to Virginia City

"*W*e're off to see Virginia City," my wife announced the next morning with great enthusiasm. She had been to the city several times and was eager to show us around.

As usual we packed what we needed including snacks (that had to be replenished due to our growing teenage girl) and our camera. After a quick breakfast and coffee, with the right amount of creamer for both Ruth and my wife, we made an early start since we wanted to spend as much time in Virginia City as we could.

My sunburned legs had somewhat subsided in their pain from the day before. It would still hurt to walk long distances or sit for any length of time, but it was far more tolerable. With any luck, I wouldn't even slow my family down from having a great time.

We followed Highway 28 through Crystal Bay and entered Nevada without any hoopla or extraordinary event except for a sign that said "*Welcome to Nevada*" and our first casino immediately beyond the sign. Our entrance into Oregon had a great view of the Columbia River and our entrance into California at least had the dizzying view of the Klamath National Forest and the Pacific Coast Mountain Ranges. Here, it was only a change from one block of Crystal Bay to another. The state line had cut the town in half and there was no real difference between one half and the other with the exception of the casino that we had passed.

We turned off to Highway 431 and started our ascent up the windy road that would take us to our destination. Up, up, up we climbed. Tall evergreens gave way to shorter, less majestic fir. Forests gave way to sporadically placed trees. Lush flora gave way to alpine meadows. Underbrush gave way to rocks, boulders and the exposure of the mountains that we were climbing.

Once we hit the peak of our climb, the wonderful view opened itself before us. It was as if we were on top of the world. We could see jagged peaks surrounding us, the great desert below us and a view that seemed to stretch on forever. This is what it must feel like when an eagle soars overhead. The cascading terrain, the changing environment, and extraordinary visuals of the great landscape were ours to capture and feast with our eyes.

We came down out of the alpine forest and into the dryer climate; its much needed water was blocked by the mountains that we were coming out of. There, before us, lay the desert basin of the Washoe Valley just south of Reno. We had come into a set of intersecting highways and all we had to do was follow the directions to our destination.

"Which way?" My wife asked as she tried to keep her eyes on the road.

Signs were pointing in all directions and there were two right turns coming up, one of which was the highway we wanted, the other led off into who knew where. It had been my turn to navigate, I would drive back, but I wasn't sure which exit we needed to take. My hand thrust into the side pocket of the door and pulled out our map. Fortunately, we had it folded to the correct place. Unfortunately I couldn't find where we were on the map fast enough. The first turn was upon us and my wife needed an answer now.

I was just about to speak when I saw her. The little girl with the "Little House on the Prairie" burned outfit and soulless eyes was right there, under the overpass that separated the two turns. Going any further to the second exit would take us right past her. I wasn't going to let anyone harm my family. I wasn't sure if my wife saw the girl or not, but my decision was made up right then and there.

"Take a right here," I said pointing at the first exit. This would take us off the highway and exit onto another before we got to the girl.

"Are you sure?"

"Yes, I'm sure."

No, I wasn't, but at this time I didn't care. We simply weren't going to go past the girl.

My wife took the exit that I had pointed to as I looked back toward the spot where the girl had been. Again, she was gone. Good, I hoped I never saw her again.

"Highway 395?" My wife asked pulling my attention back toward the road. "I don't think this is right."

I brought my attention back toward the map. 'Damn', I thought as I found the highway we just drove onto. In my desperation to not drive past a possible hallucination I had taken us onto the wrong highway. We were now in the Washoe Valley on the wrong side of Washoe Lake.

"Don't worry," I said. "I'm sure there would be a turn off soon where we can get back on the highway and head back the way we came."

I was wrong again. We ended up going ten miles out of our way before we found a place to get off and turn back around. By the time we made our way back to our incorrect turn off and went to the second exit, we had driven at least a half an hour extra.

Our road up Highway 341 gave us spectacular views. The hillside displaced splashes of hues of red and auburn and rust where iron had exposed, and of tan and brown and of slate and marble as we drove upward toward our destination. Periodically we could see the Washoe Valley, the one we had just left behind, continue to drop beyond our elevation as we continued to climb.

My wife pulled the van over to what seemed to be a minor observatory spot, one of those that seemed to only be capable of holding a few cars in its designed pullout area and although would give the spectator a wonderful view, it wouldn't be very big and after a few minutes we would continue our ascent up the road to Virginia City. My assumption had been incorrect. What I thought was only a minor pull out station ended up being the Geiger Lookout Wayside Park.

At first this lookout offered a wonderful view of Reno off to our right, the Washoe Valley and Washoe Lake below us, and the Sierra-Nevada Mountains behind them. This alone was a spectacular display of the landscape that we had left behind. The snow capped, jagged Sierra-Nevada Mountains cut into the peaceful azure blue sky. The valley displayed various colors of mountainous rock, dirt, scrub, and trees, and offered a wonderful view of the lake that centered our view.

However, once I drew myself closer to the edge of the lookout, I noticed that there was a slight descent of our mountainous observation that opened to a wide variety of paths, cleared of major debris and marked by larger rocks. The paths intertwined between desert scrub, sage, and the few squat trees that dotted this area. There were small rock structures that resembled crumbled fireplaces and perhaps even a few foundations where a couple of houses may have sat upon.

We followed one of these paths that seemed to lead to a stone wall and upon further investigation a small flight of stairs brought us to a magnificent lookout point. The panoramic view of the Washoe Valley was incredible. Of course we snapped a few shots of each other at the observation area with the background behind us for our scrapbook before going on to search the other attractions at this park.

We had ended up splitting up as my stride is much longer than both my wife and my daughter and my attention span was much shorter. I was able to take in each scene as I moved quickly from one to another. When I had turned behind a retaining wall, separating one rocky hill from another, I stopped in my tracks.

There, not too far from me, sat three men around an open fire. There was definitely enough scrub to feed their flames, that wasn't what startled me. It was the fact that I was sure that a fire was not allowed in these parts. If it was then there would be fire rings and signs that would state not to collect wood from the park. As it was, these men had a few rocks as their fire ring and I was positive that any stray spark could and probably would ignite a blazing inferno across the flora that was in such desperate need of rain.

Then my eyes looked at them closer. Their attire wasn't what I had expected. I had thought that these men might have worn jeans and a t-shirt and perhaps tennis shoes. Instead they wore cotton long sleeve off-white shirts without buttons, denim pants that looked a hundred years outdated, and boots. Two even had suspenders hooked on their jeans, going over their cotton shirts, across their shoulders and back down to their jeans again. Their facial hair as well as their hair on their head was unkempt and they looked as if they could use a bath. Their entire presence reminded me of early minors or settlers or perhaps even pioneers.

At first I thought that this might be a re-enactment or some sort of tourist attraction associated with Virginia

City. But that still didn't make sense. There was no one else around dressed up and their campfire was still a fire hazard.

The three of them turned their attention toward me. At first I thought that these vagrants might become aggressive or perhaps simply tell me to mind my own business. Instead they gave a pleading look, as if I was the only one who could help them. It was the same look that the little girl had given me, the one that had been haunting me.

I turned my head back toward the parking lot of cars to try to get someone's attention. Hopefully there was a nearby policeman or a park ranger, or someone that could give some answers. There was no one in sight. I turned back toward the men and they were gone. There wasn't any evidence in sight that announced that they had ever been there in the first place. Their fire was gone. There were no ashes, no smoke, no burning wood, it was all gone. I shook my head. I was getting tired of seeing ghosts and I wished that they would just leave me alone.

Chapter: Virginia City

*T*he large billboard sign proclaiming the world renowned "suicide table" was our first indicator that we were close to Virginia City. The sign was larger than life and was displayed upon the side of the hillside that our road was climbing. This was followed by a sign for the "Bucket of Blood Saloon."

A few more curves in the road led us to the top of our climb where Highway 341 turned into "C" Street. After a few residential houses we came across our first "old time" building named "The Way it was" museum. This was built with old, rustic wood that had been weathered over time and came complete with an old waterwheel out front.

Beyond the museum the main (old town) city began. The buildings were two stories tall and ran together taking up a whole block at a time. Each facade of every building was made to look like the old west with old wooden posts and large wooden signs. Their second story sections often had balconies that stood out over the front portion of the saloon or store. Tall old fashioned gas lamps were periodically placed. Large banners or streamers decorated various taverns.

The sidewalks had become elevated and were made of old wood and as far as I could tell were very uneven. There were wooden benches that allowed patrons and tourists to rest, but most of these were occupied and weary travelers were forced to move on and find some other form of respite.

The place was packed. There were people walking everywhere. The sidewalks were full of pedestrians and more were coming in and out of various stores and buildings. Individuals were crossing the street without regard to traffic.

Cars were parked along the sidewalks and every space had been taken. There were signs for parking that showed lots were available on streets to our left, on a lower tier of the town, but gave us no indication on how to get there. The few parking lots we did find were full and we were forced to drive on.

We passed by buildings named "Marshall Mint Inc", "Red Dog Saloon", "La Fayette Market", and "Brass Rail Saloon." We passed "Bonanza" and the "Silver Queen". We passed the "Silver Dollar Hotel" and even found the "Bucket of Blood Saloon." On and on it went with building after building.

We eventually found a place where a road from a lower tier of the town, "D" street, met up with the road we were on, turned on it and back tracked our route back into the heart of town. This tier level was full of warehouses, store facilities, and basements of the stores and businesses that were now above us. It felt more like a utility street than an actual road, although there were still some businesses here. There were also several parking lots and when we found one that suited our needs, we parked and hiked up the stairs to "C" Street.

The old west town opened up before us and what had only been a visual experience from our car was now a reality to touch, feel and experience. Sounds of the hustle and bustle of the tourists filled our ears. Smells of the shops filled the air.

The wooden walkway that served as a sidewalk was more uneven than I had imagined and proved to be harder to walk on than I had initially thought. But what made matters worse was the fact that it was all on a hill. It was only a slight incline, and we would have the benefit of going downhill once we reached the top, but it was on an incline never-the-less.

It was hotter than I had expected. The stop at the Geiger Lookout Wayside Park was warm, but now the temperature had increased as the sun had risen higher in the sky. The only shade that was available was under the eaves and balconies of the shops. The few benches that were periodically placed were full of individuals trying to find a reprieve from the heat and every ice cream parlor that we passed was very tempting to say the least.

We passed by smoke shops filled with tobacco smell and old costume shops. There was photography shops that promised the patron an old time photo dressed in the appropriate garb similar to the one we had at home, hanging on the wall that we had taken in Lincoln City, Oregon when we were dressed as pioneers from the late 1800's. There were sweets shops that smelled of heated sugar. We passed by saloons with the smell of beer and alcohol and the sounds of slot machines. We passed by a bakery with the smell of freshly baked bread, a silver store, a jewelry store, several antiques stores, and a shooting gallery. There were souvenirs, trinkets, shirts, mugs, knickknacks, and every item that every tourist trap would have to sell. There were museums, tourist attractions, and historical sites. On and on it went with many shops being duplicated with the same stuff just under a different name.

There were people from all walks of life. Many of them were tourists like us trying to make their way from one shop to another. There were couples walking hand in hand, others pushing strollers unsuccessfully upon the uneven wooden sidewalk, kids weaving in and out of the crowds with dripping ice cream or sticky cotton candy and individuals in period time costumes. There was even a group of Asians huddled closely together taking pictures of everything.

A gunshot went off and I stopped dead in my tracks. My nerves were already frayed from the ghosts I had been seeing.

"Step right up folks and see our show," the announcer, dressed as a cowboy, proclaimed as he put his pistol back in his holster. "It's an old west comedy. Great for the whole family. It starts in fifteen minutes."

Apparently the shot he had fired was only a blank and was part of the outfit and the act. No one else had been affected by the sudden explosion of his shot and had accepted it as part of the atmosphere.

A train whistle went off in the distance. It was one of those air powered train whistles, something that would be heard on a steam engine run by coal, not a modern electronic one. But it wasn't just the sound that caught my attention; I had expected a steam engine train to be around these parts. What caught me was that the sound seemed to be felt deep in my soul. It was a haunting echo and seemed to resonate within me as if I was hearing it twice, once here and now and once in a déjà vu.

We continued our trek through the town and turned into yet another souvenir shop. It had the usual items, jewelry made of silver and gold and from the semi-precious gems from around these parts, postcards, mugs, posters, maps, the t-shirt that said "My mom and dad went to Virginia City and all they got me was this stupid shirt", CD's about the town's history, art pieces from local vendors, and a wide array of other items that we had already several times over.

"Mom, dad, look at these!"

"What did you find dear?" My wife had asked as I rolled my eyes.

Ruth was able to catch an interest in anything and everything, but only for a brief moment before she moved on. If we stopped and looked at everything that she had caught her interest then we would be here all day and then some.

"Oh, those are pretty earrings. Did you want to get those Ruth?"

"Oh yes mommy. Can I please?"

"I'm sure we can pick these up…"

"Yeahhh. Oh, you're the greatest."

I didn't mind my wife getting my daughter a set of earrings. I just hoped that it didn't turn into a slew of purchases as it sometimes did. I understood that she is our only child, and would be our only child, and we could spoil her on things like this, but as long as we didn't spoil her too much.

Another stop brought us into the saloon that boasted to have the Suicide Table and since it had been highlighted as a main attraction, we simply had to see it. The table itself wasn't very big nor was it as impressive as I had thought it would be. The Suicide Table had only been attributed to three suicides and a possible fourth, though that one was never confirmed. All in all, the sign outside of town was a bigger deal than the table was. We were about to leave when my wife to turned Ruth.

"I want to show you something, Ruth. You just stay right there and watch."

My wife had instructed our daughter to stay back from the slot machines that took up the majority of the saloon. Children were allowed to come into the tavern but weren't allowed to gamble or sit up at the bar and it was customary to keep the kids back from the slots and the booze. My wife then took out a few coins and dropped them into a slot machine. She pulled the lever, waited for the appropriate amount of time and started to push her buttons. When the slot stopped and nothing had happened, she repeated the process until her full dollar had been spent. Once the dollar had been eaten up without any form of profit she turned back to our daughter.

"...And that's why you don't gamble."

I smiled. My wife might spoil our daughter periodically, but she still continued to show her pearls of wisdom and this was one of them. I just wondered what would have happened if she had actually won something.

"Ruth, come over here," I stated pointing at another machine, this one she could participate in.

The machine was one of those penny smashers. It had four different designs that Ruth could chose from by simply turning a dial. Once her choice was made, she would put in two quarters and her penny and come up with the imprint she had decided upon. This was easily the epitome of all tourists' traps, yet it was one that Ruth thoroughly enjoyed. She had a passport of sorts, a collection of these smashed pennies from all the different places she had been. This had included the Woodland Park Zoo, Seattle Aquarium, Mount Saint Helens, Snoqualmie Falls, Northwest Trek, Leavenworth, Great Wolf Lodge, the Seattle Ferris Wheel, one from the Seattle Piers, and one from the Science Fiction Museum in Seattle.

I gave Ruth the appropriate amount of coins and when she made her selection she cranked on the wheel. After a few moments her newly squashed penny appeared with her impression and she was just as overjoyed as when she received her earrings. Sometimes this girl was so easily amused and I hoped she never grew out of it.

We tried to stop in another location to have lunch but then realized that the tavern smelled too strongly of beer and that the clientele was just a little less than family friendly. We ended up stopping at a sweets shop that had a small lunch counter in the back. This had ended up being perfect. This would give us a small lunch that would stay within our already overly extended budget.

We sat at the small booths that were offered and accepted the lunch menu. My eyes were still trying to take in all my choices when my thoughts were interrupted.

"Psst, mom, do they have any corn dogs here?"

Ruth tried to keep her voice down so it wouldn't be overheard by our waitress but once she realized that she had been heard, she blushed and hid behind her menu. I had to shake my head. Although Ruth was thirteen years old, sometimes she acted mature and I could swear that she was eighteen or older. Other times, like now, she acted like she was eight. I had to remind myself that she was still a child trying to grow up and she hadn't quite gotten the hang of it yet.

Chapter: Ghosts

After lunch we continued our endeavors and moved further into town. It seemed to me that everything I was hearing now had an echo. It was curious and odd. It was like that train whistle, hearing everything once and then again in a déjà vu. It was like that movie "The Langoliers" where, near the end of the movie, everything is trying to catch up to the present time. I swore I could hear horses, carriages, and other people talking, people that weren't near me. I shook my head. I was tired, hot, and it was time to head back to our motel.

I could tell that my wife was done looking at the same shops over and over again and she was starting to look for something more substantial, something more memorable to cap off our experience here. She stopped and started to eye two different events.

"Do you guys want to do the old west play across the street that will start in a few minutes or do the tour of the haunted millionaires club?"

"The haunted house! The haunted house!"

Ruth's proclamation was animated enough to let several pedestrians know what her decision was without a shadow of a doubt. I, on the other hand, only gave a shrug. I've seen enough ghosts to no longer be concerned about someone else's version of "haunted".

There was no way that an old building full of dust could come anywhere near the haunted dreams and ghosts that I've already seen on this trip.

We paid for our entry fee and waited for several more people to join us and then waited for our tour guide. When our guide arrived we noticed that she, like many others that ran these establishments, was dressed in time period clothing to help put us in the mood. Before we started our tour she gave us a little background history of the building.

The three story brick building was built in the 1870's as a men-only meeting place for the very high class and rich travelers. The roster ended up being a "who's who" of the time and offered respite for those who could afford it. During its heyday the club was very active, but once the mining of the town had dried up, the membership dwindled until the building became all but abandoned. It was one of the few buildings that actually survived the great fire here in Virginia City in 1875.

Although The Washoe Building was a men-only Club, there was a spiral staircase in the back that allowed escorts to have access to the highest tier while remaining out of the public view. These escorts were usually a private, hand selected set of women that only offered their services to the rich and famous clientele.

Over the years, the building was subject to a couple of small fires and a few earthquakes making some of it unfit to live in. Once it was repurchased, several projects have been made to upkeep the old, historic building.

The first level has now been converted into a tavern with a small museum at the far end. Here, we were able to see various artifacts from the building but what really caught our attention were the photographs that were hanging up and the video that was constantly being played. The pictures showed still photos of clearly visible portraits of apparitions. Several showed full torso individuals in a ghostly form standing in a hall or on the stairs. The video was from a show called "Ghost Hunters" where a camera crew had caught an apparition on their cameras.

Our guide filled us in on several of the ghosts that might make their presence known during our visit. There had been a young girl that had been killed in the basement, a young, blonde prostitute named Lena who had been murdered on the third floor, and the man who had killed the prostitute who took his own life on the second floor. On top of this, the basement had been used several times to help store dead bodies of those who had died from other causes around town before they could have their proper burial.

After our brief history in the museum area, our guide led us back outside and around to the door next to the one that led us into the tavern area. The guide unlocked the door, told us to go ahead and enter and she would join us shortly.

Immediately inside we came upon a landing of a staircase leading up. The stairs were wooden, old and dusty. It was what I had expected to see from any old building and as I glanced up I could see our next guide.

He was standing at the top of the stairs in his period clothing. I smiled and nodded, but then wondered if we were to have two guides. I turned back toward the door we had entered to see our first guide return and when I looked back up the stairs, our second one was gone.

The female guide added more colorful history to our knowledge and the more I listened to her the more I realized that she would be our only guide. I shook my head and passed the man at the top of the stairs as merely someone else in the building. Yet, try as I might, I couldn't hear anyone walking around on the creaky wooden floors that would give evidence of any sudden weight shift.

Our tour went up the stairs where we came to a second landing. Here, the second floor opened up to us while a second set of stairs went higher to the top tier. My eyes took in our scene and it was only more of the same dusty, creaky, old wooden and plaster walls and floor that we started with. Some of the plaster was missing from a few of the walls exposing the wooden skeletal frame of the building. Old, thick wallpaper hung off of the walls. Cobwebs hung in some of the corners of the rooms that I could see. What little sunlight that was came through in streams to reflect the dust that was in the air.

Something was nagging at me at the back of my mind. I felt as if I had been here before. Then it struck me. I had been here before. This was part of my nightmare where I had been chased by the priest that was trying to condemn my soul. I didn't want to, and I knew I shouldn't, but I couldn't help but shoot a glance up the stairs. My heart stopped as I gasped aloud. There, to my terror and horror, was the tall, thin man, dressed in black. It was the preacher man. His eyes pierced my soul and his gaze was condemning. He was filled with hatred. I had to get out of there, we all did.

"...and in this room..."

Our guide's voice brought me out of my reverie. My eyes first darted back toward the group that had slightly wandered off into another room. I wanted to warn them about the horrible, evil spirit that was here to condemn us all but they had acted as if none of them had seen him. Then I realized my mistake, I had taken my eyes off of the specter. My eyes shot back up the stairs. He was gone. I should have known better. Now he was loose somewhere in this creepy old building.

I caught up to the crowd and kept my eyes open for this wraith but saw no more signs of him. I only saw more of the same rooms. There was dust and creaky boards, there was mold in the corners and cobwebs that tried to cover them up, there were plaster and wallpaper and exposed wood. Several of the rooms were slightly slanted from the settling foundation and I had gotten vertigo just entering them.

I had come to relax a little and started to enjoy the tour a bit more. Perhaps I had only imagined what I had seen at the top of the stairs simply because I had wanted to, or at least I believed that I would see it. I turned to my family; they were having a good time listening to the ghost stories, if only they knew. I turned to the rest of the crowd and realized that they were in the same ignorant bliss. I watched as one little girl started to reach for her mom's hand. I took this as nothing more than a child in need of reinforcement, but then she turned toward me.

My eyes went wide with fear. The little girl was the same one that I had been seeing all this time. She was still following me. Again, she gave me a pleading look, like someone in desperate need of help. I wondered if she had anything to do with the preacher man.

Suddenly my eye caught something else. The woman had pulled her hand away quickly, as if she were in pain or perhaps as if something unfamiliar had touched her and disturbed her soul. She gave an immediate look down and at first I thought that she would share the same vision that I was having, I thought that she would gasp at the ghost girl that was standing next to her.

Her reaction was only confusion and when I looked again, I could see why. The girl was gone. I wasn't surprised any more at her comings and goings. I wasn't surprised at any of the ghosts' comings and goings. I was just taking it for granted that one moment they would be there and another they would be gone. Even though I still had questions, one of them had been answered. I wasn't going out of my mind. The girl was real and someone else had noticed her. My wife had chalked up our near wreck on the highway as just me losing control of the van. I had thought that I was seeing things. Neither had been true. Now, I was certain that the "Little House on the Prairie" ghost girl, the one that was haunting me, was real. But that meant, so was the preacher man. However, I wondered about the others. I wondered about the logging truck. How was all this tied together?

After our time at the Washoe Building my wife had made it clear that we had seen all of Virginia City that we were going to see without duplicating our already prolonged visit. It was time to head back to the car. It was still a long drive back to our log cabin-like, rustic motel, including going back up and over the Sierra-Nevada Mountain Range and back into Kings Beach. It had been my turn to drive, since my wife drove us here, and I thought that it was going to be a straight shot back. However, as we started to pull out of town, my wife suggested one more stop.

"I would like to see the cemetery before we leave town", my wife said with an almost joyful giggle in her voice. "I read that this is a well preserved and massive cemetery that's worth seeing. I would love to see the old grave stones and tombstones. I would love to read their history. It's supposed to be haunted you know."

"A haunted graveyard? Yipee!"

The response from the back of the car had only reinforced my wife's desire. Now it was two against one and there was no way I was getting out of this.

I raised an eyebrow at my wife's request. I've known her for seventeen years now and I've never known her to want to walk through a cemetery. Quite honestly I've had just enough with ghosts and the haunting undead that we've been through. Perhaps she had chalked up what she had seen due to stress, but I hadn't mentioned any of the rest that only I had seen. I honestly didn't want to go through a graveyard, especially one that was supposed to be haunted.

Yet, there was only one answer that could be said, only one phrase that could be uttered. After seventeen years of marriage there may be a few things about her that still surprised me, like this sudden announcement, but there was still many that I was absolutely sure about. My only response to prevent a pout-full, cold, and distant drive back home over the next couple of days and to prevent having to sleep on the couch for several more nights was to answer with...

"Ok, how do we get there?" with as much sincerity as possible.

"It's supposed to be just down this road a bit."

Needless to say, it wasn't. The road that we were on gave no indication on how to get to this graveyard despite that fact that we could periodically see it, or at least we thought we could see it. A road that we thought would lead us there only led to a mobile park and another one led us deeper into a residential area.

'Oh, well,' I thought to myself. 'At least I tried. I was ready to make the argument to forget the cemetery when the voice to my right came up with the one answer that I had hoped she hadn't thought of.

"There's someone who looks like he lives here," came the comment from my wife while she pointed toward a man walking down the street on my left. "Why don't we ask for directions?"

I tried my best not to sigh too loudly at that. I'm a guy, I don't ask for directions. Didn't she know that? Yes, I'm sure she did and I'm also sure she knew what I was going to do next even before I did. I slowed down the car to a stop and rolled down my window.

"Excuse me sir, but we're trying to get to the cemetery. Can you direct us?"

"Sure, you just keep going down this street you're on, take a left at the dead end, then take your first right. Follow that until you see the sign. It'll be on your right."

The older man had pointed with his hand and gestured in each direction as he was giving his tour of the neighborhood. I nodded in acceptance of his directions and yet secretly hoped that he hadn't known and his answer was something more like "I don't live here so how should I know." That would have been the end of trip to the cemetery and I wouldn't have to put up with any frustrations for the next several days. I could have then said that I had tried. But no, we now had the directions and my wife was pleased and excited to be on the way.

Unfortunately for me, the man's directions had proven to be accurate. We found the parking lot to the cemetery with ease. It was nearly empty with the exception of a small, two door black car.

There was something unsettling about that black car. I couldn't tell if it was the car itself or the lonely passenger that was sitting in it, but whatever it was, it made the hairs on the back of my neck stand and a pit grew in my stomach. I tried not to think about it as I led my family into the cemetery.

That was early today. Now my daughter had gone missing and when I had finally found her she had been dead for the last one hundred years. I finally opened my eyes from the crying that I had done. It was time to face my wife and let her know what had happened to our daughter, despite the fact that I had no answers, only questions.

Book: The Past

Chapter: Virginia City Reprise

*T*he hike back down to the parking lot was longer than I had expected. My gut was in knots and shock had overcome me. I simply couldn't bring myself to bare the news and yet if anyone had to, it would be me. My feet slowly carried me over the last rise and my eyes went to our van and the woman that I had been married to, the mother to our child.

Gone.

The van, my wife, the black car, even the parking lot was gone. There was nothing but more gravel, more rock and more stone. Sage brush had replaced cars, a couple of trees had replaced where my wife had been standing. The parking lot was gone.

It was more than that, the paved road was gone. There was a dirt road in its place, but there was nothing paved. The telephone poles were gone. The satellite dishes, the sidewalks, and every car that had been parked along the street by residential buildings were gone.

My eyes continued to dart around my environment. Everything had changed. The buildings that were close to the cemetery were old, flimsy wooden structures.

This looked more like a shanty town than the residential area that we drove through.

I was in shock. The entire area had changed. My mind left the thought of finding my wife, I had to find myself.

My feet continued to carry me around and down to the nearest buildings. These buildings reminded me of something out of the old west. Yes, Virginia City had its downtown structured to look like the old west, but not its residential area.

The people were the next to catch my eye. Every one of them was in period clothing. These weren't just play actors playing a part in a small section of town. Every one of them had clothing from before the turn of the last century.

Then there was the size of the city. This city seemed to be a thriving major city, as far as an old west city went, instead of a sleepy little town feel that I had driven into. People were busy all over the place, running errands, hauling boxes and crates and wood and rope and tackle gear. They were hanging laundry between buildings, they were...riding horses?

There hadn't been any horses when I arrived. Now the cars had been replaced. There were wagons and carts. There were wheelbarrows and mining carts. There was nothing modern.

The sounds were all different as well. Instead of a quiet town, this city was bustling was noise of its activity. I could hear mining going on, workers building houses, smithies banging away at horseshoes or some other much needed piece of metal. Off in the distance I could hear a group of men singing, or at least attempting to sing, while completely intoxicated. There were people talking loudly about where once piece of cargo went and where another had belonged. A church bell rang off somewhere. A train was pulling in and I could hear its steam whistle and the clanking of its metal wheels against the track.

There were cats and dogs and children running about. There were live chickens and cows. There was a sense of controlled chaos on the verge of a complete and total melt down.

This wasn't like the old west of the early 1900's; this WAS the old west of the early 1900's. The clothing wasn't clean like an actor's clothing would be. Everyone was dirty and grungy. The streets were filthy and garbage was tucked behind alleyways. Drunkards were lying in the side roads, stench had filled my nostrils, and smoke from the incoming train, the smithies, and the mining was filling the air.

I finished my walkthrough of this shanty town area and made my way into another section. I hadn't even noticed the difference until I realized that all of the people were of the same national descent. I'm not racist, or at least I try my best not to be, I'm sure we all are to some extent, but I could see that racism was in effect here. This was the area that blacks, or African-Americans, or some other derogatory slang term that could be used during this era, would be told to live. They were huddled together in this area, not to be mixed in with any others, especially those who were white or European descent, like me. It seemed that they were welcomed here in this city, as long as they worked hard and kept to themselves.

I had to tread carefully. There was still racial hatred that spanned across all colors and I could easily be caught in the middle of a racial war if I wasn't careful. I couldn't give the same courtesy to the same people in this era as I could, and would, in mine, even though I truly wanted to. No, I wouldn't and couldn't be bigoted, but no one could know that if I wanted to blend in and right now that's what I wanted to do while I was trying to figure everything out.

If this was really the early 1900's then I could create a temporal shockwave through history, through the future and into my real present. Maybe I've read too many time travel books, but now I was living one and everything I did had to be carefully thought about including how I treated people.

I came to an abrupt stop. The large figure of a man had stepped before me and had interrupted my reverie. I was about to sidestep him and continue as if nothing had happened but then I realized that several others had come up beside him. All were very dark colored skin. My blood ran cold. It wasn't the fact that I was nearly surrounded by men of a different color; it was the fact that I was surrounded by very angry men that were very big. No one knew that I was here and if they decided to squash me like a bug then no one would come looking for me.

"We ain't want no trouble with ya." The man's voice was as big and burly as he was. His voice seemed to come somewhere deep within his soul and reverberated within in chest before coming out with a life of its own.

I had been bullied before when I was younger and knew exactly how to handle bullies. I couldn't back down even if I had the living tar beaten out of me, I wouldn't stand being bullied. I looked this man deep into his eyes.

What I saw reflecting back at me wasn't anger at all, despite my initial thoughts, it was fear. He was more scared of me than I was of him. Apparently if he or his friends hurt one white man, even out of self defense, than they would all be punished, probably hanged. I hadn't thought about that. They would receive no justice, only punishment. Suddenly I felt sorry for him, but I couldn't let him know that, it would hurt his pride. Again, I had to remember to tread lightly.

"And I want no trouble with you. Just walking through, minding my own business."

"Ya lost den?"

"I'm new in town," I said as I gave a little shrug.

He nodded. That seemed to alleviate any sense of trouble that he thought that I was trying to cause by being in the wrong side of town. It was a simple misunderstanding, one that could easily be justified by someone lost and new in town. At least that was kind of true. If I was going to lie, I was going to keep it as close to the truth as possible.

"Ah'm Thomas. Me an me boys, and me kin and theirs all live 'ere. You'll be lookin' in dat dere direction."

His chin pointed further down the street. He gave one more glance at me and then moved so I could pass. I tried not to show fear and did my best to calm my heart from beating through my chest as I continued on my way.

The road led further into town and my environment changed. Instead of a shanty town, the buildings had more of an eastern Asian atmosphere. They still had a shanty feel but there were Asian symbols and words on the buildings. There were restaurants with Asian foods and shops with exotic medicines and herbs,

One building had a couple of individuals walking out of it, or rather half stumbling and hardly aware of their surroundings. It appeared to me that they might be stoned or high or...then it dawn on me. This was an opium den.

My eyes continued to scan the area. There was a very large population of east Asian, probably more Chinese than any other culture, but I could tell that there was a definite mix. This was the city's "Chinatown".

My feet continued to carry me through the area and into another where the buildings had more of an adobe feel to them. Words written on buildings were in Spanish, some of which I could read and I read enough to know that I had entered a predominantly Mexican section of town. Looking about the area my suspicions had been proven to be accurate; there were a lot of Mexicans here.

I continued to move from one section to another. There was a large Irish section and even a section that seemed to isolate Native Americans. It dawned on me, back in Seattle our "Chinatown" might have started due to racism but now it had become an area to freely express and maintain a culture rather than creating isolation. Here, there was still racism. These areas weren't here to express culture, these people were forced to live in their respective locations and any deviation would only barely be tolerated at best. But it wasn't just racism, it was fear. Cultures stuck together out of fear of reprisal from other cultures, especially from whites, like me. This had explained the cautious looks of fear and hatred that I sometime received as I walked through areas where I didn't belong.

I continued my circumference of the town, hoping to get a better perspective before I walked into the heart of it. My journey took me into area that initially felt more "comfortable". The signs were all in English, the inhabitants were white and I was getting far less stares, although I was still getting quite a few since my clothing made me stand out like a sore thumb.

The buildings had changed. These were now two story businesses made of wood. It reminded me of downtown Virginia City with large print on their buildings and wooden raised sidewalks. Large wooden pillars held up balconies. People were still dressed in their 1900 clothing.

Suddenly I was aware of where I was. I was sure I was in Virginia City circa 1900, that much I was starting to accept. However, I was now simply aware of what part of town I was in. There were several bars and saloons but there were other buildings, buildings where a lot of women were going in and out and some with male escorts. There were a lot of women in this section and I could hear quite a bit of giggling from one bar, and some sounds of "entertainment" from an upstairs open window. I had stumbled into the red light district and from the looks of things it was very prosperous. And why shouldn't it be? If I was right then the Millionaire's Washoe Club wasn't too far from here, there were many investors that came to town to spend lots of money, and there were plenty of miners that were drunk and lonely.

It was time for me to leave this place post haste. It wasn't the fact that prostitutes made me uncomfortable. This may be circa 1900 but I was still a happily married man and I could easily refute any approach. It was the fact that this line of business had a habit of being very risky. Jealousy and drunkenness often lead to violence. The tales of the Washoe Millionaire's Club already had one story of a prostitute being killed and if I recall there was a famous Madam that was killed as well. On top of that I didn't want to be accused of standing between a potential customer and his favorite patron which would lead to even more violence. Yes, it was time to leave.

I turned the corner and headed deeper into the heart of the town. I could see several opera houses, comedy clubs, and theaters. I could see various bars and saloons offering billiards, gambling, food, drinks, and even target practicing. I could hear a piano being played from one saloon and a large group of drunken men singing in another. A fight broke out in a third that spilled into the street that I easily avoided. There were clothing shops, a postal service and several banks. There were general goods shops, and barber shops, a sheriff's office and a printing press.

I tried to keep my route on the uneven, raised, wooden sidewalk. It was more uneven than during my era at Virginia City. If I wasn't careful I could twist an ankle.

I continued to take in the sights before me. A stagecoach pulled by a team of horses rolled down the main street. Several riders on horses were riding in the opposite direction. A few chickens came running along chased by a little boy. Now I knew why the chicken crossed the road. I almost laughed at that.

People continued to pass me by dressed in their 1900 attire with the men wearing dusty and dirty jeans and a simple long sleeve pullover shirt. The women either wore their dresses or a simple blouse and skirt combination. Each of them continued to give me a stare.

I paid no attention to them; there was something else I needed.

I needed information without causing too much attention. If I had the internet this would be a lot easier. The best thing to do was to swing into this era's version of the internet, a library. But since I hadn't seen one, and wasn't sure if this town had one, I took the next best thing, I chose the printing press.

As I walked in, I could hear the "ca-chunk, ca-chunk" as the various individuals were working the large printing press, slapping their machine down upon the paper, making their imprints. In some regards this reminded me of a UPS store or some other mailing business where workers were busy with their machines rather it be a computer, a scale, a printing labeler, a copier, a laminator, or anything else. The technology had drastically changed, but in some regards not much had changed. Unlike my era, the store smelled of ink, paper dust, sweat, oil, and some other chemicals that I was sure was used to wash their equipment.

My eyes scanned the area until I caught a stack of papers sitting beside the wall next to me. I discreetly grabbed one and gave it a quick glance until I found the information that I wanted. The year of the paper said 1875. My initial guess at my temporal displacement was off. Not only was I not in the twenty first century, I wasn't even in the twentieth century.

"Hey, ya payin' fer dat? It ain't fer free readin' ya know. We all gotta make ah livin'."

The shop owner's protest brought me out of my reverie. What had initially started out as a quick glance turned into a several minute endeavor. I guess it was the shock of the final proof of my new reality.

I immediately reached into my pocket to pull out some change and then stopped. What change I did have in my pocket wouldn't work. I put the paper back where I had retrieved it, gave a quick apology, and went to leave. My quick spin had been too fast and I hadn't looked to see where I was going. My body crashed into the person directly behind me.

"I'm sorry. My apologies. Let me…" I stopped mid-sentence.

The metallic star badge on his vest caught my immediate attention. The man looked similarly dressed in the fashion with most of the other men with the exception of a vest, one of those cowboy hats on his head, the highly polished star badge that was on the upper left of his vest, and the gun that was in his holster on his belt.

"Heard that some stranger was in town, thought I'd check it out myself. I've been followin' ya. Name's Elijah, Sheriff Elijah, or just Sheriff to you."

He gave me a quick look over before proceeding.

"Where are you from?" He asked accusatory.

"Seattle," I quickly said. Although I wasn't really from Seattle, I was from an outlying smaller city that most people don't bother knowing about. Saying "Seattle" was easier.

He gave a curious stare. I had to remember my history. The landing of the Denny Party, the very group that the street was named after, on Alki Point wasn't until November 13, 1851 and that was a forced landing during a rainstorm. The corporate seal of the City of Seattle wasn't until 1869. It was now 1875 only six years later. News didn't travel very fast. There was no internet, cell phones, and we were three to four states away. This was an inland mountainous, desert mining town. No one here would care about a coastal city about 730 miles away. Sure, those who paid attention to the telegraph or even the trade routes through the railroad would be more up to date. But a sheriff in a landlocked state whose only concern was about the safety, security, and the upkeep of the law in Virginia City probably wouldn't be concerned about a city in Washington.

"It's In Washington State, on the coast," I said quickly.

I knew it was on the Puget Sound, but that would be difficult to explain. This person has probably never seen the ocean and would probably never see the sound. It was close enough to the truth without having to explain myself further.

He gave me a scowl as if to suggest that my remark seemed to explain a lot.

"Well, where are you ya stayin'?" Again his question seemed accusatory. The sheriff was trying to fish for information. He obviously didn't trust me and he was trying to find an excuse to validate his suspicions.

"I don't have a place to stay yet."

"We don't take kindly to vagrants. We got too many o' them as is."

"I'm not a ..." I was trying to correct him.

"You don't have no place to stay, no job and don't have no money neither. Ain't that right?"

He did have a point. I had no plans for the night. I did have money, but none of it was valid any more. The credit cards were useless. I couldn't use anything I had on me as identification. I guess I was a vagrant. I had to think of something fast.

"I'm hoping to get a job as a ..."

"Let meh guess, you want to try your hand at minnin. We'll there's plenty o' opportunities. Ya go see Sam down at dah mines. He'll fix ya right up. Though I doubt ya'll be able ta handle it. There's been folk that've been 'alf yer age an they coulnn't 'andle it. Plus, theres cave-ins all da time. Ah doubt you'll be lastin' more dan a few days, a week tops. When dat happens I don't expect ta see yah on the streets beggin'. It won't be tolerated."

I nodded at that, gave him a courteous "thank you" and started to make my way to the mines. I wasn't sure if that was what I really wanted to do, but I wanted to

196

make good on the sheriff's offer. Last thing I wanted to do was wind up in jail. No one would know that I was there and no one would care.

I still had no idea what I was going to do even if I did find a job. I was still stuck in Virginia City in 1875 and my mind was wandering when I stopped dead in my tracks. The sound that I heard froze me to my core. There was no denying what had I heard, I had listened to it for thirteen years.

"Daddy?!"

Chapter: Ruth

"*D*addy? Is that really you?"

The voice was slightly deeper, more confident, and more mature, but there was no denying what I had heard. My only question was, was I hearing what I wanted to hear or was this really her? I turned to face the location from where the sound had come from.

The form that I saw standing not too far from me wasn't what I had expected. The individual was about twenty years old and more of a young woman than my little girl. Her hair was golden brown, almost blonde, and was shoulder length and curly. She wore dark brown jeans with dark brown boots and a light brown, long sleeve shirt, unlike the majority of the women who wore some form of dress or blouse and skirt. Her frame was tall and her shoulders were set firm with confidence as was her stance and her face. No longer was this the timid and shy little girl that had hid behind a menu. She was a proud and confident woman. Much had changed about her, but there was no mistaken her eyes. Her eyes were the same, deep dark blue. They were the reflection of mine with the shine of recognition.

"Daddy...It is you! It's really you!"

Before the reality of meeting my daughter, my grown up daughter, had a chance to sink in, she ran toward me and threw her arms around me. I could hear her start to sob with relief or joy, I couldn't tell. Perhaps it was a little bit of both. I put my arms around her to comfort her, and to ensure myself that what I was experiencing was real. It was then that I had realized how tall she had become; she was almost as tall as I was. When she was done sobbing she pulled slightly away from me and did her best to compose herself.

"Come. Come on inside. There's a lot to talk about."

She directed me into a nearby saloon. It looked like any other. It was a two story building with a portion of the upper floor sticking out a little and propped up with wooden pillars, covering the wooden sidewalk. The doors were only half doors on hinges which allowed them to swing inward as we made our way inside.

The inside seemed typical for a saloon at this time period, or at least what I had seen in the movies and TV shows. There was a bar at the far back that took up the whole wall. A bartender was busy arranging glasses and washing them, although I was sure that he was in violation of several health codes by the way he was washing them. There was a wooden stairway on the left wall that led up to a balcony that overlooked the saloon below. I could see several doors beyond the balcony and was sure that these were bedrooms that were either lived in or rented out. There were several round tables scattered about the lower level, where we were, with about four chairs each. There were only a few patrons in the saloon, all quiet and docile, sipping whatever they had in their glasses. To me, it seemed as if someone had died and those that were here were afraid to say anything to break the silence and wake the dead. This was nothing like the other taverns that were full of singing either with entertainment girls or a room full of drunken men. The other taverns also hand dancing, drinking, and fighting that sometimes spilled out into the streets. This tavern had none of those.

Ruth directed me to a table and we both pulled up a chair to sit down. As we sat there I could get a better close up look at her. She was wearing the earrings that we had bought her in our era, in the small tourist trap shop that we had entered. Around her neck was a silver chain necklace that held a penny attached to it. This was the penny that we had squashed near the suicide table. I wondered if anyone had taken a real good look at the date of the penny. I would have loved to see their reaction if they had.

I was about to say something, although I wasn't sure what. I didn't know to say really. It was all too surreal. However, before I was able to put two words together, Ruth started a stream of questions and comments that ran together like she usually did when she was overly excited. Despite everything that had changed about her, this had remained the same.

"How did we get here? How do we get back? Why did I come first and have to spend all of this time without you? What's going on? What are we going to do?"

The questions came so quickly that I wasn't sure she really wanted an answer and she gave me no time between questions to give one, even if I did know any of the answers.

"Ruth," I said.

"Did you know that I just missed Samuel Clemens, you know, the guy that wrote as Mark Twain. He was here, you know. Anyway, the last time he was here was to witness the hanging of a man that killed Virginia City's famous prostitute, Julia Bulette."

Did Ruth just say "Julia Bulette"? Where had I heard that name before?

"Did you know that Yellowstone National Park was created only three years ago? Yosemite won't be one for another fifteen. Didn't mom talk about going to Yosemite National Park and Bodie California next year, which is the year after we went to Virginia City seven years ago?"

"Ruth."

"Did you guys go to Yosemite? How long has it been for you? You don't look any older than when I came here. Aren't those the same clothes you wore when I came here?"

"Ruth," I said again.

"Did you know that the telephone won't be invented for another year? I've lived all this time without my phone. Not that it would do me any good. There wouldn't be any connection out here."

As Ruth continued to talk, ignoring my attempts to interrupt her, her eyes were becoming wider, her speech was becoming more rapid and her words were running closer together. I had to get her attention.

"Ruth!" I said with a little more force. This had gotten her to stop talking.

"What?!" She asked.

"You're getting overly excited again. If we were back...back where we came from, I would give you your medication. I'm sorry, but I don't have any on me."

She looked back at me wide eyed. At first I thought she just might start to argue, like she used to when she was younger. However she simply gave me a nod. I could see that she was doing her best to compose herself. I wondered how she had managed to not drive herself and everyone else crazy. When she was thirteen she couldn't or wouldn't see these episodes by herself. When I saw them coming on I did everything I could to help her, including remembering to give her the medication that she was on. She would never remember to do it for herself. Now, she had been without it for seven years. When she had done her best to settle down she excused herself from the table and made her way toward the bar.

"Coffee. The usual." Her voice had a sense of forced calmness.

I watched as the bartender moved toward the back of his area and pulled a metal coffee pot off of a wood burning stove. He poured the liquid that had been brewing into a metal cup that he pulled out from under the bar. The sludge that came forth was thick and dark. It reminded me of "cowboy coffee", a brew so thick that when a cowboy tossed in a spoon and it stood up, then it was done. I couldn't see anyone drinking this kind of stuff, and yet my daughter took the cup and tossed the liquid down. Gone was the girl that drank a quarter cup of regular coffee and three quarters of creamer. My little girl wasn't my little girl any more.

I waited, knowing what would happen next. Caffeine had the reverse effect on Ruth, instead of speeding her up, it actually calmed her down. The stimulant allowed her body to catch up with her brain; this allowed her to become stable and reduced her mood swings. I watched as her wide eyes started to settle down.

Now that she had calmed down I remembered her saying something about a woman, Julia Bulette. Then it struck me where I had heard that name before. It was the name of the woman that I had met outside of my motel. This was getting creepier by the moment. But, if she had already died in this present's past, then what did she want with me in the here and now? That was something to think about later, right now I needed to talk to my daughter.

"Are you alright?" I asked with a bit of concern in my voice.

"Yes, I'm fine. The caffeine will…"

"No, that's not what I mean. I mean, how are you doing? How have you taken care of yourself? Are you eating well? Do you have a job? A boyfriend? What has your life been like?"

Now it was my turn to ramble off questions as quickly as I could.

"I'm doing fine dad. No, I don't have a boyfriend. Life has been tough, but I've managed. I've found work here, as a bar maid, server."

I shook my head. "No. You shouldn't be working here. People die in places like this and women are given a bad time in the time we came from. Here, I'm sure things are worse. We should get you a better job."

"Doing what? I didn't even get a chance to finish high school. Besides, you've got to remember dad, this is 1875, and women don't get to vote for almost another 45 years. I'm still expected to do all of the dishes, the laundry, the housecleaning and that's about it. I don't get to have a better job."

"And don't tell me what I should or shouldn't be doing. I've been here for seven years. Seven years! I had to live on my own, find work, make a living. I did this all without you. You weren't even here. I depended on you, I needed you and you weren't here!"

The words stung. Some of the worst words that a father could ever hear were how he had failed his child.

"I'm here now," I said softly reaching for her hands.

She shook her head. "Well, I don't need you anymore. I can do this by myself."

"I will always be there for my little girl."

"That's the problem. Dad, I'm not your little girl any more. I'm all grown up."

"You will always be my little girl." I paused to consider her words before adding. "But I will do my best to treat you like the young woman you have become."

For one moment I thought that I would get another emotional blast, or perhaps that she would storm off and I would run the risk of never seeing her again. I've already faced that fear once; I didn't want to face it again. Yet, despite the emotional outbursts, she threw herself at me and held me as if she were afraid to let me go. I put my arms around her and gave her comfort as her tears started to flow.

Once she composed herself she asked, "What are your plans?"

"Well, the sheriff made it quite clear; I need to get a job and a place to stay. If it's ok with you, I can stay with you until I can get my own place."

She put her hand on mine. "You can stay with me, here, upstairs, for as long as you need."

I smiled. I had taken care of her while she was younger, now she was taking care of me. I guess that's how family works.

"What were you thinking in lines of work?" She asked.

"I hear they have an opening at the mines."

"The mines? Dad, no, you can't. It's too dangerous. People die there all the time. There is hardly a week that goes by that someone isn't buried under a ton of rock, they hit a gas pocket or that there's some other accident. Besides, you're..." she stopped as if she were afraid to say what was on her mind.

"I'm what?"

"You're old, that's what. You're not as young as these men, most of which are half your age. And you're not as strong as you used to be. I'm concerned about you."

I smiled at that. She was in fact concerned me, I could hear it in her tone, and I did appreciate it, but I had something that might just change her mind. I pulled out a piece of paper from my back pocket, unfolded it, and gave it to her. I watched her eyes as she read the piece. I wasn't sure if she remembered writing it, but it slowly brought tears to her eyes. It read:

Dads are awesome!

My dad is so awesome that I feel like I just want to hug him so tight that his eyes pop out super far and go back inside of him because I love him a lot. He is funny and he is a great artist and he loves dragons and he loves to play "Lord of the Rings" and he even has their characters too.

My dad, Stephen!

My dad's name is Stephen and he just loves to paint, play on his computer, fix things, watch cartoons, Wright stories on his computer and read a scary book called "Stephen King a novel: Bag of bones and The complete works of Edgar Allen Poe "and he is on chapter 25 page, 590 and he loves it and the other book, he is on chapter 10, page 28.

Get to know Stephen

Stephen is a great guy, a great dad I should say and he is great to be with and hang out with. He is 42 years old... I think that I should make a list about him.

Favorite color: Blue
Favorite book: Stephen King a novel: Bag of bones and The complete works of Edgar Allan Poe
Favorite food: Ice cream: Rocky road
Favorite game: Lord of the Rings
Favorite hobbies: Painting

Well, that is about... oh wait a minute! I have one more thing about my dad or maybe two or three things. Stephen is 6 feet tall and he likes Cancun, Mexico and he loves to be silly all the time.

His hobbies that he loves to do a lot

Stephen loves to paint little figures from "lord of the rings". He has over 100 and I said over 100 of them.
Me and my dad love to go boating and have fun with me too and that also reminds me that I could do another list but this time, I could make a list what he likes like this.

He likes:

Dragons
Painting
To be funny

He also loves to read and play on the computer a lot (like every day!!!! :). He even likes Star Wars the Clone Wars and for one Father's day, I got him a light saber and the color was blue and he was my softball coach and now, he isn't any more because some of our players were being mean because he was trying to keep them safe and that is not working so he stopped being coach and he is only watching us playing our games.

What a great guy my dad is!

My dad is so strong that he could carry a dozen logs at once and that is how strong he is.

"You've...you've had this all this time?"

I smiled. "Yes, I carry it around with me every day."

"But this is why I don't want you to go work in the mines. Don't you see? You mean so much to me."

"And that is exactly why I will go. This is the daughter, now a young woman that has inspired me to take on any and every challenge to help you become the best person you can possibly be. So yes, I'll take the job at the mines, at least for now, until something better opens up. Well get through this crisis together and I will do everything possible to make sure that we do, including taking this job. Besides, according to this note, I'm quite strong. See?"

I flexed a muscle to show her.

My little speech nearly sent her to tears. She wrapped her arms around me and we embraced for the longest time.

She took a little time to compose herself before changing the subject.

"We can crash at my place tonight and head to church tomorrow morning. Then you can go see Sam down at the mines."

We continued to talk until evening at which time Ruth paid for a meal for the both of us since she had a discount here. I was almost reluctant to eat seeing how the bartender was washing his glasses, but when my stomach protested I ate my fill.

She told me about when she had arrived and how things were since she had been here. She told me a lot about her life and her experience. I was jealous to hear these since I hadn't been there to help see her through them. Yet I continued to listen. I just couldn't believe how grown up she had become.

Ruth's room was a small bedroom upstairs with a single cot and a small dresser. Her clothing was scattered about the place and only reminded me of when she was younger. I guess some things never change. She was able to clear a space on the floor and toss a couple of blankets down. It wasn't the most comfortable rest I would ever have, but it wouldn't be the most uncomfortable either. I've had worse. I wouldn't complain, after all, this would be temporary and I was doing it for her. I would do anything for her. I would walk through hell for her. Sleeping on the floor would be a piece of cake.

Chapter: Saint Mary's-in-the-Mountains Catholic Church

*T*he preacher's voice boomed from the front of the church.

"And in Psalms 11:6 it states '*Upon the wicked he shall rain snares, fire and brimstone, and an horrible tempest: this shall be the portion of their cup.*'"

The preacher was reading out of an old copy of a King James Bible. He was one of those "fire and brimstone" preachers that were certain that everyone except him was going to hell and it was his personal job to scare everyone to death through God's holy wrath. His look seemed to fit the proverbial bible thumping preacher man. He was tall and thin. He wore the traditional missionary clothing of all black with the exception of a white undershirt which was mostly hidden under his black priestly jacket and a black thin tie that was more like a preacher's collar than an actual garment that any man would actually wear. His hair was raven black and slicked back. His eyes were dark and sunken. He looked like a dark version of Ichabod Crane and he gave me the creeps.

Ruth had taken me to this church, Saint Mary's-in-the-Mountains Catholic Church, for a Sunday service. I had agreed although I had to admit that the invitation to attend mass took me by surprise. Neither Ruth nor I had been to church in years, well at least the Ruth that I knew. I don't really know how long she has been going to this church while she was here.

The church was wooden, like most of the buildings here. It was plain looking, rather square-like with a steeple and a cross on top. Inside was just as plain looking. It had wooden pews that were the most uncomfortable piece of furniture that I had ever sat upon. I guess this version of heaven wasn't supposed to be comfortable. There was a modest raised dais up front where the preacher paced back and forth upon, waving his bible in one hand directly at the crowd as if the word of God would leap from the pages at us and his other hand was held up high as if to draw forth some divine intervention.

The church was rather full. It was mostly men, since there was less women here in Virginia City than men. All of the people were seemingly enthralled by the preacher man. However I was sure that this wasn't because of the message. There was enough sin here in this city that periodically individuals needed their conscious clear so they could go back out and do the same thing all over again. I doubted that anyone here really heard what was being said, or at least trying to be said.

Ruth and I sat in the back where we could find room. To tell the truth, the preacher made me feel uncomfortable. Perhaps it was his method of preaching or perhaps it was the fact that I hadn't been to church in a long time, or perhaps it was because I was uncomfortable in larger groups of people.

"And in Revelation 9:18 it states '*By these three was the third part of men killed, by the fire, and the smoke, and by the brimstone, which issued out of their mouths.*'"

Speaking of which, it was already sweltering hot in here. It was uncomfortably warm outside in this Nevada mountain desert, but in here there wasn't any ventilation. The heat had just built up in here and I was afraid that about a half of a dozen women or so were going to pass out. I was also sure that if they did then the preacher would see it as a sign that his message was getting across to his flock and that he was driving out unholy demons and cleansing souls.

"And in Revelation 20:10 it says '*And the devil that deceived them was cast into the lake of fire and brimstone, where the beast and the false prophet are, and shall be tormented day and night for ever and ever*'."

The preacher was building himself to a fever pitch and was bringing his sermon to a crescendo. I couldn't wait for this to be over and from the look of things neither could the majority if not the entirety of the audience.

"And in Revelation 21:8 the word of God is very clear '*But the fearful, and the unbelieving, and the abominable, and merderers, and woremongers, and sorcerers, and idolaters, and all liars, shall have their part in the lake which burneth with fire and brimstone: which is the second death'."*

I turned to Ruth and whispered, trying not to interrupt such a display of self righteousness and condemnation toward everyone else.

"Why would you want to come to this church?"

"There are two kinds of women here in this town, those who go to church and the prostitutes. It doesn't matter if a woman really isn't a prostitute; if she isn't at a church early Sunday morning then she is labeled as one."

I had to remember when I was. During this time women still didn't have any rights and a rumor or an accusation was all the proof anyone needed to condemn her.

"The sin in this town needs to be purged and cast into the fire so it may be cleansed."

Now the preacher was becoming scary. He no longer seemed like a man that was talking about changing people's lives, he seemed to be the type of man that would actually take some action and I didn't like where he was going with this. I've already seen this town. There were the sick and the poor; there were those who were sexually harassed, and others who were racially discriminated. These people didn't need condemnation, they needed compassion.

Suddenly the preacher turned his attention toward me. I was sure that he was trying to burrow his eyes into my soul. Perhaps it was my yawn that made him look my way, I couldn't help it, it was rather warm, stuffy, and he was rambling on a bit. There was something familiar about him that I just couldn't quite put my finger on, something that made the hairs on the back of my neck stand up, and it wasn't just his fire and brimstone, holy-than-thou preaching.

Then it struck me. This was the man I saw in the burning building in my dream. This was the thing that was under my bed. This was the man that grabbed my ankle and tried to drown me. This was the man at the top of the stairs in the Washoe Building. This was the man that had declared war upon me and my family.

The feelings of initial fear and terror had shifted. The feelings of displeasure at his condemnation of others had changed. I no longer had a discomfort about this man; I had a full blown, hostile, feeling of hatred and loathing for this man. I hadn't done anything to make him haunt me, at least not yet or perhaps never would; I don't know how these temporal shifts work. But whatever I did do, or was about to do, or he thinks I might have done or will do, or not do no matter what it was, wasn't a reason to haunt me and my family in my time. Probably the best thing to do was to stay away from him, and then there wouldn't be a reason for him to haunt me later, that is it would be his later and my earlier.

I was getting a headache from trying to figure this out and it was only made worse by the lack of air in the church. Fortunately the preacher had wrapped everything up and had dismissed us. I made a beeline for the doors to try to get them open, not only for my sake, but for the sake of all those who had to put up with the environment.

The fresh cool air would have been a comfort, if there were any. Instead the heat from the desert only blasted us with an arid waft of its midday sun. At least the air wasn't stagnant any more. I moved aside to let everyone out and made my way toward one of the corners of the building, away from the door. If this preacher was like most that I have known in my lifetime, he would do his best to make his way toward the front door to try to greet everyone as they left. I wanted to be as far away from him as possible. All I had to do was to wait for Ruth.

My eyes scanned the door and I noticed two things immediately. The first was that I was right about the preacher. He had been not too far behind me and was holding up the congregation from leaving too quickly by speaking directly to everyone that attempted to walk out.

The second thing that I saw was that Ruth had tried to follow me, but we had become separated. The existing congregation had ended up pushing Ruth towards the other corner of the church. This didn't bother me too much. She would just make her way through the crowd and meet me...

All thoughts of meeting up with Ruth had come to a sudden and immediate halt. A man had cornered her and from the looks of things she was trying to, very politely, move along. Unfortunately he kept putting an arm in her way as he leaned against the wall of the church, blocking her every attempt to make an escape.

I was sure that Ruth would be able to take care of herself; after all, she had done so for seven years. However, two things crossed my mind. The first was that during this time, women didn't have many rights, if any at all. She could get into trouble if she tried to defend herself. A woman's word just didn't carry as much weight as a man's words and if a fight did start out, she would probably be the one in jail. The second thought that went through my mind was that I was a very overprotective father. It didn't matter if the preacher was standing between the two of us, or not I was going to put a stop to this man's unwanted and unsolicited advances.

My straight shot through the exiting congregation was less than cordial. My shoulders had clipped others as I cut through the crowd and I'm sure that my slight, and only slight, shove was not appreciated. However, I didn't care at this point.

My left hand shot out and grabbed the offensive and intrusive man by his arm and slammed him against the side wall of the church. His body hit was a great "thud" that I'm sure that it was heard by all who were present. My right hand reached up and caught him by his throat and kept him pinned there. I could have easily pounded his head into the wall or crushed his throat or perhaps even raised a knee to his groin if I wanted to, I was tempted to do all three simultaneously.

"I believe she said 'NO'. Do you know what the word 'NO' means? I can easily explain it to you."

The answer that the man tried to give was only garbled by the pressure I was applying to his throat. I was getting the gist of his response through his eyes. They weren't pleading, like I had hoped that they would have been and they weren't even full of understanding. Instead they were filled with hatred and were challenging me to go through with my intentions. Yet, I wanted to hear it through his voice. I slightly let go of his throat so he could talk.

"...and who are you?" He asked full of spite. "Some other lover that she's banging? I bet she's had plenty and if she's resorting to old men like you…"

I reapplied my pressure and slammed him against the wall hard. I could hear his head strike the wood behind him and from what I could tell, his back had hit as well. He was having trouble catching his breath. I hoped that was enough to catch his attention.

"I want to you to listen, and listen very carefully. I am her father. I will not tolerate you insinuating that she is some form of prostitute and I will not stand for it. Secondly, if you ever touch her again, I will break your arm and any other part of your body that I see fit. Do I make myself clear?"

The response from his eyes was all that I needed to hear. He continued to challenge me as if I hadn't the will to follow through with my threats. I was about to show him that I was when I suddenly realized, I had seen this man before.

I had been mistaken. I realized that the truck that almost ran us off the road did have a driver and that the truck that almost ran me over in my nightmare did have a driver. I had been in too much shock, in too much horror to realize or register who or what I had seen. It was easier to accept that there hadn't been a driver in each case, now I realized I was wrong, there had been. I remembered because I was now looking at his face.

This man, this man that I had pinned against the wall was the same man that had tried to kill me a hundred years from now. It was like with the preacher, another individual that had tried to kill me in my present, his future. What did these two have to do with each other? Did they know the little girl?

"That is enough!"

The voice was commanding and haunting at the same time. It was easily recognizable and I didn't need to turn around to know who it was. The preacher had made his presence known.

"I totally agree," I stated as I slammed my hostage against the wall. "He simply doesn't understand. I will not stand for …"

"No, it is you that doesn't understand." The preacher's tirade was directed towards me. "I will not stand for violence here upon this holy ground and I will not stand for violence perpetrated upon members of my congregation. This man, Luke, is a righteous man with a righteous name and you will do well to leave him and my congregation alone. He and his father have been upstanding members of this church, which is the least I can say about you and your daughter. Neither you nor she are welcomed here in God's house anymore."

"And who do you think you are?" I asked with a bit of anger.

I had just about enough of this man's sanctimonious attitude. I was about to tell him that I also had a righteous name and could easily quote as much scripture as he could, if not more.

"I am Abraham Smith, and I am God's right hand. I will not have you act in such a manner."

"And I will not have men approaching my daughter in such a fashion."

"Well, if you daughter were to dress more appropriately…"

That was it. I was about to let go of Luke and punch out Abraham. However, the voice caught my attention.

"I hope I'm not interrupting anything. Or, should I start taking people into the station?"

That was another voice I had recognized. Sheriff Elijah had just come upon the scene. Why isn't there a policeman around when you need one and when he does show up its at the most inopportune time? Before I had a chance to explain, it was Ruth who had spoken.

"No sheriff, I think my father has rectified the situation. We shall have no more problems with this gentleman. Isn't that correct, Luke?"

I could feel the man's eyes try to bore into me if only for a moment as if to tell me that this wasn't finished. Then he gave a quick, non-convincing nod. I took my cue and let go of him. Again, he gave me that look as if I should keep a look out over my shoulder as he slowly walked away. Abraham also gave me the same look as he made his way toward his congregation that had stopped to watch the spectacle. I had also turned to take Ruth and make my leave, but when I turned I came face to face with the Sheriff Elijah.

"Ah know ya'll new in town an' all, an' I've been lenient with ya, but it won't last long so let me give ya some friendly advice. First, keep yar nose clean. I won't hesitate to take ya in, an' the only reason why I didn't was 'cause of Luke, which brings me to my second piece of advice."

"Luke, there, is no good. He's the son of a very rich land owner around these here parts who gives a bunch of money to the local church, this one to be exact. Luke is one of those that think because he has a rich daddy means he can do anythin' he wants. I've been looking for a reason to bust him hard, but can't get much on him. An' even if I did, his pa would be raisin' hell. I didn't bring ya in cause I wanted to watch ya beat the livin' snot out of him, but ya didn't hear that from me."

"Now, my gut feelin' is that ya just made some enemies, so I'd be watchin' my back if I were you." The sheriff gave a slight tip of his hat toward Ruth before turning to move on.

I had expected that this was the end of our spectacle. We would go our separate ways and do our best to stay away from each other and that would be the end of that. It was a large enough town, and neither I nor Ruth needed to stay here anyway. We could make our way to Seattle if we wanted to and put all of this behind us. Of course we would still be locked in the past without knowing how or why. However, the commotion behind me caught my attention and I simply couldn't ignore it.

As I turned around, I caught sight of one of the women start to faint. A few people around her had caught her and were trying to lay her on ground. She was having trouble breathing and was slightly trembling.

I dashed over to her and pushed a few people away. The woman was very pale, and her breathing had become rapid and shallow. Her eyes fluttered and she was barely conscious.

"Begone demon. I command you to exit this woman's body and leave her be. By the power of Christ Almighty, I banish you. Get behind me Satan. You will not possess this woman."

Now I was really going to punch this priest. He had absolutely no idea what he was doing but as long as he was the center of attention, he was going to do it. What he hadn't realized was that he was actually half of this woman's problem.

I ignored him and went straight to work. I pushed a few others aside so I could get closer to her and immediately started removing some of her top layers of clothing. I heard gasps of shock as the others around her came to their own realization that I was trying to disrobe her for my personal pleasure.

"Unhand her you beast," yelled the preacher. "You will not touch her."

I felt a couple of strong arms try to pull me away.

"She isn't possessed, you idiot!" I protested. "She has heat exhaustion, probably having heat stroke! She doesn't need an exorcism; she needs to cool down, water, and shade."

"Blasphemous. Sheriff, I need you to remove..."

"My father knows what he's doing," my daughter challenged back. "Let him finish."

The crowd had silenced and all eyes turned toward the sheriff. I could tell that he was trying to decide who to side with. Suddenly he nodded toward me.

"Let him try."

Although Abraham said nothing, I could almost hear him seething with rage. I guess the sheriff was still siding with me since I almost buried Luke into the church wall. I felt the hands around me let go and I fell back into removing her top layer of clothing.

"She's too hot. All of these layers are keeping the hot air trapped. Here hold this, and this," I said as I started to hand out the woman's blouse, skirt, and boots.

I didn't disrobe her all the way down, just down to her very tight corset that was over her undergarments. Quickly, I turned her over and loosened her corset, but didn't take it off. No wonder her breathing was shallow, the corset was too tight and was already crushing her ribs. As soon as I had loosed it, she was able to take deeper breaths. As oxygen started to come into her lungs she started to open her eyes a little.

"Water!" I demanded. "Anyone have water?"

I heard a slight murmur and then realized that a flask had been passed through the crowd. Once I had gotten a hold of it, I raised it to her lips and let her drink. At first I let her sip, then let her drink more. She started to guzzle the water as if her body was in such desperate need and it was her only life saving opportunity that she could cling to. I guess, perhaps both were the case. After she had drunk the water, I could tell that she was feeling much better, but still weak. Despite the fact that I had almost completely undressed her in front of strangers, she had a smile of gratitude on her face.

"Now, get her to her home, put her in some shade. Keep the windows open enough to allow a draft. If you can get her in a cool bath, that would be better. Make sure she stays in loose clothing and keep giving her water."

Some of her friends around her started to help her up. The advice had been taken and would be followed and I was sure that they would take her away as quickly as they could, but they stopped.

"Wait…" the woman said weakly.

The two other women that had hold of her and her clothing stopped for a moment. The woman turned to me and continued to speak.

"Thank you. Thank you, I feel much better already. I don't know what would have happened if you hadn't been here."

"You just need to cool down," I said. "Get plenty of water and stay cool. Also, have the local doc come and check up on you."

"We'll make sure she gets that bath," one of her friends said as they started up again to take the woman home.

I turned to catch up with Ruth and found Abraham, the preacher man, the right hand of God, staring at me with complete contempt and hatred. The very person I was trying to avoid, the very person that I was trying to

ensure that our paths didn't cross, now had a personal
vendetta against me.

Chapter: Reflections

"*T*wo root beers please."

I had come up to the bar in the tavern where we were staying and placed my order. This only inspired an odd look from both the bartender and from Ruth. I was pretty sure that they had root beer so I wondered why they were looking at me in such a fashion.

"What?" I asked.

"First of all, I've had real beer. I do have an occasional drink."

That was hard to accept. Only a few days ago she was my little girl that would never touch alcohol. Now she was all grown up and didn't know how to handle it.

"But I don't," I said hoping that it would end the conversation. I should have known better. She may have my eyes, but she had her mother's personality, strong and independent.

"But I do," she snapped back.

"Just humor me…. please."

"Ruth?" The voice came from behind the counter. "Is anything wrong? Is this man bothering you? I can have him thrown out."

I turned to the bartender. "Do you mind? This is a private conversation."

"Now look here," he shot back. "She's the best waitress we have, I've known her for years and I don't take kindly to strangers that think that they can…"

"William," Ruth interrupted, "I would like for you to meet my overly protective but well intended father. Dad, this is Will."

I gave a slight scowl as I narrowed my eyes at him. What father isn't overly protective of his daughter?

"Dad, don't be that way. He's a sweet guy, really he is. He took me in and gave me a job here. If it wasn't for him I'd still be on the street."

Now I really didn't like him. He had filled in the gap that I couldn't. He had been there when I wasn't.

Ruth turned to me and whispered so she couldn't be overheard. "Secondly, there isn't any root beer. I've tried. No one's heard about it so my guess is, is that it hasn't been invented yet, or at least it's not for the general public."

She was right. Root beer may have been invented by now, but won't be available to the general public until 1876, another year from now. Even then, it still might take another year or two before it reaches Virginia City. Once it did, it would only be available through the local pharmacy, not at a tavern. The main ingredient of sassafras would prove to be carcinogenic and would eventually be banned, that was until the safrole could be removed and that wouldn't happen for many years. In other words, I was in the wrong year, the wrong place, and the root beer would be poisonous anyway. A sarsaparilla would fall under the same category. I wondered what they did have good to drink that I could order.

"Two beers," Ruth said as she ordered the drinks.

I looked at her to protest, but decided against it. She knew that I didn't drink but perhaps I needed a beer after all of this. Perhaps I needed two. Ruth paid for the two beers and we went outside to sit on the bench on the wooden raised walkway under the eaves.

I took a sip of my beer and almost spat it back out. I never did like the taste of alcohol and everything I had tasted had been very refined. This was strong and thick. But it was worse than just an odd taste that I had never acquired; it was the fact that it was warm. That was another thing I had to get used to, there was a lack of refrigeration out here.

That was yet another realization of when I was. It was going to be difficult to get used to. I looked at my beer. This wasn't going to help, but it might make me feel better. I took a gulp, and then another. I could feel it hit my stomach and start to enter my blood stream. My mind started to calm and I started to become more relaxed.

"So, that's it I guess." Ruth's remark had broken the silence between us while she continued to sip her warm beer.

"I've been able to live here quietly for seven years without any problems and yet you've managed to get us both kicked out of church, piss off the local sheriff, the local clergy, and the local son of a wealthy business man all in one day. Now you've almost ticked off Will. Good job, dad."

"Ruth! Watch your language."

"Don't give me that. I am twenty years old dad; I can say what I want."

Damn. Where was the little girl that I used to know? I wondered what else she did that I didn't know about. Then again, I really didn't want to know.

"Yeah, I know," I consented, "I just miss my little girl that's all. I've missed seven years of your life. I've missed you growing up. I would have taken you out to your first beer, once you hit twenty one of course. I would have taken you to your prom. Damn this whole time warp, thing."

There was a moment of silence as we sipped our warm beer. It was Ruth who spoke first.

"How did we get here? How are we going to get back? Why are we here?"

I shook my head. I usually had an answer to every question she had ever asked, I had always prided myself that she could come to me for answers. Now, I didn't have any.

"I don't know. But we'll find a way and we'll see this through together."

I hoped so, I had seen her grave and I would do anything to ensure that this wouldn't become a reality. However, the place of Virginia City and the year 1875 rang a bell in the back of my mind, but I couldn't place it. If I could figure it out perhaps I would have a better idea of why we were here or if there was something that we were supposed to do.

"In the meantime," I continued. "We have to be careful with what we do and say. We can't mess with the past. Who knows what consequences might happen if we cause something to happen that wasn't, or if we don't do something that is supposed to happen."

"You mean like saving Ms. Willows? Or by ordering a root beer? Or by upsetting a good number of people?"

She had a point. I had to be more careful. I may have already changed the future. What if Ms. Williams was supposed to die? But then again what if I was supposed to save her?

"I'll try to be more careful myself. However, there are times that I simply just can't sit by and not do anything, but we'll both have to use more wisdom from here on in. As far as the root beer is concerned, I doubt that will cause any ripples in time. William will get over being slightly upset, and you're right, he's a nice guy. The others I've upset? That's too bad. I won't stand for bullies, no matter who they are, especially if they bully you. I won't stand for it."

Ruth was about to speak, but my nod caught her attention. She turned to look and understood what I was directly her toward. Now was not the time to speak about being out of time. The sheriff had made his way toward us.

"Mornin'," Sheriff Elijah stated as he gave a tip of his hat. I suspect that it was more towards Ruth than me.

"Mornin'", we both answered back in unison.

"What brings you here sheriff?" I asked.

"Just makin' my rounds, checkin' up on ya, makin' sure you're stayin' out of trouble. Did ya' look into a job at the mines?

"Yup", I said. "I start tomorrow. You can ask Sam if you want."

He shook his head. "Ya seem to be an honest man, but if ya lying I'll find out sooner or later."

"Ah also wanted to come by and give ya some gratitude an' thanks an' all. Seems Ms. Willows is makin' a great recovery and doin' much better now.

Doc gave her a clean bill of health this mornin'. Much obliged."

"Seems ta me that ya made an enemy with the preacher, Abraham Smith. I've seen that look in people's eyes before. If I didn't know better, I'd think that he's lookin' to get a lychin' party after ya. Ya just be careful. Same goes with Luke."

"I'll do my best to stay clear of the both of them while I'm in town," I replied.

The sheriff tilted his hat again toward Ruth and was about to make his departure when the both of them seemed to tense at the sight of the stagecoach that was pulling up across the street.

Chapter: Alexander

*T*he stagecoach that pulled up was pulled by a team of six pristine looking horses. The chestnut colored steeds looked very muscular and well trained, but not necessarily what I had expected to see in these parts. I had seen some strong looking draft horses and some mules, but these looked more like show horses than anything else. They had a high stepping precision that seemed to show off both the set of horses and the occupants of the coach.

The coach itself wasn't like any other coach I've seen in these parts. Instead of a large, beat up stagecoach similar to the Wells Fargo coach, this was a smaller version, almost like a carriage. The top half was jet black with red trim while the bottom half was bright red. Two gas lanterns hung on the coach, one on each side. There was a section behind the carriage part where a footman could stand. Two men were driving the team of horses while another stood in the back. The entire mode of travel seemed to scream money.

"Who's in the stagecoach?" I asked.

"Ain't no stagecoach," the sheriff said. "It's called a park drag. Not that I be known' the difference, mind ya, 'cept that it's smaller and lighter, but ol' Mr. Jacobson over there will be the first ta correct ya if ya' callin' it a coach. An' them horses? Ah ain't seen a breed like 'em. He calls 'em Hackney or something like that. If ya ask me, they don't be lookin' like some draft horse that would be carrin' a coach load around these parts. My guess is that he's got them on some ranch near Carson City and drive them up here just to look fancy an all. He probably gets around mostly by railroad if he wants to travel further. Not many coaches come up this way anyway; most people just take the train, 'less they want ta show off."

"Anyway, that there's one Mr. Alexander Jacobson. He's the richest guy around here, makes Luke's pa look broke. Now, them two get along like oil an' water if ya know what I mean. Like you've noticed, I don't mind anyone that can put ol' Luke in his place, buy ya want to steer clear of Mr. Jacobson there. He's one guy ya really don't want to mess with. He's rich and he's powerful and he don't mind rubbin' it in. Don't like him one bit. Been wantin' to find some reason to haul him into prison myself. Wouldn't mind watchin' what would happen if he and Luke were put in the same cell. Now that would be entertainment, but ya didn't hear it from me."

"He comes up here to buy out some foreclosed business or home an' toss out the occupants Soon he'll have the whole town and probably da mines as well. Rumor has it that he's been forcin' the foreclosures himself an' if anyone can prove that, I'll be more than happy to drag his sorry hide in. 'Till then, all I can do is watch as he drags this city under."

I watched as the man in back stepped down from the coach, came around, and opened the door for the coach's occupant. He had chosen the door that faced us, away from the side of the street that was closest to him. This not only let me get a good look at who this "Mr Alexander Jacobson" was, but it also allowed him to be seen by a wider range of people. From his grandstanding attitude, I could tell that he wanted the whole city to know that he was here.

The man wore a three piece suit complete with black pants, white shirt, black vest and back jacket. He had a black thin tie. In one hand he had a black top hand that he immediately put on his head. In his other hand was a walking stick, or perhaps a cane, with a metal cap on the top. He looked like he belonged in the big city of New York and definitely out of place here. I initially wondered what had brought him here, but then I remembered the Millionaire's Washoe Club. However, that building was several blocks from here.

Mr. Jacobson waited briefly and scanned the streets to make sure that everyone was watching him and from what I could tell, they were. Everyone had stopped to see what he was doing. But it wasn't out of respect or even idle curiosity. It seemed that the town was afraid of this man. Then, when he was sure that he was the center of attention, he made a grand sweeping gesture with his arm as he put on his top hat and turned toward the shops that were behind him.

Alexander went straight to the shop he had in mind. I had thought that perhaps he had gone into the wrong store. The seamstress and fabric shop didn't seem like a place that he would frequent and it seemed to not be as upscale as I thought that he would prefer.

Suddenly we could all hear yelling and screaming from inside. An argument had commenced and from what I could tell, it was rather heated. The few words that I could make out weren't very flattering to the woman that was answering back.

I couldn't believe what I was seeing. No one was coming to this woman's rescue. She was simply being belittled and berated in a tone loud enough for the entire town to hear. This had to stop and I didn't care about any temporal anomalies. I got up from the bench. Someone had to stop this.

To my surprise, the sheriff put his arm out and stopped me. I looked back at him and was about to protest, but he only shook his head. When I turned toward Ruth, she only gave a downcast look.

"Ain't none of your business."

I was about to correct him. I was about to tell him that yes, it was my business. It was always my business when people were ill-treated. It was also his business. But then I had to remember. Women don't even have the right to vote yet. They were still considered lower class and could be treated with great disrespect and it would be tolerated. Yet, I still couldn't just stand by. If the sheriff had to arrest me, then so be it. I brushed aside his arm and went to step forward.

Suddenly both Mr. Jacobson and the woman business owner came into view. He had her by her left upper arm and was escorting her out of her own shop.

"...and stay out!"

I was shocked. I thought that this was her shop. Perhaps he had owned it. Then I remembered what the sheriff had said. This man had just bought out this woman's shop and had tossed her out on the street in front of everyone, publically humiliating her and destroying her income in one swift move. I turned toward Sheriff Elijah.

"Are you just going to stand there? Aren't you going to do anything?"

"Nothing for me to be doin', He's got the legal right. It ain't right an' twists my gut ta watch it, but ain't nothin' I can do about it. An don'cha get any notions that ya can be doin' anythin' either. He's got his rights."

I could hear Alexander Jacobson continue his tirade and belittlement upon the poor woman that was still lying in the street. She was sobbing from the verbal abuse that he was heaping upon her.

"Women have no right running a business! This is a man's world and you and your kind need to stay out! If a man was running this place then it wouldn't have failed! You are a pathetic excuse of a human being! What in the world ever got into your head that you can be a good as a man?! Someone should beat you into your place and if no one here is man enough to do it then it shall be my honor and privilege to do so. You need to be taught a lesson. All women need to be taught a lesson."

I watched as Mr. Jacobson raised his cane into the air, tighten his grip and tensed his muscles.

"...and ya can just stop right there Mr. Jacobson."

Sheriff Elijah was already halfway across the street before he spoke. His long, fast stride had allowed him to move quickly, to the point that I hadn't even seen him move. His right hand fell toward the gun in his holster, but he hadn't drawn it yet. He seemed to be more relaxing his hand upon the weapon as a show that he did have it but didn't want to pull it out unless he had to.

"Don't you dare interfere, sheriff. I've got my rights."

Mr. Jacobson had swung his cane down and around and started pointing towards the sheriff's direction. At first I thought that the rich man was going to be stupid enough to actually try to hit Sheriff Elijah. I was hoping to watch the local law enforcer draw his weapon and fire and that would be the end of the rich tyrant. However, he did something even worse. He eyed his footman and the closest driver and I could see the two of them get off of the coach and start to make their way toward the pending conflict.

I wondered what I could do, then shook my head. I couldn't do anything. I had to let time and these events run their course without me. I might have already done too much by saving Ms. Willows from heat stroke. However, standing here and watching this happen was only twisting me up inside so much. My mind had been racing back and forth between staying out of things and interfering. No, I had to do something, despite the consequences.

I was willing to go help the sheriff. I was sure that the two of us could take down Mr. Jacobson and his associates. However, now that Sheriff Elijah had a tighter grip on his pistol, I thought that I would pass. I wanted to stay away if bullets were starting to fly. As it was, the two henchmen only drew close, but kept a respectable distance. It seemed to me that they didn't want to be involved if bullets started to fly either.

"I have a bill of sale. I bought up her debt and took over her deed. I own this shop now and everything in it."

Mr. Jacobson's voice had increased in volume so that it could carry to all those that had stopped to watch the scene unfold. He thrust his free hand into his pocket and pulled out a piece of paper and began waving it about proudly as if it were the most important accomplishment he had ever succeeded in life.

"Yes, yes I can see that an' so can everyone else here. I'm sure everythin's in order. But dat don't mean you can jus start hittin' anyone ya want with that cane of yours. So ya can either be puttin' that away right now or ya can come with me and I'll be puttin' you away."

Mr. Jacobson gave a look toward that sheriff as if to say 'go ahead and try it.' I was secretly hoping that it would come to that and I was sure so did the majority of those standing around. Unfortunately we never go to see our desires come to fruition. Mr. Jacobson lowered his cane, gave a sneer toward the woman on the ground and made his way back into her, now his, shop.

Movement near the back of the coach had caught my eye. I had been too focused on the scene before me that I hadn't kept track of everything else going on around me. Ruth had stepped forward to help the poor woman off of the street. I guess if I had seen her, I would have tried to stop her. I didn't want her anywhere near this area. But, despite the fact that the two henchmen constantly gave her a cautious stare, a stare that stated that they would be willing to do anything if they were directed by Mr. Jacobson, Ruth didn't back down. She wasn't intimidated one bit by these two and gave her own "just try it" look in return. I guess I hadn't been more proud of her than right then. She was willing to take on the world to help someone else.

Sheriff Elijah gave a nod toward both Ruth and the other woman once he realized that neither was in any further danger of being harmed before he took his leave. I kept an eye on the henchmen. I was sure that they would try to make a move as soon as the sheriff was out of sight or that the odds were more in their favor. However, that hadn't proved to be the case. Ruth had helped the woman back to where I was and finally into the saloon that we had come out of, leaving the street empty of any more potential victims.

Mr. Jacobson came out of the shop some time later. I watched as he went to the back of his carriage and pulled out a chain and a padlock from the small chest of a trunk. He then proceeded to lock up the newly acquired shop with some pride. He could have easily let one of his henchmen do such a menial task, but I was sure that he wanted the prestige all to himself and probably also wanted to continue to make his public announcement.

It seemed to me that this Mr. Jacobson had managed to catch everyone's attention, now it was time to let him know that he had received my attention. My gut told me that this man was up to more than just buying up a few shops and it was time to find out. However, it struck me that this Mr. Jacobson was a very intelligent man. He had made sure that he had everything in order before he made his move. If I wanted information from him, I would have to outsmart him and hit him at his weakest spot, his pride. Every move would have to be calculated. I put my thoughts together quickly and made my move.

I made my way toward the horses and reached up to pat one. I got the response that I had anticipated. The last carriage driver pulled his whip back and snapped it forward toward me. Immediately I stepped forward and thrust my left hand straight out. The whip snaked around my arm and I gave a quick yank. The entire processes happened so fast and so unexpectedly that the carriage driver wasn't prepared. The whip was pulled from his grip and I tossed it aside and behind me. Now all I had to do was to wait for the outburst.

"If you touch my horse again, or even try to touch it, I'll have your horsewhipped."

It was perfect, almost down to the exact words that I had suspected. I now had his complete and undivided attention and there was one less weapon for me to worry about. On top of that, I was no longer a mere nuisance that would be dealt with by his lackeys; he would personally deal with me. That momentarily took the three henchmen out of the picture.

I wanted to say 'I'll like to see you try.' But I had to be careful and keep my emotions in check. I had to continue to play up on his pride.

"Nice horses. I haven't seen any like them around."

"And you won't either. They are called Hackney and very popular in Europe, but only for those who can afford them. And I can afford them. I brought them over myself and as far as I know, I'm the only one here in the states that have any."

"They must be expensive then."

He gave a slight laugh. "For you, perhaps, but not for me. I deserve the best so I get the best, no matter the price."

"And...that fabric shop? That's the best one in town?"

He scoffed. "Hardly. But it's what I want, for now. So, I took it."

"And...what do you want...later?"

He gave another slight laugh. I could tell that he was enjoying himself; playing up to the fact that he could and would take anything and everything he wanted and he wanted everyone to know about it.

"I'll take the whole town. Perhaps I'll name it after myself. Alexandria or something similar."

"And...when everyone leaves town because you own it all?"

"Then I'll take the mines."

So, that was it. The mines were holding this town together. It was worth a fortune if he could claim them for himself. The thought that he could buy the mines was preposterous. However if he started small, say a few shops then he could slowly build equity and leverage. There would also be less resistance once he made his move. Let's see how badly he really wanted those mines.

"You know, I've seen those mines." This was a lie. I hadn't really been inside of them yet, but he didn't know that. I did, however, know their history, or at least their future. "There isn't much left in them and I'm sure, and have even heard talk to verify my suspicions, that they will dry up in a few years."

He shrugged. "It doesn't matter to me. I'll have the whole town by then and suck it completely dry. Then, I'll move on the next town and then the next. I'll take them all. I'll even take Carson City and Reno. I'll control the entire fertile land of the Washoe Valley, the farms, the ranches, the silver mines, the gold mines, and every railroad that passes through here. People will pay me just to move their goods through here. I will control the price of gold and silver. I will control this entire area. It will be mine. Do you hear me? Mine! And there is nothing you or anyone else can do about it."

I had insulted his pride by getting too close to one of his prized possessions. I had goaded him into telling me his plans. Bad guys with plans seem to be all the same. They have over inflated egos and want to tell the whole world how smart they are. I guess he took the time to tell me since I was probably the first to ask, but I was sure that he would brag to anyone given the right circumstances.

The problem to his plan was that I already knew that he would fail, history had already dictated this. Or, would he fail because I interfered? Was I here to stop something from happening that should never come about?

He had moved closer and closer until he was about an arm's length away. When he had finished his announcement of his delusions of grandeur, he brought his cane up and thrust it toward my direction as if to drive home his point. I had also anticipated, expected and hoped for this. Mr. Jacobson was so predictable. He had meant to personally bully me with his intelligence then personally bully me with his stick, something he wouldn't do while the sheriff was still around. I was also sure that he wasn't happy about not being able to beat the poor woman he had thrown out on the street. He wanted, needed to show his superiority by making others feel inferior. He was going to find out that I've already had my share of bullies in the past and I knew exactly how to take care of them.

Quickly I stepped forward and reached out. My hand caught hold of his cane and I pulled hard. Like the driver that I had disarmed, I had caught Mr. Jacobson by surprise. His cane went flying out of his hand and was in my possession before he knew what had happened. I snapped it downward and gave a sudden kick out. My foot connected with enough force to snap his walking stick in half.

"My cane! You broke my cane! That was an expensive cane! You will pay..."

"Oopsy. Did I do that? I am so sorry. It was a total accident. They don't make these like they used to."

"I'll get the sheriff..."

"To do what? Arrest me for breaking a stick? Do you really think that he has the time, effort, energy or even concern over the simple matter of a stick? Do you even think that he likes you enough to even care? Besides, there are enough witnesses here to say that it was self defense. If he does show up, I'll simply say that you tried to hit me with it and he'll haul your rear end into prison so fast that it will make your head spin, and I'm sure he's looking for any excuse to do that."

"Then I'll take care of you myself."

Mr. Jacobson pushed the cuffs of his shirt and jacket back as he moved toward me. Good, I had made him too emotional to think straight. I took another step forward and thrust what was left of his stick, the top half with the metal cap, just under his neck. This made him stop immediately.

"Let me make this clear," I stated. "I don't like you. No one likes you. No one will care if you simply disappear off of the face of this Earth and I'm sure I can find a good number people that can help me do it too. I doubt that the sheriff would come looking for you. So let me say this once. If you cross my path again I'll make sure that you are dealt with appropriately."

I could see his blood start to boil. If I was correct, he would start to make more mistakes, but not now. All I had to do was have him mess up once and the sheriff would take care of him and then I wouldn't have to worry too much about timelines being disrupted, or at least I hoped so. I tossed what was left of his cane aside, turned and headed back toward the tavern I had come from.

"Don't you turn your back on me! Come back here! Coward! Face me like a man! You'll rue the day you crossed me!"

I ignored him and slightly chuckled to myself. Now he was simply publically humiliating himself, like some two year old child throwing a fit in the middle of a store. I knew that he wouldn't attack me. I had already proven that I was faster than he was and I had already taken away his primary weapon. He only wanted me to come back so that his henchmen could be brought in, but he wouldn't initiate the fight with the threat of being tossed in jail.

As I approached the saloon, I could see Ruth standing there, waiting for me by the pair of swinging doors. She had that little smirk on her face, the one that only slightly gave a disapproving look while trying to tell me that she was proud of me.

"Did you really have to do that? I mean...you've only managed to tick off yet another person here in Virginia City."

"He got what was coming to him, and don't give me that look of disapproval. I could see by your initial reaction that you've crossed paths with him before."

She gave a nod. "In case you haven't noticed, the bar hasn't been very busy as of late. Will's been a little behind on his payments to the bank and Mr. Jacobson has threatened to collect on the debt. I can't let that happen. Not only will I be on the street, but if it wasn't for Will, I would have been there already. He could have used the money that he gave to me to pay his bills, he could have rented out the room I'm in to pay his mortgage. Will's in this mess because of me, and I won't let him go down because of it."

I shook my head and put my hand upon her shoulder for comfort. "No. I have a feeling that Mr. Jacobson would find some way to go after this place sooner or later, even if you weren't here. We'll have to keep an eye out. I'm sure he'll target this saloon next and when he does, he'll start making his mistakes. We'll be there to stop him."

"Aren't you worried about hurting the timeline? After all you had said...."

I put a finger to her mouth. "I know what I said, but now I'm not so sure that I agree with it. There's a possibility that we are here to stop something from happening. I can't live my life second guessing all of my actions. If my heart and gut tell me that I need to act then I will, and that includes putting a stop to Mr. Jacobson so Will can keep his bar. We'll see this through together, no matter the outcome."

Ruth gave me a hug that seemed to last an eternity. I guess I was still her number one dad, even if I had missed seven years of her life.

Chapter: The Mines

*T*he morning came way too early, like it always did when I had to get up to go to work, and today was no exception. Usually I would at least have the comfort of a good night sleep on a nice comfortable bed. Then I would be able to fall into my familiar routine at work, pushing papers and clicking on the keyboard.

Today, however, was a different story. I still wasn't sleeping well on the makeshift bed that Ruth had set up for me. It wasn't her fault; it was the best she had. Still, my body wasn't used to it. But that was the least of my worries. I would be facing yet something else that my body wasn't used to, hard physical labor. Not just any physical labor, but body aching, back wrenching, laborious, physically demanding work that would break any man half my age. What was I thinking?

I looked over at my daughter, still sound asleep. There was my answer. I would do anything for her and I would keep that in mind as I performed the tasks at hand.

I got dressed as quietly as I could without waking my daughter. Will had lent me some of his clothing; I guess he was a good guy after all. However, he probably would have been nicer had he gained a few more pounds and was a little taller. His clothing was very snug. I would have to be careful not to rip them while working in the mines. My first purchase after getting paid would be a new set of clothing, but until then I would have to borrow from Will.

I also grabbed the canteen that Ruth had set aside for me. She said that one of the problems with mining was that the workers continued to forget about rehydrating themselves. In this desert terrain it was easy to lose a lot of water, and fast, as I had witnessed at the church. However, hard, intensive labor would sap much needed hydration out of an individual that much faster. Most of these young men were too prideful and arrogant and believed that they could push their bodies beyond their limits and no one really understood the importance of staying hydrated. The water in the canteen would be a life saver. She said she would even come down to the mines, during a break in her shift, to swap out a full canteen with this one after I had finished it.

She was very thoughtful. I almost gave her a kiss on the forehead before I left, but decided against it. I didn't want to wake her.

"You're late."

The mines were already a beehive of activity. Mining carts were being pushed in and out of the mines. Workers were coming in and out. Lumber was being hauled into the caves for support while ore was being hauled out. There was a steam engine close to the entrance that seemed to be pumping water, from who knew where, down into the shaft through a series of pipes. Water was leaking out from where some of the pipes where joined leaving puddles of mud. Mining carts were being unloaded on to wagons that were being hauled away toward the railroad station where I'm sure that it would find some processing plant.

Sam was standing, at the mouth of the mine giving orders as the workers were coming and going. He was the only thing keeping this chaotic mess from spiraling out of control.

I could hear the clanking of metal wheels of the mining carts against the rails. I could hear the banging of pick axes and shovels against the rock walls and the ore that was being pulled out. I could hear twenty different conversations going on all at once. I could hear the steam engine chugging away. I could hear the train off in the distance.

Dust was being kicked about. Dust and dirt and ore fragments were everywhere; it was amazing that anyone could breathe. On top of that, everyone was covered in the stuff as if they were rolling around in the ground.

"I'm sorry; I thought you said we started in the morning." I gave a yawn to show him how early it was. The sun was barely coming up and I wondered what time it really was.

"Yup, an the sun started comin' up some time ago. You're late."

"My apologies. I'll make sure I get up earlier."

However, I wasn't sure that showing up earlier would have made a difference anyway. He seemed to be one of those bosses that were annoyed at everything and nothing would ever please him. Hopefully I wouldn't run into him too much. I would show up, do my work, collect my pay, and keep an eye out for a better job.

"Now, since ya don't 'ave much experience and ya'r older an all, I'll send ya down to help in the eastern section. Ya just follow the tracks to the right. Meet up with Tom, you'll know him when you see him. The miners down there will put ya to work."

I glanced over toward the mining carts that were being unloaded onto the wagons. That seemed like an easy job. Then it struck me. He didn't want me to have an easy job. He probably took one look at me and decided that he didn't want an older person who couldn't pull his weight. He probably sent me to a tougher job, probably one of the toughest, so I would quit. I gave a nod of recognition in his direction that he only barely caught as I went about my way.

I followed the tracks and passed by branching tunnels from the main one. I could see many hard working miners digging away at the veins that ran through here. Some were taking pick axes to the tunnel walls, others were shearing up wooden beams, and some were hauling the ore out of their smaller tunnel into the main tunnel where I was and loading carts.

I kept looking for someone that I couldn't possibly miss, and yet despite everyone that I saw, none really stood out more than any other. Most of the men were young, or at least young in my opinion. I had to remember, the lifespan of people during this time was a lot shorter than in my time. The twenty year olds that were working here in the mines were considered older while I considered them younger. However, there were still much older men down here as well. I periodically saw the typical '49er worker with the longer beards, unkempt hair, and bent backs. They probably came here after finding that their proposed claim had nothing to pan out.

The tunnel became very dark very fast. My eyes were growing accustomed to the lack of light to some degree, but what really helped was the lanterns that some of the miners had. They were placed every so often to help give some light to some degree, yet it was still difficult to…

"Ouch."

I was too busy looking at the light sources that I wasn't watching where I was going. I probably wouldn't have run into the metal cart if it wasn't so dark in the first place. I wondered if Sam didn't give me a lantern so I would end up getting lost or wind up running into so many things that I wouldn't come back. If I really wanted this job, I was going to have to make my own opportunities. I waited until no one was watching before I snagged one of the lanterns for myself.

My route continued to go deeper and deeper into the tunnels and further down into the Earth. I had lost the network of pipes a long time ago and I hadn't realized until now that it was getting hotter and hotter the further I traveled. There was less ventilation down here and the air became stuffy. My hike became less strenuous and far easier and I was sure that it was because I was heading downhill. I wasn't looking forward to having to hike back up.

There were less and less workers down here and I was wondering if I had made a wrong turn somewhere or if I was had been sent on a wild goose chase. My guess was that Sam really didn't want me working for him. This was finally solidified when the mining cart tracks ran out.

I stood there, in the dark, with no one around, at the end of the tracks, holding my lantern, trying to figure out what to do next. I felt like I had been abandoned and almost lost. The tunnel did run further down but I wasn't sure if I should continue or turn back. It wasn't sure what to do until the sounds of metal banging against the rock wall reached my ears from further down the tunnel did I come to the conclusion of where I needed to go. I turned and continued my venture.

I wasn't sure how much further I had walked but I was sure that once I reached the spot, I knew I had found where I was supposed to go. The rough cavern-like area wasn't very wide. Rubble was starting to pile up in the center of the cavern, making the cavern look smaller than it really was. It was lit by a couple of lanterns on the ground placed in a circle around the area. The light of the lanterns flickered and weren't much help in giving enough light to see, but what little there was gave enough illumination to see the men that were at work here.

There were about six men hard at work. Sweat glistened off of their bodies and it wasn't necessarily because they were working hard, it was sweltering hot down here. The lack of airflow and the many tons of rock above us had made the air almost unbearable. On top of that, the heat generated off of the men was adding to the already stifling conditions.

Here, I couldn't help but notice racism at its finest, or at least its continued ugliness. All of these men were black, and I didn't mean because they were dirty from working in the mines. These African-Americans were placed down here to work by themselves, away from the other white men. I guess they were welcomed to work here in these mines, as long as they kept to themselves and away from everyone else. On top of that, these men didn't have the luxury of having the mining cart nearby. The tracks had stopped some time ago and these men would have to haul their ore up by hand until they came to the tracks.

"Err...um...Excuse me. I think I'm supposed to help here."

The men stopped their work at the sound of my voice and turned around to see who had violated their work space. The men were big and muscular and for one moment I thought that would be squashed like a bug.

"You that fella that was lost de other day. Never thought I would see ya again."

I looked at him curiously until the light of the lanterns caught his face and I could see him better. Suddenly I recognized him.

"Thomas? It's Thomas, right?" I had asked as I stepped forward and reached out to shake his hand.

He immediately retreated from my gesture. Again, I had to remember that this was a different time. I had to be careful how I treated people, but I was sure that a simple handshake down in the depths of these mines, where no one else was watching except for those who wouldn't say a word, would hurt. I left my hand forward in its initial gesture.

Thomas thought about it for a moment and then, when seeing that I was genuine, offered his in return.

"So, what did ya do ta tick off ol' Sam ta have him send ya down here with us?"

"I guess it's because I'm the new man on the block. So, what can I do to help?"

Thomas seemed to be floored by this. I guess he was expecting me to start making demands and telling him and his men what to do, not the other way around. Once he realized that this was how things were going to be, he put me to work.

"Ok, well we got ta get this here ore out without takin' too much of da rock with it. It ain't easy an hard ta see. If you were more experienced I'd let ya.

Probably be better leavin' that to us, if that's alright. It's really hard work, probably the slowest an hardest way to get to da ore, 'cept the water pipes don't run this far down. Whenever they open a new tunnel an the pipes and tracks ain't been laid yet, they send us."

I nodded. I think he was trying his best to be diplomatic to make sure that he didn't offend me in any way, shape or form. Since I really didn't know what I was doing, there really was no offence to be taken. I also realized a tone of pride in his voice. He and his "men" might have been discriminated against and had been given the hardest job to do, but they had taken it with pride as if only they could be called upon to do the heaviest work where others would fail.

"Any way," he continued, "It would sure make things go a lot faster if ya could haul the ore up to da carts so they could be hauled away. Me and me boys would truly appreciate it."

"It's a deal," I said thrusting my hand back out again. This time he wasn't so reluctant to accept it.

I found the buckets that were set aside, filled two and carried them up to the long shaft until I found a cart to dump them into. This I did over and over, again and again. It was hard work. The rocks were heavy, the hike was uphill and the heat and lack of fresh air was playing havoc on my system. It didn't take long before my leg muscles started to hurt from all of the walking and my shoulders and arms from all of the hauling. I was sure that I would have blisters on my hands from the handles of the buckets.

Yet, I kept my mind focused. I was doing this for Ruth. This would add to our income and I wouldn't drain her resources. We would see this through together.

I didn't know how long I worked but it was good for my soul. I found that the physical labor had relieved my stress about my financial and temporal problems. This gave me a focus and outlet. On top of that, I had gained the respect of Thomas and his friends each time I returned with empty pails. I was sure that they had expected me to run off, but now that I had shown that I could be counted on, they treated me as one of their own kind, an individual unwanted and tossed aside.

We took a break a few hours in and didn't say much, it was too exhausting to speak. Besides, there wasn't much to say. We knew our job and we were doing it. I drank from my canteen and was about to take another sip when I heard a familiar voice.

"Lookee lookee, what do we 'ave here?"

I looked up to see the man I was hoping I would never run into again, well, one of the three that I hoped to never to run into again. There, standing in the cavern entrance, silhouetted by the lanterns was Luke. The young, pompous, rich kid had decided to pay us a visit. I doubted there was anything down here to pique his interest except to antagonize everyone here.

"Luke," Thomas said in a dull flat voice. "Ya know you're suppose ta be makin sure the beams are set properly. Ain't nothin about givin us a bad time."

"Well, I'll tell you what," the hot tempered, young punk started in. "I'm the one to tell ya'll what to do and ya ain't gonna give me no lip about it neither. My pa's one of the richest guys around here, an if it ain't for him than ya wouldn't be havin' no job. He's the one supplin' da timber for this here mine, an' don't ya forget it."

Thomas took a stand and started making a step toward the smaller, younger boy. I could imagine Luke being squashed in an instant. The big man got in his face and looked down upon Luke. There was mean look in his face as if he was truly contemplating, and barely resisting, the urge to take Luke's head in that big paw of a hand and snap Luke's skull right off. For a moment, I thought that he might actually do it. Instead he raised his voice and made his words very clear.

"An' da only reason ya got a job here is cause of yar pa. You ain't done no good here. The timber you've placin keeps collapsin, makin' it dangerous for us all."

'Wait a second', I thought. Luke's father brought up the timber for the mines? Luke was in charge of setting up the support beams? Now the lumber truck incidents made sense.

"Dat's your opinion. Ain't no one goin' ta believe you over me," Luke said. "And don't go believin' otherwise. Ya pass dat story around and yar likely ta get yourself hanged an ya know it."

I could see Thomas's body start to tense. I could see the others around him start to get up. If I didn't do something fast, Luke was going to be nothing but a splatter on the wall. Despite what Luke had coming to him, I interfered.

"Thomas! No."

The words were flat, not condemning nor authoritative. It was a simple statement. I was sure that if I tried to "tell" Thomas what to do, he wouldn't listen. The tone was more a pleading toward his rational mind, at least what was left of it.

"He's not worth it." I continued.

For a moment I thought that Thomas wasn't going to listen to me and that he was going to squash Luke anyway. But then I watched him back down, and I thought that the danger had passed.

"Finally, someone down here with some smarts," Luke said as he reached over and grabbed my canteen.

"Whatcha drinkin' there? Gimme."

"Water," I stated flatly. Now it was my turn to start to build resentment toward this individual.

He gave me a snide look as though he didn't believe me and took a gulp. Immediately he turned and spat his whole mouthful into my face.

"Funniest tastin' 'water' I've ever had," he said with disgust.

"That's because it IS water," I snapped back as I grabbed my canteen, and what was left of my water away from him.

"Well, you can keep your 'water'. I'm keepin' this," Luke said as he reached down and grabbed one of the fist sized silver nuggets from the ground and put it in his pocket.

"Hey," Thomas snapped, "you can't take that! That's part of da haul!"

"An who's gonna stop me? You? No? I didn't think so."

With that, Luke left the seven of us in such a state that I was sure that if he had stayed any longer, he probably wouldn't make it out of the cavern in one piece.

"You know," Thomas said once he was sure that Luke was out of earshot and when he had calmed down a bit. "If that dere man were to disappear, an there's a lot o' tunnels to disappear into, I don't think anyone would mind."

"I know what you mean," I responded. "But he's not worth it. The cost would weigh down on your soul for the rest of your life. There's another way, there always is. All we have to do is find it."

I wasn't sure if Thomas believed me or not, and I wasn't even sure I believed myself. Whatever the case was, we went back to work hoping that we never saw hide or hair of Luke again.

Chapter: Cave-in

*M*y arms, legs, back and shoulders were screaming at me and I wasn't sure how much longer I could work. I was going to be sore tomorrow and yet I knew I had to push on.

After I emptied my two buckets into the cart, I stopped to take a breather before heading back down to fetch another load. I was about to go, when I stopped. Something wasn't right. I turned back around and took in my environment.

Gone. They were all gone. All of the other workers that were up at this end, where the tracks ended were no longer working in their respected tunnels. I listened and couldn't hear any form of working. There weren't any pickaxes against rock, any shovels being used, or any carts being pushed. All the lanterns were gone. If it wasn't for the one I was carrying I wouldn't have any light. I guess I was just too caught up in my work to have noticed.

"Their gone," I said once I returned to our cavern. "Their all gone. Are they on break or...?"

The others looked at me then at each other. Finally Thomas gave a disappointing shake of his head.

"Naw. They've just gone home an' forgot to tell us...again."

"I assume that they do this often?"

His silence told me volumes.

"Well," he finally said breaking the silent tension that was growing, "Ah guess it's quittin' time. Why don't you take another load up while we pack up here? We'll meet you at the tracks and help you push the cart to da surface."

I gave him a nod at that and filled my buckets. I figured the six of them wanted to blow off some steam at being left behind again and they were probably ashamed at the choice words that they were about to say around their newly discovered friend. I would give them their peace.

Just as I started to dump my last load into the cart I noticed that the sound was louder than expected. At first I thought nothing of it until the ground started to shake. Then I realized that my worst nightmare to happen down in these tunnels was happening. It was a cave in.

The ground shook and the walls buckled. I could hear the tunnels ahead of me roar like some great beast. Dust blew in my direction and I could hear rock and rubble falling up ahead. The sounds were coming closer and closer.

I had frozen. I didn't know what to do. If I ran, would I be able to find any safe place? I had to think of something quickly.

My mind raced fast as I watched debris start to fall near me. Rock was piling up ahead of me, blocking my way and building a wall of earth that would crush me in a heartbeat. Quickly I understood what I had to do.

I threw myself at the cart sideways as hard as I could. I knew it was either life or death and I had nothing to lose. The blow was hard against my shoulder and I felt something give. I knew that I would either have the worst bruise in the history of my life at best or a dislocated shoulder at worst. Either way, the pain would hit in a few minutes. Right now I was too full of adrenaline to care.

My blow was enough to knock the cart, and its load, off of its tracks, spilling it ore onto the ground. My hard work was no longer a concern. Rocks started falling all around me. The ceiling was caving in right where I was. Huge boulders just barely missed me. Large beams snapped and broke as if they were kindling. Pain shot through my back as a good sized rock struck me. I saw stars as another hit my head. I could feel warm blood start to trickle down my face.

I was trying to move as quickly as I could. Despite my best efforts at attempting to dodge the falling debris, I was still getting pummeled. My body flew across the overturned cart in a desperate attempt to reach the open part that was now facing away from me. My foot caught the underside of the cart, hung me up, and sent me cascading into boulders and falling rock.

I did my best to ignore the pain and to subdue the panic that was trying to well up inside of me and burst forth. With all due haste, I climbed inside the sideways metal container and curled up as much as I could. With the ore that I had already put inside and some of the falling rocks that had bounced inside, it was a tight and painful fit.

The collapsing tunnel rained dirt, rocks, boulders and timber beams upon the cart and all around me. The sound was like hail striking against the metal and it rang in my ears with each blow.

Rocks continued to fall and smash against already fallen debris. Pieces shattered and were sent flying in all directions, including into my reprieve. I was being pelted by shatter shots. I did my best to cover my face with my arms, but even then I could feel my arms being blasted by debris.

A sharp pain shot through my leg. I was sure that I was as curled up inside my metal container as much as was possible, but there was no avoiding the rock that ricocheted off of the piling boulders and shooting right at me. It was like a bullet. I wasn't sure if I was heavily bruised or if something was broken.

Large boulders continued to fall. I could hear the metal of the cart start to give way. The cart would only take so much before it, too, collapsed.

On top of the rocks, I could hear the timber snap and break all around me. Large pieces of wood smacked against the cart.

Dust was being kicked up. What little oxygen that was down here was now being saturated with dirt making it more difficult to breath. I was either going to be squashed in my metal coffin or I was going to suffocate.

After what seemed like an eternity, the barrage finally stopped. I waited a few moments. I could feel my heart beating through my chest. I noticed that I had stopped breathing. I had started holding my breath some time ago out of fear. Now I was able to start breathing.

A couple of rocks fell further down the tunnel and I froze out of panic. Nothing more came; it was just some shifting that had occurred. The collapse was over.

I opened my eyes and then realized that they were already opened. It was simply too dark to see. My lantern had been smashed and destroyed, taking with it the only source of illumination.

My body only slowly reacted to my wishes as I started to try to make my way out of the sideways, beat up, smashed, dented and buried cart. I found places for my hands to snake through the rubble and push one rock and then another. Wooden beams had fallen in such a way as to keep most of the bigger boulders from pushing against the cart. I squeezed my way through small openings and pushed more debris to make more room.

Weight shifted and fell. More pain shot through my legs as rock collapsed upon them. My yelps of agony went unheard and unanswered except for the echoes that came back.

It took some doing as I shifted the debris to free myself. Once I managed, I was able to crawl on top, but the question was, where to go from there? My mind wandered and then I came to a conclusion. I shifted left and crawled.

My progress was slow, difficult and arduous. The rocks cut into me and I often bumped into the ceiling, walls, or larger boulders. I would be bruised from head to toe if I ever got out of this. I felt my progress go downward and I hoped that I hadn't crawled into a different tunnel that had opened up due to cave-in. I could easily become lost down here and that was before all of this rubble.

I came to a stop. My trek ended and any further progress was hindered by fallen rock. I could feel gaps between some of the smaller rock and knew that if I spent the time, I could clear some of this out. However, I needed to know if it was worth it.

"Hello? Anyone down there?"

Nothing. There wasn't a response.

"Hello?" I called again.

My heart sank. They were gone. The little time that I had spent with Thomas and his friends had brought peace and strength. They were good, decent men. They were strong and strong willed. They had families. They didn't need to be treated like they had been and now they were…

"Hey….is someone up there?"

The words were weak and seemed far away. Perhaps they were further than I had thought.

"Yes. It's me." I had raised my voice in hopes that they could hear me better. "Is everyone alright?"

"Thomas. His leg is caught. Can't move him. All this rock blocking us. Can't get out."

"You wait right there," I commented back. 'Like, right, they could go anywhere else.' I thought. "I'm going to get help."

I turned back around as best as I could and started to make my way back the way I came. My climb was hard. Sharp rocks cut and slashed into me. Hard boulders banged against my body. Jagged wooden beams sliced at my skin. The terrain was completely uneven and very difficult to crawl through. I had to push debris out of my way in the darkness a few times and had to circumnavigate barriers.

There was no telling how long I crawled. Time had no meaning here, only one precarious placement of my hands and knees after another. Yet, despite the lack of air, the superheated atmosphere, the dust that I had to breathe, the hard rocks and the sharp beams of timber, I pushed on. This was a matter of life or death. This was survival. And it wasn't just for me; it was for the six other men trapped further behind me. If I didn't make it back then neither would they.

A push of yet another rock out of the way resulted in a curious noise. Instead of sliding to one side, I could hear the rock bounce off of other debris and continue its descent. Its sound echoed throughout the tunnel ahead of me. I stopped. I was probably at the end of the caved-in portion. I had to be careful or I would…

The pile of rocks collapsed under me and slid downward. My body followed suit. I was in a freefall, tumbling weightlessly in the dark.

The sudden impact was harder than I had thought. My back had struck a couple of the rocks that had fallen before me and I was sure that I had broken a rib. The rocks that tumbled with me struck my fallen body and debris rained down on top of me.

It took a while before I was able to move again and when I did I was in agony. My body protested to every move. Nothing wanted to move. Yet, out of sheer desperation I pushed on.

The ground was more level here. My pace picked up. I could almost see light up ahead, as if the night sky was shining into the tunnels, welcoming me, guiding me. I could hear voices, no, just one familiar voice and some sobbing.

"And I looked and behold a pale horse."

Why was the preacher man quoting from Revelations? I didn't know and didn't care. I simply continued to follow his voice.

"and his name that sat on him was Death."

He had no idea. Really, he didn't, but not today. Today death could be cheated if only I could make the next few steps and exit the cave.

"and Hell followed with him."

I heard gasps as Abraham Smith finished that last piece. At first I thought that those that had surround him to hear his sermon, to grieve for those who were buried, would be too sensitive to hear such an incantation of the harbinger of Death. Then I realized. They weren't gasping at what they heard, they were gasping at what they saw and the timing of which it had happened.

I must have been a sight to see. My form was silhouetted by the dust that was still falling. My body had come from the pits of deep darkness. My presence had announced its arrival from impossible odds. The expression on my face was an indication of my sheer will. Blood had caked on my face. My clothing was ripped and blood could be seen from where I had been cut and scraped. For all intents and purposes, I was sure that I looked as if I had brought death and that Hell was following close behind.

"Daddy?"

The sobbing had stopped. Now I knew who had been crying. It had been my little girl, my daughter now grown up. She threw herself upon me and held me as if she would never let go and if she did then I might simply disappear and her fear would become a reality. She let her tears flow from the emotional stress she had been feeling.

Chapter: Decisions

"**D**on't ever do that to me again," Ruth whispered wiping her tears away. "I thought you were...oh I couldn't lose you. Not again. I thought I had lost you when I came here so long ago."

Ruth started to cry again, but when she finally composed herself, she continued. "I came looking for you, to give you more water, but couldn't find you. Then I heard the rubble and thought..."

"You're...you're alive."

It was Sam who had interrupted Ruth's emotional melt down and had broken the silence that had come over the crowd of people that had formed a semicircle around the entrance to the mine.

"Yes, I am, and so are six others trapped further down."

The others started looking at each other as if they had no idea what I was talking about. Surely they must be aware of who all of the miners were. Then I noticed, Thomas's family wasn't here. Of course they weren't, they wouldn't be allowed to be here.

"Luke and the others are trapped," I said as I turned to Sam. "We've got to get some men down there to save them."

Sam only shook his head. I understood what he was trying to say. These men were expendable based upon the color or their skin. However, it was Luke who spoke up and stated what no else wanted to admit.

"Ya can't expect anyone here to go help those…"

"Those men…" I corrected Luke before he said something that I would make him regret. "Those men are honest hard working men that keep this mine alive. They have families. They are people that live and breathe. If you don't save them, then I will."

"You might have been able to escape God's wrath," Abraham, the preacher man stated. "But they won't. It's God's judgment, his punishment upon the unrighteous. There is only one thing left to do…"

"The Lord is my shepherd; I shall not want. He maketh me to lie down in green pastures: he leadeth me beside the still waters. He restoreth my soul: He leadeth me to the paths of righteousness for his name's sake. Yea, though I walk through the valley of the shadow of death, I will fear no evil: for thou art with me; thy rod and thy staff they comfort me. Thou preparest a table before me in the presence of mine enemies: thou anointest my head with oil: my cup runneth over. Surely goodness and mercy shall follow me all the days of my life: and I will dwell in the house of the Lord forever."

I couldn't believe it. Abraham Smith, God's anointed man of the cloth for this area was simply going to give these men their last rights and walk away from them. The man that was supposed to inspire hope and love was simply doing nothing more than condemning these men to a prolonged, slow and painful death. I turned and headed toward the mine once again. However, I was stopped by a single touch upon my shoulder.

"Dad? You really can't be serious about going back in there, are you? I mean, it's noble and all, and yes they need saving, but the mine might not be done collapsing. You can still be killed."

I took her aside so no one could hear us. "I've had some time to think while I was in there. I should have died several times over, but I didn't. The only thing I could come up with is that we are here for a reason. I don't know what yet, but I'm sure we're not going to die until that reason happens; at least I hope I'm right. Until then, I'm going to continue to do what my heart tells me to. I'm going back in there to save them."

She took one look deep into my eyes and knew that my heart and mind was set. There was no turning back. She gave me a long hug, smiled, and nodded. This was why she loved me, not just because I was her dad, but because I was able to stand up for the right thing, no matter the cost. I hoped that my assumption about not dying yet had been accurate; I also hoped that I would be in time to make a difference.

I squared my shoulders and headed back in. I could hear the murmuring of those I had left behind that only faded as I continued my journey. After a short distance, I stopped and let my vision get used to the darkness.

It wasn't too difficult to find where the cave-in had first announced its presence. The rubble stood almost as high as the ceiling and I had to take a moment to appreciate just how high I had fallen. Then, with resolution, I began my ascent.

I knew that there was no way I could clear enough of this rubble to make a difference. Even if I started with the hope of the others catching on, it would take some time to clear enough rubble to help those that were injured and give them safe passage. Besides, who was to say that even if a few did become inspired that they would continue to be inspired? The last thing I wanted was a helping party to give up because the people on the other side weren't "worth it". No, what Luke and the others needed first was medical attention and that meant that I would go to them. This would, hopefully, inspire others to come get me.

The climb was harder than I thought and I received more bruises and cuts to add to my already growing collection. Even when I did manage to get to the top, my crawl across the debris continued to give me abrasions, cuts, and bumps.

My return trip was longer than I thought it would take. Perhaps because I was getting tired of all of the new sensations of pain that I was receiving or perhaps it simply was because I was just getting tired. My muscles didn't want to work anymore, my body wasn't responding the way I wanted it to.

"Hello? Anyone there?"

I guess my approach was louder than I had expected it to be, either that or the others had become so accustomed to the silence that anyone approaching would have been heard.

"Yes, it's me. I'm back."

I found my way to the spot that had initially blocked my way to the men and started moving some of the debris. I needed to be careful not to start an avalanche effect and bury the very people that I was trying to save. When I was done, I carefully picked my way down their side of the rubble. It was steeper than the climb from the first side. There was no way I could climb back up without help, no one here could. We would need rope and probably tackle and a lot more debris cleared from the top. I sure hoped that someone was coming to get us.

There was a little light here. One of the lanterns hadn't shattered in the cave-in and what little illumination it offered was barely enough to see everyone.

"What cha doin' here?" Thomas asked while wincing in pain. "They ain't goin' to be savin' us. We ain't worth savin'. Don't know where you come from, and I can tell it ain't from around here, but here's different. They ain't comin'."

"Yeah, well, now they have to come and save me, don't they? That means they would have to save you in the process. Right?"

"You sure know how to stir things up don't you?" Thomas asked. "I heard you got yourself in trouble with the preacher man, Alexander and then again with Luke earlier, and then even with Mr. Jacobson. Seems you like to get yourself into lots o' trouble. An' trouble's what you're gonna to get by comin' down here to help us an' riskin' your life."

I shook my head. "No, I usually don't like to get myself into any trouble and do my best to not even get involved. But I know what it's like to have been wrongly treated. I just can't sit back and watch as other people, any people, are treated like this. No one deserves this."

I could see that my little speech had moved him, had moved them all. An awkward silence overcame us. I wondered what else could be said.

"What's that sound?"

Now the silence between us was because of tension. Everyone was straining to hear the sound that I had heard. At first they didn't heard it, but when they did, horror came over their faces.

"Water!" Thomas announced.

"Water?"

"Yes, you've seen da pipes haven't you? Well that's to cool the mines else they would be too hot to work in. Only we get sent to the areas where pipes haven't been laid yet. Sounds like the pipes are broken, and that the water has found its way here. Probably gathered from all of the areas above us. We'll drown if we ain't rescued."

I waited with horror. I stood, anticipating the blast of water that would come from above us through the clearing that I had created. I prepared for …

A trickle?

Only a small amount of water trickled from overhead and down the side of the rocks. There was nothing to worry about. This would never amount to much, at least that's what I thought until the water started to pool at my feet. Apparently we were at the lowest level; there was no other place for the water to go. It wouldn't be a gush of water but a slow death from exposure and exhaustion before we drowned. The water wouldn't fill up fast enough to the top for us to swim out. We would lose our strength before it was even half way up.

I looked across the cavern at the others. Each one of them had a stoic look upon their face. It seemed to me that they had already accepted death a long time ago; it was only a matter of time. Now that time was slowly coming upon us. I hoped that I wasn't wrong about the people outside, yet I heard nothing to tell me that I was right.

We stayed there, in peace and waited. The trickle picked up a little, but not enough to make a difference in our accent, just enough to speed up our demise. The water continued to pool around us. First it was at our ankles, then our knees and then our waist.

The temperature dropped dramatically. What had started off as being almost unbearable hot was now cold. My body was shivering with the chill and I could hear teeth chattering from the others. We were trying our best to stay warm, yet I know understood that hyperthermia would add to our inability to leave.

The water climbed higher and higher, to our chest and then our necks. Our lantern went out when we could no longer hold it above the water line. It was shortly after that when we started to tread water. We would be too tired and too cold to keep this up for too long. Even if it were possible to ride the water to the top, the small passage that I had taken of cleared rubble would be underwater. There was nowhere to go.

"Here, catch."

The sound of the person's voice echoed off of the chamber walls and brought our attention to the top of the debris. There we could make out a lighted lantern being held by our would-be rescuer. It was another miner that been working down here and had seemingly had a change of heart on his desire to be part of any rescue party. From the sounds of things, it sounded that there were others behind him moving more debris, making the crawlspace wider.

The rope that he tossed down was a godsend if I had ever seen one. I had let one of the other men go first and when I was given an odd look, I told them that I would be the last one out. It wasn't just out of selflessness, it was out of a childhood habit when I was placed in the back of us kids to keep an eye on all of them and make sure that everyone kept up and that no one got lost. I had been the rear guard. I guess I continued to be that rear guard.

The trip back through the debris was easier than I had initially traversed. The crew that had come in to save us had done a great job in clearing some of this out. At no time did anyone mention anything or complain about having saved a man of a different color. For this one moment in time, we were all the same.

 Once we had exited the tunnels it was pushing morning. The sun was starting to rise and I wasn't sure if I was happy to see it and see another day or if I was disappointed that we had stayed underground all night. Either way we received a warm welcome from the townsfolk that had been there. They offered us blankets and hot coffee.

My daughter had come up and given me a hug. "I'm so proud of you," she said. "You know I couldn't just let you go in by yourself. As soon as you were out of sight, I started in on these men about courage and what was right. It didn't take long before everyone felt guilty enough to chip in."

I smiled and hugged her back. She may have been proud of me because I had gone back in, but I was equally proud of her for doing her part. Other miners were receiving hugs from their families and even Thomas's family was there welcoming him to the land of the living. Everyone seemed happy, well, almost everyone.

I caught sight of Abraham. He had given me the worst "I hate you from the bowels of hell" stare that I had ever seen before turning away in disgust. I could only smile.

"Ruth, I would like you to meet Thomas."

I had moved over toward the large man and had introduced my daughter to him. His eyes had gone wide. It seemed that my gestures of being a human being never ceased to amaze him. At first he didn't know what to do, but when he saw my daughter reach out her hand in a gesture of friendship, he awkwardly extended his.

This had done several things. First, it was to show my daughter that I wasn't burning every bridge that I was crossing. I wanted to let her know that I was trying to make friends. Second, it was to continue to build trust in Thomas. He had been nice to me, an initial fair warning perhaps, but he hadn't shown any reason to not like him. He was an honest and hard working individual with no other alternative motive. Third, it was to further tick off the preacher man, Abraham, and from my follow up scan toward his direction I had been accurate.

I continued to look at the crowd at all of the happy people. Kids had welcomed their fathers back from helping in the rescue. I guessed that my daughter wasn't the only one who was proud of her father. I was about to turn back when I saw her. I saw the little girl holding her father as Ruth was holding me. That was the little ghost girl that I almost ran over on the highway, that's the "Little House on the Prairie" girl that came to me at the hotel and that's the girl in the Washoe Millionaire's Building.

I wanted some answers and I wanted them now. I wanted to know who she was and why she was haunting me. But how was I going to get that from a little girl? I would look like some kind of perverted stalker or a predator of children. The best I could hope for was scaring the kid, having her scream for her life and being shot by the local deputy.

I had to calm down. The answers would come; at least I hoped that they would. But now I knew all of the ghosts that I had encountered. They were all here, except for the prostitute who had died years ago. Something was about to happen, something that would tie all of these people together and I was in the middle of it all.

"Alright everyone," Sam stated from a nearby table that had been pulled up.

The table was just an average wooden table with Sam sitting on the other side in a chair. On the table, a small chest was placed and I could tell, from the lid being open, that it was full of coins. Two men were behind Sam, flanking him, with what I could tell, sawed off shotguns; obvious hired muscle.

"We'll investigate the cause of the cave-in later. It's payin' time so go ahead an line up."

"No need to investigate, boss man, I know what happened."

All eyes turned to the one man that had broken the silence, Thomas.

"It's the wood braces," he continued. "Ain't been placed right, hasn't been for some time. It's why we've been havin' the cave-ins lately. Only was a matter o time 'fore someone got hurt."

Sam had to think about that for a short bit and seemed to weigh the implications before making any statement. "Alright, who's in charge of…"

"Now hold it right there," a familiar and annoying voice said, cutting off Sam's inquest as his form cut through the crowd. "Ah don't like what he's sayin'. An ya can't prove it neither. 'Sides, ya gonna take his word over mine. Ya know me pappy…"

"We know who your pa is, Luke," Sam said shutting him up. "But you're right. Without proof…"

"You may be right about not having proof about the timber," I said cutting off Sam again as I approached the scene that was unfolding. I stood beside Luke so everyone could see us. "But there's something else you should know."

There was a hush that fell over the crowd. I had a feeling that everyone here was starting to hang on to my every word. Word had been spreading about how I saved one woman from heat stroke, had stood up to Alexander Jacobson and now had went into a caved-in mine shaft to help rescue six other men that were left for dead. I seemed to have everyone's attention. Once I knew that I had it, I suddenly, and as quickly as I could, reached into Luke's over coat pocket, the same overcoat he was wearing the last time I saw him deep in the mines. Before Luke could object, I pulled out the fist size silver ore that he had put there and tossed it to Sam.

"I don't think the owners of this mine are inclined to theft," I concluded.

Sam caught the rock, and then looked at Luke. "Luke, you know what this means."

"In all the confusion, it must of fallen into my pocket."

Sam gave a disbelieving scowl.

"But my pa…"

"Right now I don't care about you or your pa. Get off of this here mine and never come back or I'll have the sheriff drag you into a cell. Now get, 'fore I shoot you for trespassin', claim jumpin', theft, an' anything else I can think of."

Luke seemed to stand there, stunned, as if he had been slapped. He went to say something, but I could see

286

how the two men behind Sam started to tense and bring down their fire arms. I wasn't so sure that they would have fired, considering how they would hit everyone else, but it told Luke that they were serious.

Luke broke through the ground and ran off as if death was chasing him.

I didn't know what events I had set into motion, but both Luke and Abraham seemed to be set upon revenge. I was sure that I hadn't seen the last of either of them. My only question was, what would they do next? I would have to keep an eye on them, and Mr. Jacobson, and, yes, even the little girl.

After Luke had made his hasty exit, the rest of the miners lined up at the table single file. Surprisingly there wasn't any pushing or shoving, and then I understood. Those that did show such actions would probably get a warning from Sam and his henchmen. One warning would be all they got. Sam ran a tight crew, and I could understand why.

If I remembered the literature, these mines produced about 700 million dollars worth of gold and silver by their economic standards. In my time it would be well above that mark. The investors that owned these mines took their income very seriously. Just like the scene with Luke, nothing out of the ordinary would be tolerated.

I slowly made my way up to the front of the line. My body was in pain and all I wanted to do was sleep. As soon as I received my pay I would head to bed and come back the next day. I had heard that the mine would shut down for today and everyone would come back tomorrow and start to clear out the collapsed section. That was fine by me, I needed the rest.

Once I was at the front, I put my hand out like everyone else had before me. Sam found my name on his roster gave a slight check beside it with a pencil and reached into his small chest of coins. His hand then pressed a coin into my hand. I looked at it.

"One dollar? All that for one dollar?"

"One dollar for one day's work," Sam answered flatly. "Do you have a problem with that?"

I could hear the two henchmen start to tense up. I had to remember when I was. I was used to being paid a considerable amount more than this. This was something that I had to get used to and wondered how a minimum wage demand would go over here at this town, with these men, with these guns. Employees either took what they got paid and liked it or they could move on to somewhere else. There was no argument, there was no strike, there was simply being paid or not.

"No, no problems. Thank you."

I gave Sam a slight nod, took my payment and headed toward the saloon where Ruth was staying.

Chapter: Tavern

I woke the next morning to arguing.

"I want you all out of here immediately!"

The voice was familiar and so was the tone. It wasn't difficult to recall almost the exact same words from several days ago and now it was coming from downstairs.

I had to hurry up and get dressed and get down there. My body wasn't responding as I hoped that it would. Every movement was a new sensation of pain. Fortunately I had gotten a full night's rest...no wait, now I remembered. I went to bed as the sun was rising; it was still morning of the same day. I had only gotten a few hours of sleep at best.

I got dressed as quickly as I could and turned to wake up Ruth. She wasn't in her bed. I probably would have noticed this sooner if I were more awake, not in pain, and less focused on the ruckus downstairs. My mind wondered where she could be.

"We aren't going anywhere, and I don't care what you say! I'll fight you no matter what it takes or how long! You will not throw anyone out, not here, not now, not ever! Your reign of terror ends here and now! Now get out before I toss you out!"

There's my little girl. She was already up and berating Mr. Jacobson. From her tone I was sure that she would, indeed, physically pick up and toss out the rich tycoon. I wasn't sure if I wanted to watch that or try to stop it for fear that she might get hurt in the process. Either way, I had to get down there fast. As I opened the door I heard the conversation continue.

"Oh, no. I have every right to be here and if you don't leave then I'll make sure that the sheriff sends you packing. You see, this establishment was behind on its payments. It had a debt, a debt that I bought. Now I own this place and it's you who will be tossed out. Now you can either pack your things and go quietly or I will take matters into my own hands."

"I would like to see you try it!"

As I descended the stairs, I could see Ruth standing toe to toe with Mr. Jacobson. Her face was right in his and she was not only verbally daring him to try something, she was physically daring him. Unlike the other women here in Virginia City, Ruth wasn't going to back down. Ruth may have had my eyes, but when it came to strong will, she had her mother's.

I watched as William stood, almost helplessly, behind the bar not knowing what to do. I think if it weren't for Ruth, he probably would have headed upstairs to pack his bags. Now, he wasn't sure. I watched as Mr. Jacobson started to tense with a new cane in his hand. I was sure that he would try to hit my daughter with it. I had to do something fast before someone got hurt. My only question was where were his three thugs? They were probably just outside, waiting for his command to come in. If a fight did break out, there would be four of them to the three of us and I doubted that William would put up a good fight. Even then, if Mr. Jacobson was correct, he now owned this establishment and the sheriff would have Ruth and I arrested, not the rich man or his goons. I had to think of something else.

"How much does he owe you?"

My voice cut through the silence of the tavern like a hot sharp knife. My arrival seemed to surprise everyone. I was sure that Ruth wanted to take care of this without involving me, believing that she could stand up for herself and that I needed the rest. I was also sure that Mr. Jacobson didn't want to wake me since I had already demonstrated an ability to outsmart and outwit him let alone demonstrate my ability to be faster and probably stronger than he was.

I watched as his eyes darted out toward the main doors and beyond. I'm sure he was thinking about trying to call in his henchmen and then trying to decide if they could come in quick enough. Then he seemed to notice my lack of aggression and a seemingly sincerity to my question. Suddenly his face went from concern to curious.

I heard a bag of coins hit the table in front of Mr. Jacobson. I didn't have to look to see who had tossed it but I did any way. Ruth was ready for this individual's greed, or so she thought. He hardly looked at it.

"It's all I've got…"

Ruth attempted to not only appeal to Mr. Jacobson's greed but also to his sense of compassion. I had a feeling that the rich investor's greed knew no bounds and as for compassion, I doubted he had any.

"It's not enough," Mr. Jacobson replied as he picked up the bag of coins.

Ruth almost gasped in horror. The man had taken her coins without counting them and had already said that it wasn't enough. On top of that, it seemed as if he wasn't going to give them back. She was ready to lash out at the man, but since I had moved close enough, I put my arm between them and held her back. This was not the way to take out this man.

"How much more would you need?" I asked.

"One hundred dollars."

I was sure it probably wasn't this amount and I doubted that William was even behind on his payments by this much and by the look on William's face I was probably right. I was also sure that this amount was set high enough that none of us could pay it off, not even if we combined all of our incomes. The smirk on his Mr. Jacobson's face seemed to allude to that.

"And how do I know that once we come up with said amount that you won't come back asking for more? What proof do you have that William owes anything and what receipts can you produce for any payment?"

Mr. Jacobson, who had a smug smile up until now was slightly taken aback. He was ready for us to cave in, say that we couldn't come up with that kind of money and then leave. Now, however, with the seriousness on my face, I could tell that he was seriously thinking about calling my "bluff" and seeing if I could actually produce that kind of money right now. I was sure that he had a lot more than a hundred dollars readily available to him and that he didn't need it, but he seemed to be the type of man where money was money and that he would take it if given. After he thought about it for a moment, he reached under his vest pocket and removed a document.

"It's a receipt for payment of debt. It's not, by any means the mortgage, but it does show that all debt is caught up. I will give you this for one hundred dollars...plus the financial deposit already made." He patted his lower left coat pocket where he had put Ruth's money. "Call it a convenience fee."

Ruth nearly jumped over my arm as she went to rip off Mr. Jacobson's face. I was sure she would too, if I wasn't holding her back and I was only just barely doing that. Once she calmed down, I turned to the investor.

"Fine."

"Dad! You don't have that kind of money!"

I ignored her and reached for my wallet in my back pocket. I opened it and found what I was looking for. There were two bills.

"This is the new one hundred dollar bill," I said showing most of the bill that I was presenting. I watched as his eyes went wide.

"Dad! You can't..."

"Where did you get that?" Mr. Jacobson asked as he started to reach for it.

"You are not the only one with connections. I just don't want attention being drawn upon myself, at least not yet."

"You have a funny way of showing that," he retorted.

I merely shrugged. "Is it a deal?"

I could see his eyes calculating his next move. I had just insinuated that I had access to more, all he had to do was come up with more unpaid debt and my good hearted nature would swoop in to save the day. Of course he would continue to do this until he found my source or until he bled me dry. It was all in his eyes. He smiled with a plan written across his face as he went to hand me the paper he had in his hand.

I took a step forward and lost my footing. My hand went to his chest, caught myself and then stood up again. I was tired and my muscles weren't responding as well as they should have. With disgust to get me away from him, he simply grabbed the bill, shoved the receipt of debt into my hands and left with a huff.

"Dad?! What were you thinking?"

I ignored her again and moved toward William who had stood motionless and speechless behind the bar.

"Four things: first, never fall behind on your payments again. We will help drum up business but if you can't make your payments, let us know. Second, burn this." I handed the slip of paper that I had just bought with my money. Once he had put it in his log burning stove, never to be seen again, I continued.

"Third, you didn't see or hear anything that transpired here today. Do you understand? Not a word for any reason." His nod let me know that he understood.

"Fourth, two cups of coffee black and keep it coming."

"Dad! Are you ignoring me? Didn't you hear me? This man will be back time and time again. He'll stop at nothing to bleed everyone dry. And now you've simply caved in and gave him the money?"

I turned to her and handed her a cup of coffee. "Oh? Didn't you try to pay him off?"

She looked horrified that I had called her out on her own actions. I guessed it was alright for her to make personal sacrifices but not me. I only smiled. Suddenly she gave me that look, the look that told me that she realized that I had a plan, the "what's really going on" plan. I pointed toward a table, sat and waited.

I watched as Ruth periodically got up to take care of a few patrons that came and went. She did her job with a smile on her face and at times seemed to forget our incident with Mr. Jacobson but then remembered between customers and returned the look that she had given me earlier.

I would have gone back to bed, Ruth had everything covered here and my body could use the rest, but I wanted to watch the fallout that was about to happen and I was sure it would happen soon. I simply sat, enjoyed my coffee to keep me awake, and continued my wait.

"Ok, everyone out!"

The overly broadcasted vocalization announced the arrival of the scene that I knew would happen and by the sounds of things he wasn't too happy. As I turned toward the door I saw the people that I was expecting to see. There, framed by the doorway was Mr. Jacobson in full rage and fury and standing beside him was the sheriff who look disappointed. I couldn't tell if he was disappointed with me or with the fact that he had to deal with Mr. Jacobson and from the looks of things he was going to have to defend his case.

I watched as all six of the patrons were escorted out of the tavern. Sheriff Elijah seemed to take his time and be apologetic to each one while Mr. Jacobson only continued to stare at me with evil and murderous intent in his eyes. William had come to his usual stand still, frozen from unwillingness to involve himself in any confrontation while Ruth sat down next to me.

"Something I can help you with sheriff?" I asked.

"Seems ol' Mr. Alexander Jacobson, here, has been caught passing out counterfeit money…"

"It's not my fault…." Alexander shouted.

"He's accusing you of given' the bill to him. I've come 'ere to clean this up."

"I see…" I stated dryly.

"And don't you deny it! You gave me this bill. He gave me this bill." The second half of Mr. Jacobson's statement was directed toward the sheriff who only put up his hands and patted the air as if to placate the investor.

"And what bill would that be?" I asked still playing ignorant.

"The one hundred dollar bill, the 'new' hundred dollar bill. The one I didn't have time to look at before you gave it to me. Your clumsiness had me recoiling out the door too quick to look at what you handed me!"

"And why would I give you a one hundred dollar bill, and a fake one at that? Surely you can't claim that I'm giving out money out of the goodness and kindness of my heart."

"You gave it to me to buy off the debt he owes." Mr. Jacobson gestured toward the bar where William was. He was now furious and had crossed the room. His body was practically leaning against my table in an attempt to get into my face.

"I see. So...I gave you a hundred dollars to pay off someone else's debt?"

"Yes you did!"

"and...I used a fake bill?"

"Yes, you did! It had the year of 2010 on it!"

"Wouldn't it have just been better for me to pay William with any fake money for the rent of his room and for the purchase of his food? For that matter, if I had counterfeit money, why would I be staying here? Heck for that matter, if I had one hundred dollar bills that I could just pass around, fake or real, I would be dressed better than I am now and staying at the Washoe Millionaire's Building. And ... if I could pass around this kind of money, fake or not, why would I be working down at the mines?"

I could see Mr. Jacobson's face start to redden and I was sure that he would explode at any given moment. My eyes darted over toward Ruth who was now starting to understand what I had planned and she was doing her best to hide her chuckle.

"YOU GAVE IT TO ME! DON'T YOU DARE DENY IT! STOP LYING!"

"So, let's get your story straight. You mean to tell me that I gave you a hundred dollar bill that doesn't make sense to give you even if I did have it, from a year that hasn't happened yet, for a bill of sale that doesn't exist all in front of witnesses that didn't see anything?"

I heard a snicker from my left and knew that Ruth was just shy of completely losing it. Alexander, on the other hand, just stood there, mortified. He finally realized what was going on, or at least he thought he did.

"Mr. Alexander Jacobson," the sheriff stated. "Do you have any proof of your allegations? Are there any witnesses?"

I watched as the sheriff scanned the room to try to get confirmation or denials from both Ruth and William, but neither said a word.

"No. No, I guess I don't," Alexander said through gritted teeth.

"Perhaps I can help with that sheriff."

My comment caught the attention of everyone present. All I had to do was keep my mouth shut and the investor would probably be hauled off to jail for possible counterfeiting charges and possible slander. But I wasn't done with him, not yet.

"I'll tell you what. If I, or anyone else for that matter, made one counterfeit bill then it stands to reason that I or anyone else would make more. So whoever is counterfeiting bills would have more of them."

When the sheriff nodded at my logic I started to turn out my pockets one by one. When that was done, I took out my wallet and fanned through it. I had nothing.

"So you think that I can't prove the same? If all it takes is a quick search of my pockets to clear me of this...this conspiracy then so be it."

Mr. Jacobson started to follow my lead. Pocket by pocket was pulled out showing that he had nothing to hide. His usual smirk came across his face as he reached for his last pocket on his upper right of his vest. Suddenly his smile turned to horror as his hand came out holding a bill. He desperately attempted to put it back in but the sheriff reached over and caught his hand.

"Looks like you have another one. You're already in trouble for havin' one an' now you got more. I was almost ready to give to the benefit of the doubt, but now...now I gotta take you in awhile I investigate this."

"Don't you see? He planted it on me! It was his I tell you! I'm innocent!"

Sheriff Elijah ignored the man while he produced a set of irons and slapped them on his wrists. Despite the echoes of protests as Mr. Jacobson was being hauled away, I could hear the echoes of snickering coming from Ruth.

I gave a yawn and excused myself from Ruth's company. The coffee could keep me awake for only so long before my lack of sleep and sore muscles pushed my endurance over the limit. It was time to get some sleep.

I don't know how long I had slept, but it was dark outside when I finally woke. My body was still screaming at me and I wasn't sure if it would ever quit. All I knew was that I had to go to work later in the morning, if it wasn't morning already.

At first I had wondered what had woken me. I was sure that I would have slept throughout the night and wasn't sure that I would be able to wake up early enough to go to work. Yet, here I was. I lay there for a moment before it dawned on me; there was noise downstairs, a lot of it.

I went to wake Ruth, but then realized that she wasn't in her bed. I wondered if she had even made it to bed or if she had gotten up because of the noise downstairs. Either way, the only way I would be able to get any answers was to see what was causing the ruckus. I dressed and opened the bedroom door.

There, in the saloon, was a vision that I thought that I would never see. The bar was filled with people. They were all having a great time, eating, drinking, laughing and some were dancing. This was the fullest I've seen the saloon since I've arrived and from what I've gathered, for a long time.

I made my way down to the festive crowd and made my way to the bar, I figured Ruth would make her way here eventually since she was taking orders. I was proven accurate.

"Dad. Dad, isn't this great? Look at all these people."

"Why are they here? I mean it's great and all, but what's changed?"

"From what I could gather two things have happened. First, news got around how you sent Mr. Jacobson to jail. No one knows how you did it, and the tales grow wilder by the moment, but they all have you involved. Seems like you're a hero again, dad. Oh...I'm so proud of you." She gave me a hug with that last statement.

"Second," she continued, "Mr. Alexander Jacobson made bail, took his goons and left town. It seems that his henchmen, at least from the stories that I've heard, have kept customers from businesses to deliberately drive down their income. Without customers, shops were going out of business and Mr. Jacobson came in to scoop them up. Now, everyone thinks he did it through counterfeit money. What was once a group of business owners that were frightened and in debt to this bottom feeder, are now an angry mob ready to lynch him if he ever shows up again."

"This is a celebration. People can get back to their lives, all because of you. You drove him out."

I smiled. Not at the fact that "I" did something, but the fact that something had been done. These people were truly happy, probably for the first time in a long time. I wondered if some of the shops that had been bought out would be able to start up again.

I also had to think about Mr. Jacobson's reaction. I had thought that he would want to stick around and prove his innocence, and then I remembered. There was a Samuel Upham in the mid 1860's that started producing counterfeit money. His production had caught the attention of congress that in turn made it so that anyone caught guilty of said crime could be given the death penalty. This would be a harsh punishment during my time, but this was during the civil war and the country was already suffering from economic hardships. Counterfeiting money was a blatant statement against the government and a direct attempt to undermine its economy.

I was sure that Mr. Jacobson would probably be found innocent or be given only a short amount of time in jail for possessing counterfeit money, or at least I hoped that the judicial system wasn't going to make an example out of him. However that wasn't his fear. The old west had a way of serving up its own type of justice and I wondered if the sheriff would look the other way.

However, something else was stirring in the back of my mind. Perhaps I was too broody, anti-social, or had a tough time feeling happiness and needed to have an excuse to look at the dark side of things. Either way, I simply couldn't view a man like Mr. Jacobson as someone who gave up so easily. I doubted that we had seen the last of him and his henchmen.

Chapter: A Bad Man

*M*orning had come too early and my body continued to protest from the previous day's and night's encounter in the mine. My muscles still screamed at me, bruises were still evident and sore, and I was fatigued beyond all get up. Yet, I would go back to the mines, despite it being before the crack of dawn.

From the looks of things, Ruth, who was still asleep, also had a long night. I wondered how long the patrons stayed keeping her up and awake serving them drinks. It was probably the longest night she had ever put in, yet I was sure that it was also probably the most satisfying. Business would pick up and she would be able to feel as if she had paid off a debt to the man that had brought her in and rescued her. I gave her a quick kiss on her forehead, tucked her in and made my way off to work.

I had arrived at the mines about the same time that everyone else had and reported in to Sam who still gave me the look that told me that I was late again. I doubted that anything would make him happy even if I were the first person to arrive.

Our task was to split into groups. Most of the groups would go about their mining procedures if their tunnels weren't collapsed. He still had a schedule to keep and a quota to produce. He wasn't going to let a little thing like a cave-in stop his production.

The rest of us were going to split into sections according to the tunnels that had their cave-in. I was still assigned to Thomas and his crew and that was alright by me. I wondered if Sam was still trying to get rid of me by placing me with the minorities of his mine. It didn't matter. We had grown accustomed to working together and I figured that we would probably out work any crew, and I had an idea on how to do just that.

I set us up in a line of workers where the front person would remove a rock and hand it to the next, all the way down the line until we could put it in a cart that hadn't been crushed. While we were doing this, I had dismissed our first worker to a ten minute break. Of course everyone was confused until I further explained my plan. After ten minutes, the person at the front of the line would take a break, everyone would move up one and the person on break would get to be in the back of the line. After working for about an hour, the last person in line would get a ten minute break while the rest of us continued. This would ensure that our production line would continue to flow in the narrow working conditions that we had. Alright, so it wasn't really my plan, I had stolen it from the Romans when they fought in their line formations.

I was able to catch a glimpse of some of the other working teams as they all tried to haul rocks out one by one while stumbling over each other since there wasn't enough room to maneuver. They wasted so much time and energy trying to get away from each other's paths that their production was far less than ours. On top of that, their breaks were longer since they were working harder. A little bit of brain muscle was sometimes better than a lot of physical muscle.

We worked all day like this with our production line going non-stop. We had outworked crews with twice the amount of people and had cleared a significant amount of rubble, so much that we had even impressed Sam.

Payment was like last time. We all lined up outside at quitting time at the table without pushing or shoving. We were marked off on Sam's book and were each given a single one dollar coin for our one day of labor.

"Good job."

The words took me by surprise. Sam hadn't said a word to anyone one else. He had passed out payment in complete silence but when it came to me he gave his praise as he handed me the coin. I smiled and nodded not knowing what to say.

I caught up with Thomas and his friends before they left the site and told them that I would see them again tomorrow. This was really a small gesture for me, but I could tell, and knew that it would be, a large gesture for them to receive. At first they were slightly taken aback by my approach but then accepted it with a smile.

My trip back to the saloon was uneventful and I couldn't wait to find my set of blankets on the floor that I was using for my bed so I could get the much needed rest that my body craved. I just hoped that the saloon would be quiet enough for me to get said rest so I would be able to get up early the next morning and start all over. My hopes were quickly dashed.

As I got near the tavern, I could hear the same sounds that I had heard the night before. The place was in full swing again with everyone having a great time. Every table was full of patrons and there were more walking about, talking, dancing, drinking and singing. All were having a great time. I was sure that if this building had one of those maximum occupation signs up then this would have reached said capacity and then some.

I started to make my way upstairs when I suddenly stopped. There, halfway up the stairs, was the little girl, the one that had been haunting me. At first I thought that she was out of place here or perhaps her father was downstairs sharing in the jubilation, but then I noticed, this wasn't the same girl that I had seen at the mines. That girl was alive, and full of life. She had emotions and fluidity in her form. This version had neither.

This wasn't the living girl, this was the ghost girl. This was the girl with the soulless eyes, the far off stare and the burned clothing. My blood ran cold and a chill ran down my spine. I thought that I might be done with these episodes but her presence had proven me wrong. Suddenly she did something that her apparition never had, she spoke and when she did it was haunting, like some voice of desperation off in the far distance trying to reach my ears. It was mixed with fear, despair, distress, and even a bit of anger.

"He's a bad man."

It was like a set of fingernails across my soul. It was like the death cold embrace of a wraith reaching into my chest and pulling on my heart. But despite the fact that I wanted to run, despite that fact that my skin was crawling, despite the fact that my heart was pounding through my chest as if it would burst, my heart still went out to this girl. She was in fear, in pain, and in distress. She needed my help and for the first time since I've met her, I could now get some answers.

"Who? Who is the bad man?"

She started to raise her hand and pointed toward the front of the room downstairs. I turned and looked. At first I saw nothing out of the ordinary, everyone was having fun, laughing and drinking like the night before. I turned back to validate where she was pointing but I should have known better, she was gone. She was gone like she had never been there.

I was about to dismiss the whole thing. I was about to just go upstairs and forget that I had seen her. I was about to chalk her up as a figment of my imagination based on the exhaustion of my body. Yet something didn't seem right. I simply couldn't ignore the plea of a little girl, even if this was an undead specter of one. I turned back to try to make out where she was pointing.

Again, my eyes saw nothing out of the ordinary until I saw Ruth. I thought about making sure that Ruth was alright. I would give her a signal that I had returned and that all was fine. When she finally spotted me, I waved. She went to wave back when she was suddenly pulled backward on to the lap of one of the nearby seated patrons.

Despite my desire to go to sleep and rest my aching muscles, I shot across the room with all of the speed that I could muster to where I had last seen my daughter. I pushed aside strangers as if they were nothing. I was going to find out what had happened and nothing was going to stop me...I stopped dead cold again, the second time in as many minutes.

There sitting in a chair with a smug look on his face was Luke. The young punk of a kid had pulled my daughter on to his lap and was trying his best to keep hold of her. If there was any time that I wanted to completely strangle this man, this was it.

"Get your hands off of her!"

My tone had the threat of murder in it as I pulled his arm away from my daughter allowing her to pull free. However, this didn't seem to bother him one bit. He only sat there with his big smirk on his face.

"My pa..."

I wasn't in the mood for this. My muscles hurt and I was cranky. All I wanted to do was go to bed and get some rest. I really didn't want to put up with some spoiled rich kid who thought that he was better than everyone else because his father was rich.

"I don't care who your pa is..."

"Well, I don't care if ya care of not, I'm sure he cares about you."

"If he can't teach his son some manners, if he can't raise his son properly with some respect toward others, then I wouldn't mind giving him a piece of mind."

"Well, funny you should be sayin' that 'cause he's right behind ya."

I stopped dead silent. I should have known better. I did have a habit of sticking my foot into my mouth at the most inappropriate of times, especially when I was upset. By the smug look upon Luke's face I could tell that he had a feeling about this and that he had set me up from the start. It was then that I realized that he hadn't grabbed Ruth until I had walked into the bar. He, in fact, had set the whole thing up. I probably would have guessed this had I not been so tired or so emotionally charged by Ruth being grabbed. Now, I had fallen for it hook, line, and sinker. The only thing left for me to do was follow this out to its entirety, and I could already see the next several series of events before they unfolded. There was no getting around it. With a sigh I turned around.

The man was big and I mean he was huge, and I thought that Thomas was large. This man had lots of muscles, especially in his arms and chest. If this went where I thought it was going to go, and I was pretty sure that it was, then I was in for a world of hurt.

I quickly made a turn toward Ruth and whispered in her ear so that no one else could hear, "We'll probably need the sheriff. Scratch that; he'll need some back up. Get Thomas as well."

I hoped that Ruth would obey and run off immediately. At first her eyes went wide with the knowledge of what was about to happen and I could see the pleading in her face. Yet I stayed firm and when she understood my response, she took off as quickly as she could.

I turned back toward the big man. I would do everything to avoid this, but I couldn't back down when it came to the safety and well being of my child, despite how much it would hurt. I only hope that Ruth came back as quickly as possible.

The big man got into my face and I realized that there was no turning away. The moment I turned to walk, he would strike. The best I could hope for was to stand here, not back down, and hope that he would see that it wasn't worth what he was pushing for. If that didn't work, my next hope was to stall long enough so that the sheriff and Thomas would arrive.

"I will not tolerate you laying a hand on my son!"

The big man pointed his finger into the center of my chest while he got into my face. Darn it, that hurt. The man could knock me down with just his finger.

"And I will not tolerate your son laying his dirty, stinking paws on my daughter!"

I heard the tavern grow quiet. Our conversation had gotten the attention of everyone in the room. At first I thought that this might be a good thing. Many of the patrons here were happy about me driving out Mr. Jacobson but then my eyes took in the whole scene. While there were plenty of those that I was sure would help, I noticed several others that came behind this big man to give him support.

'Oh great,' I thought. 'He brought reinforcements.'

"Well, maybe if your daughter wasn't such a cheap…"

My knee immediately found his groin. I had some idea of what he was going to say and no father needs to hear his daughter being called such a word. There was only so much that I could walk away from and that wasn't one of them.

The blow wasn't as powerful as I had hoped. He had only slightly bent down instead of dropping to the floor. I had done the proper thing with a follow up to his head twice before he was able to get his senses back. The quick rise with a backhand across my face, knocking me to the ground, told me that I had only upset him.

I tried to get back up, but I felt the man's left hand grab hold of my shirt and haul me up off the ground. I could catch a glimpse of his right hand balled into a fist, ready to punch me in my face. And he probably would have too, if it wasn't for the shattering of wood across his back. A chair had been picked up and smashed over his body.

The big man let me go and I was able to catch a glimpse of my surroundings. All hell had broken loose. The entire tavern had broken out into one major brawl. I could see chairs flying, bottles being smashed, and tables were being shattered. Chaos had erupted. I could see one person get hit in the jaw, another hit in the stomach. One of Luke's men went down; one of the regular patrons went down. I thought I heard a bone break near me, someone's nose was hit hard and blood was starting to drip.

I felt a blow on my side and without even finding out who it was; I spun and lead with my right hand. The shift of my weight with my blow knocked the man sideways. A cheap shot across my blind spot caught me off guard. My knees buckled, but only for a moment. I spun back to my other side and again let the weight of my body carry my blow.

These men may be younger and have more muscles than I had, and perhaps even a bit quicker, but I understood physics. I taught my daughter how to play baseball and that meant how to swing a bat. I told her it wasn't in the arms, but in the legs, thighs and then hips and waist. I told her to step into her swing and let momentum do its job. Only at the last moment did the arms come into play. I applied these techniques into my swings. The blows were staggering. No, I doubted that the blows would have floored these men, but they were off balance with their swings and other men were getting in the way. It didn't take much to knock them down.

I felt a kidney blow from behind. I just about yelled out in pain. With a quick step backwards I let my elbow follow and was satisfied when I felt the connection it made upon my attacker.

I did another quick look around to see where I could help. If I could just get to Luke or his father, perhaps I could end this fight before someone got seriously hurt. From what I could tell, the intruders, those that had come in to help Luke, were winning. Maybe if the sheriff or …

The swinging doors burst open and from my initial thought, I believed that Luke had more support coming to help. These men were also big, very big. Where did they grow these guys? My heart was about to sink, until I caught sight of one of the men. It was Thomas. He had come to my rescue as I had come to his.

My assessment of the situation had cost me. I felt the body tackle knock me to the ground. I hit the ground hard and my breath was knocked out of me. A quick turn brought my face around to see…

Luke. It was Luke. Good, I now had the opportunity to end this madness.

Luke's fists started to rain down upon me. I did my best to keep his fists away from my face until the palm of my hand caught him under his chin. I pushed with all of my might; I had to get him off of me.

Suddenly his right hand shot around to his back hip as if to reach for something and when I was able to see it again, he was holding a knife. It was one of those simple dagger-like hunting knives, nothing special and didn't even look sharp, but it was still metal and a good push would still cut into me. Both of my hands shot out and grabbed his wrist as he started to push his blade toward the center of my chest. I probably had more strength than the young kid, but he had leverage. All I could do was watch as he slowly made progress toward piercing my ribs and shoving his weapon deep into my heart.

"Blam!"

The sudden explosion of a gunshot froze us all in place. I pulled myself from the grip of the man that held me. Blood was running down my face and my eyes were puffy. It would be hard to see out of them for a while, yet I could see clear enough.

There, standing in the middle of the swinging doorway, was Sheriff Elijah with two deputies as backups. The sheriff had his hand on his gun, although it was still in his holster. The two deputies behind him were each carrying shotguns and by the looks of things one of them had shot a warning shot into the air.

"Alright! Break it up! Everyone go home!"

"He started it, sheriff an' I'm aiming to finish it." Luke's father was pointing towards me.

I could see Sheriff Elijah just shake his head. I think that he was getting tired of me being in the middle of everything, good and bad.

"Did you hit him back?" The sheriff asked.

The silence spoke volumes.

"I thought so. You each got some good licks on the other, now your fun's over. Time to head home."

There was a little bit of pushing and shoving as everyone started to untangle themselves from each other. However, it didn't take long before everyone left for the evening. The sheriff could only give me a glare as if saying "I don't want to come back here again" before leaving with the last guest.

The tavern was in pieces and shambles. Tables were broken, the remains of chairs were scattered all over the place, bottles were smashed, broken glass littered the floor, and dishes were sprawled everywhere. It looked like a hurricane had hit the place and left nothing untouched.

"I'll start cleaning and will try to get more items from the stock," William said once everyone had left.

His voice was somber. I was sure that what profits that he was initially making would now be eaten up by the bar fight. I almost wondered if Luke's desire to stir up trouble was the true culprit of this fight or if it was Mr. Jacobson who had organized it to make sure that this fight happened here to ensure that William's new profits would be destroyed.

I watched a little as Ruth and William started cleaning. I wasn't going to join since it would be a whole night's work and I still had to get up early tomorrow morning and head to the mines. Besides, it seemed to me that the two of them were becoming "friendly". I didn't know how friendly, and I wasn't sure I wanted to know, and I wasn't sure how long I wanted to leave them together alone, but they seemed to need a moment, at least some space, so I stepped outside for some air to relax before retiring to bed for the night.

I could hear other taverns in full swing. There was plenty of giggling, laughing, partying, and singing. People were coming and going as they should be. My gaze caught a few people until one individual stole my attention. It was a tall thin man escorting a very young girl. This was completely odd. No young child should be in this side of town, especially this time of night. Then, at the corner of my eye, I saw another man approach them. This was not settling right, not at all.

However, as the individuals came into the spotlight of a nearby gaslight, I could see who they were. The thin man was the preacher Abraham and he was escorting the young girl from my dreams, from my nightmares, to her father.

The man that had been coming out of the nearby bar was picking up his daughter from Abraham. This wasn't the ghost girl, this was the living girl. It was the same girl, but not the dead one. Why didn't he leave his daughter with his wife at home if he was going to go out and visit a bar?

I again had to remember my history. The average life expectancy around this time was less than forty years old since so many people died in their earlier years due to complications that my time had figured out how to deal with. It was very possible that his wife had passed away and now he was a single dad trying to raise his only daughter.

As I watched the father pick up his daughter, the little girl turned to me with almost pleading eyes before she quickened her pace and hid behind her father. From what I could tell, her father simply passed it off as being shy. I wondered if the child was going through a phase or if she simply couldn't get away from the preacher fast enough.

After both the dad and the little girl turned and disappeared into the night, Abraham turn to go as well, but then stopped. He caught me staring at him. His eyes bore back at me with hatred and loathing before he turned and went back to where he had come from.

'He's a bad man.'

The words echoed in my mind and I realized who the ghost girl was talking about. It wasn't about Luke, it was about Abraham.

Chapter: Stampede

*W*ork continued for the next several days till the end of the week. We continued to pull the rubble from the cave-in. Since this area had already been mined, there was no need to process this rock, it was all junk. It took us the rest of the week before we could clear enough to start up mining again; even then there was always more rubble to clear.

I had looked forward to Saturday night. Apparently the mines closed down in observance of Sunday so everyone could go to church. After being around such foul language, adult situations, physical violence, and drunkenness, one would think that going to church would help change these men, especially deliberately shutting down the mines so the workers could go attend. Yet, there was no redemption, no change of behavior and no soul saving miracles by going to service. I knew that these men would all come back Monday morning unchanged and untouched by whatever spiritual message that they would hear on Sunday morning.

Not me though. I wasn't going to any service. Since I had already been thrown out of Saint Mary's-in-the-Mountains Catholic Church by the preacher Abraham, news had traveled that neither Ruth nor I would be welcomed in any church. That was fine by me. I was looking forward to the chance of sleeping in and giving my muscles the rest that they needed.

However, I couldn't find rest despite the fact that my body was screaming for it, not since the bar fight a few days ago. It was nothing physical; it was what the ghost girl had said.

'He's a bad man.'

This continued to echo in my head as I thought of the church service that I was not going to. Despite that fact that my body didn't want to get out of bed, despite the fact that I would not be welcomed, despite the fact that I didn't like the man, there was still something stirring in my soul. I wanted to be at church just to keep an eye on the preacher man, Abraham Smith. I needed to know the connection between him and the little girl.

My mind and my body wrestled between getting up and staying in bed and this was what kept me from getting the rest I needed. It wasn't until I promised myself that I would swing around the church later in the afternoon, just to poke around a little, did I finally start to really drift off to sleep.

The sound was akin to thunder, the vibrations to that of an earthquake. My hopes and dreams of sleeping in were dashed aside by the horrible sounds off…

Cattle?

Was someone driving a herd of cattle through the streets of Virginia City? People were walking on the streets, horses could be spooked, and people were doing business. What selfish, self-centered, thoughtless, idiotic, individual would attempt such a thing?

Blam! Blam!

The two gunshots followed by the yelling and screaming told me that this couldn't be a cattle drive. No one was guiding cows through the streets to a railroad that would have been more easily accessed further down the hill toward Carson City. No, these "herders" were causing the cows to run wild, to run scared in sheer terror, to stampede.

I scrambled out of "bed" and looked over toward Ruth. What had always been a task and a nightmare of itself, the job of waking up my daughter, was now done without effort. The sounds of the stampede and the gun shots followed by the yelling of the herders and the citizens that were trying to get out of the way was enough to wake her from her deep slumber.

The both of us made our way toward the window and looked out. It was earlier than I had thought. The sun had yet to come up and darkness had still enveloped the city. Yet, despite the lack of sunlight, we could still see the cows that were being pushed through the streets.

Periodically one of the men on horses that were herding them would ride by one of the gas lamps that dotted the town and we understood that these men weren't just being reckless, they were enjoying themselves. They all had red bandanas that covered most of their faces, yet the rest of their body language showed nothing but excitement as they pushed the cows onward.

A dust cloud had risen from all of the cows and the few horses. It would have been hard to see anything if one were on level ground, but since we were above it; we were able to see enough.

Despite once watching a show that proved that a bull in a china shop was a misnomer and a myth by showing that a bull would do anything that it could to not knock over anything and was actually a gentle and graceful beast, the sight before me was of legend. These panicked bulls were slamming into everything that was getting in their way. Benches, wagons, barrels, carts, benches, and even pillars to upper floors were slammed into and each item was sent to the ground in shards and pieces leaving it unrecognizable. Once a pillar was shattered, the balcony that was being supported would sway and buckle until gravity took over and that piece of the building would collapse not only doing extensive damage to the shops, but it put the people that were in that section of the building at risk of being hurt.

Bulls weren't just herded down the street; they were being herded into buildings, shops, and taverns. I could hear glass breaking and tables being shattered. I could see people trying to run for their lives but getting caught by the bulls and were run through with their horns or trampled on with their hooves.

People were getting hurt out there. Some were already dead while others were wounded and if they didn't get help soon, they would die as well. Yells of pain mixed with screams of terror. Panic and pandemonium had run wild.

I stood there, looking out of the window, dumbstruck. I had no idea what I could do. I wasn't sure that I would have done anything knowing full well that anything I tried to do would have been suicide, yet I was torn. Shouldn't I at least try? I tried with those that were buried alive.

Out of the corner of my eye I watched as one of the herders lowered his pistol, after shooting a couple of rounds to keep the cattle in a panic, and shot at one of the storekeepers that was trying to run for his life. The shopkeeper seemed to freeze before his knees buckled and he dropped to the ground.

Murdered. The man was shot in the back and murdered right before our eyes. I stood in shock, trembling; I didn't know what to do...

The next gunshot scared me into action. The loud explosion was near my ear and had startled me so bad that I had jumped. I could have sworn that the gun was fired right next to me and when I looked, I could see why.

Ruth was holding a pistol and pointing it out of the window, a second weapon lay on a small table near the window. Both were six shooter revolvers, nothing fancy, but they were still guns and still capable of killing. I was shocked and dismayed. I couldn't believe...

The sound of a bullet ricocheting off of the window seal made me drop. Obviously Ruth had been able to draw their fire away from innocent bystanders. It was a smart move to save people, but now our lives were in danger.

"You're going to have to tell me how you managed to pick up a couple of guns," I shouted over the noise from below us.

"That's a story for another time," she shouted back as another bullet broke the top half of the window that couldn't be opened. "Take the extra pistol."

I have shot guns before when I was younger, but I've never shot them at people. Even if I were to try, I was afraid that anything I attempted would be useless. One of my eyes didn't focus very well and it messed up my ability to aim. Even when I had tried at carnivals I couldn't hit anything. Even if I were to aim and hit my target, I wasn't sure that I could take a life. But if I didn't, if I didn't at least try, more innocent people would be killed.

I waited for a couple of rounds to bounce off of the window before I sprang up. My eyes took in the vision before me quickly, as I knew that I didn't have much time before there would be a return shot. In a matter of a heartbeat I had found my first target, a man who was hiding his face with a bandana riding a horse. Without giving myself a chance to think I took my shot.

My shot went short and hit the cow in front of him. The bovine took a short stagger and fell sideways, into the man's horse, knocking over the horse and his rider. For a moment I saw the rider try to stand and for a moment I thought that he could try to get back on his horse or at least try to move out of the way.

The bull cow hit him hard, sending his body crashing through the air. When he landed, he landed hard upon the unforgiving ground. I could have sworn I heard bones being crushed under the impact of the stampede.

One of the herders turned his horse into a small section of the cows and herded them straight under us, right into the bar. We had only recently put everything back together and just barely at that, and now the stampede was going to destroy everything all over again. I could hear the sounds of broken tables and chairs that only confirmed my suspicions. But I wasn't too concerned about a bunch of cows, we could rebuild again and again. What I was more afraid of was that these "cowboys" were deliberately hurting and killing people and now that they knew that we had guns, at least one of them would try to come up here to take care of us.

I made my way toward Ruth's door and gave it a slight shove open. I could hear cows down below trampling through everything, but all of that was immediately forgotten about when two gun shots rang through air. The bullets pierced through the door and lodged themselves somewhere in the wall on the opposite end of the room. My thoughts went out to Ruth who wasn't too far from where the slugs had hit. This man was going to kill us both.

I rolled out through the door one way and then back another. Another shot rang out, striking the wall where I just was. My roll had brought me to the top of the stairs where I tried to come out of my maneuver and onto the stairs so I could make a mad dash down them. I had hoped that the railing, my speed and the cows between us would distract his aim and I hoped that my presence would stop him from firing into the room where my daughter was. My plan was flawed. What would have been a great move in the movies almost got me killed.

I rolled out of my somersault later than I had expected and my momentum took me over the edge of the first step. My body continued to roll unceremoniously down the stairs. My head banged against the wall and I saw stars. A couple more shots rang out as I tumbled, barely missing my body.

As I lay there in pain I could hear the man trying to make his way through the cows in an attempt to get a better shot at me. The cows pushed and shoved against each other in the already overcrowded space that they had been jammed into. There was nowhere for him to go.

I pulled myself up off of the ground and came up with my gun raised, poised, ready to fire. He had his ready first. For a brief moment, a span of a heartbeat that seemed to go on forever, we stared at each other. Then the silence was shattered by a single shot.

To my horror, I realized that I hadn't been the one who pulled the trigger. I waited another moment for the shock to wear off, for the pain to kick in, for the blood to start to spill and pool at my feet. There was nothing.

I looked across the room, full of cows, to the shooter at the other side. He, too, looked surprised as if he was also waiting for the pain to kick in. His eyes went wide once he found out that he was the one that had been hit. He stumbled back a little. His arm dropped, his gun fell from his grasp. Blood seeped from his shoulder as he dropped to ground.

I looked back to my left and up the stairs. There was my daughter holding her pistol, its smoke was still coming out of the barrel.

Chapter: Answers

*R*uth and I had managed to restrain our shooter and slowly move the cows back outside. We had found that the sheriff and his two deputies had come on the scene and had traded a few shots with the cowboys themselves. Most of the herders had been shot, knocked off their horses and trampled, or had ridden off as quickly as they could leaving a mess of cows behind.

It had taken a while and was a mass effort, but the cows were eventually rounded up and slowly driven off. However, the damage had been done. Many people were hurt and a few were dead. Shops and businesses were torn up or destroyed outright.

"They've been driven hard," Sheriff Elijah stated as he turned to me. "Ain't no way to drive cattle."

I looked at him curiously.

"Been a cattle driver at one point, don't ask. But I can tell you that we could drive them cattle about fifteen miles or so on any given day an' that's with stops so the cattle could feed an' rest. It took us two months sometimes to herd them cattle from one place to another. If we drove them any harder, they would lose weight and be too sickly and tired and not be healthy for sellin'."

"Anyway I know when cattle have been driven too hard, even for a full day, an' these cattle are them. The closest ranch would be in Carson City and that's about fifteen miles, only that's all uphill from there to here. The cows would have been pushed all night else they would have been seen and heard. An' the biggest thing is, there are closer trains to be driven to. Ain't no reason to be up here. No feed for them cows neither."

"So, what you are saying, sheriff," I stated. "Is that this wasn't merely a cattle-drive gone wrong. These cattle were specifically driven, here, to stampede. I agree, I saw a couple of the herders shoot down bystanders in the back. The entire thing was a cover up from the start."

I looked around and considered the damage. The stampede wasn't directed toward the residential section where it would do more damage. It had been directed here, in the business section.

"Well," he said. "If I could get me some answers, like who's responsible, who hired the men, why this was done in the first place. Someone's gonna answer to all of this an' someone knows something an' I plan on findin' out. So, if you know anyone, or know someone who knows someone..."

I knew he was grasping at straws. He had no leads to go on. The statement was more out of pleading. I smiled, he had no idea and it was my pleasure to give him what he needed.

"You mean like the one Ruth and I have back at the saloon?"

Now it was his time to look at me curiously.

"One of the men tried to come into our tavern and bring us to an early demise. Ruth was able to wing him. We have him held up back at the tavern. I thought that it was safest that he stay there until this mess was dealt with first. Ruth is 'taking care' of him. I was wondering when the best time to bring up this conversation would be. I guess this would be it."

The sheriff gave me one of those disapproving looks, as if to say 'you should have told me sooner.' I merely shrugged. With all of the excitement I had honestly forgotten about him.

Sheriff Elijah followed me back to what was left of the tavern. It was reminiscent of when we had the bar fight. Everything was knocked down and in shambles. Wood pieces were everywhere. Tables were broken and chairs were demolished. The only difference was that on top of everything, there were now freshly laid cow pies as well. We were going to need some major cleaning before anyone could come back in as a customer.

I led the sheriff to an offshoot room that had primarily been used for storage. We had cleared the storage items out in hopes to use them in the clean up and had secured our hostage for further interrogation. Actually, I was going to find an excuse to slap him around a bit before turning him over to the sheriff. The guy would have had the worst case of "falling down" that anyone had seen.

We found the man right where Ruth and I had left him. He was still locked in the room that we had put him in and was tied to the chair that we had placed him on. His wound was taken care of and bound so his bleeding had stopped. For a man that tried to kill me and my daughter, it was more than he deserved.

"What's yar name, boy?"

"I ain't tellin', sheriff. I ain't tellin' nothin'. Now you let me go and stick me in your cell, 'cause I'll be out in a day or two."

"You're gonna to tell me who you're workin' for. Now don't look at me like that. First of all, you ain't got the intelligence to pull this off; I know a hired hand when I see one. Second, you already hinted as much when you said you would 'be out in a day or two.' Only way to do that is if you make bail and I doubt you got that kind of money. But I'm not after you. I'm after your boss. You tell me who he is and I'll be prone to look the other way as you ride off and out of town on your own, no questions asked."

The man seemed to think about that for a moment but then shook his head.

"Nope, not worth it. I'll take my chances in your cell."

The sheriff's rage started to build and for one moment I thought that he would strike down our prisoner right there. I'm pretty sure that he would have, since this wasn't my era and my judicial system. Plus, there wouldn't be any witnesses. However, I couldn't let this continue. I doubted that our suspect would talk no matter what happened to him and this would get us nowhere. I put my arm up and stopped the sheriff from moving forward. When he gave me the look of 'I know what I'm doing', I shook my head and spoke.

"Actually, you don't need to tell us anything. Your boss is going to think that you have already told us. We'll put the word out with the local paper that you'll be testifying and I'm sure that he will show up very quickly, but not to post your bail. I doubt that you would live long without our protection. However, if you really did give us the information that we need, I'm sure we can get you a horse so you can ride off to wherever you want to go."

"You...you can't do that," our hostage stuttered.

"No, he can't do that," I replied pointing at the sheriff. "But I can, and I will."

This really made our prisoner pause. Then he spoke with hesitation.

"Give me some time ta think about it, will ya?"

"I'll give ya five minutes," the sheriff stated. "After that I gotta take you in, one way or another."

We left him where he was, bound to the chair and closed the door behind us. He wanted time alone; we were going to give it to him. After all, where was he going to go? At least that I was thought. The sheriff had other ideas though.

"He's going to try to escape."

I turned to the sheriff and gave him a look of confusion.

"I've seen his look before. He'll do his best to wiggle out of those bonds, not matter how much he's hurtin'. He'll probably go for my gun and will either succeed in gettin' away or force me to shot him. Either way, he ain't goin' to jail. You've scared him, scared him too much. Don't give me that look; it was worth it, every last word you said. But he's more scared of someone else..."

The scream pierced the air and stopped us dead in our tracks. We had wandered away from the storage room and had made our way to the other side of the tavern. We didn't need to be near a door that we had locked to hold a person that was tied to a chair. The screams told us otherwise.

"I'm not tellin' ya nothin'! No, no..Pleasssee! Noooo!"

There was someone else in that room with him despite the fact that there was no way to get inside. Sheriff Elijah and I rushed to the door and started to unlock it.

"Ok! Ok! I'll tell….It was Mr. Jacobson. He hired us! He did it! It was his plan to run everyone out! It was his idea to…no, no. NOOO!"

Sheriff Elijah had managed to get the door open and I was the first to step inside. The temperature had dropped dramatically, so much so that I could see my breath. And it wasn't just a temperature drop, it felt as if someone had walked upon my grave. I had come to know and understand these feelings. This was a haunting, only this time, I wasn't the one being haunted.

My eyes caught movement out of the corner of my eye near the back of the room. I turned to look and I saw her and recognized her right away. The woman had her hair pulled back, giving her a sharp, stern look. Her dress was period clothing, from this time period, all black. It came up to her neck, went out to her wrists and covered her ankles. This left a cold, unappealing look and it was hard to believe that she could have been in the profession that she was. This was Madam Julia Bulette. She may have died several years ago, from this present year, yet here she was or at least what was left of her.

The physical body of the woman seemed to stand there for just a moment. The look on her face was part satisfaction and part concern. However, before the sheriff could take one step to follow me into the room, Madam Julia Bulette's body turned transparent and then faded away as if she had never been there.

"Dear Lord, what happened to him?"

The sheriff's exclamation brought me out of my reverie. I looked over at our prisoner and almost gasped out of freight.

The man was slumped forward in his chair, unmoving. The restraints were the only thing holding him upright, and that was just barely. My first guess was that this man was now dead. His hair had turned white, his skin was pale and clammy, and there was a look of absolute terror upon his face now frozen in place by his demise. He had been scared to death,

"We heard him! He was talkin' to someone. But no one's here. How did…" The sheriff's confusion had left him speechless.

He might not have known, but I did. I doubted that he would have believed me if I had told him. I doubt that he would have believed me if I said that the ghost of a prostitute had been here and killed him.

She might be dead, but she was here to protect her city. However, she couldn't do it alone; she still needed someone's help. Now I understood. When I first met her, I thought that she was trying to pull me to an early grave. Now I knew that this wasn't the case. She was trying to get me to come here and help. But help with what? Was a stampede that did very little damage, comparatively, really warrant her soul to reach out from beyond the grave and travel through time and space just to reach me? Somehow, I doubted this. Suddenly I was left with more questions than answers.

Chapter: Prelude to a Disaster

*T*he warm air felt good upon my body. The sand beneath my towel curved and molded to my form. It was wonderful soaking up the sun on the beach of Lake Tahoe. A light gentle breeze blew across the beach, keeping the heat from becoming unbearable. The sky was azure blue, without a cloud overhead. The water was crystal clear. The boats bobbed lazily to the rhythm of the waves as the lake softly lapped against the shore.

It was good just to lay here, under the sun, putting my nightmares behind me. The stress of just getting here had given me some of the worst nightmares that I thought I would ever have. It had all been a dream. The undead, the blood river, the haunting ghosts, the little girl, the ghost prostitute, the preacher man, even the time travel back to the old west with the cave-in, the stampede and gun fight was all just a dream.

I rolled over on my back to feel the sun's rays upon my face. It was such a comfortable feeling. All of my troubles seemed to fade away.

"Hey, you're in my sunlight."

The shadow fell upon me, blocking the sun's warmth. I was sure that it was my wife's as she stood over me. I expected a snappish come back, perhaps even a sexy one, or perhaps a glass of cold water playfully splashed upon me. What I didn't expect was…

"Help….please…"

The sound of the voice was familiar, but it wasn't my wife's voice. It was feminine and young, like my daughter, only younger. I remembered the voice and my eyes opened with horror to the realization of what I was going to see.

The young girl, the ghost girl, the "Little House on the Prairie" girl with the burned dress and the soulless eyes was standing over me. But that wasn't all that had stirred horror in my blood. The air grew cold, cold enough to make my breath visible. It wasn't just a chill that caressed my skin and gave me goose bumps; it was a soul chilling, permeating, frozen blast of icy cold that took a hold of my inner being like a vise. It took my breath away and grabbed at my heart and lungs. On top of this, the sky turned from an azure blue to a blood red. The lake reflected the sky and became turbulent as if some storm had blown in. Its waves were slapping against the shore and rocked the boats so violently that I was certain that most of them would tip over. Then there was the smell. It smelled of fire and burning wood. It smelled of charcoaled flesh.

"He's going to kill us. He's going to kill us all. You need to wake up. You need to wake up. Please, you have to help."

It dawned on me in a horrible realization that I was actually dreaming that all of the horrible and terrible things that I have encountered so far were real. I was still back in 1875 in Virginia City. It had all been real and this was the nightmare.

Only, I realized that it wasn't. Yes, I was still dreaming about me on this shore with the ghost girl and blood sky. But this wasn't a nightmare. This was a plea for help. It wasn't meant to scare me, to terrify me, this was just how the plea was coming across. The ghost girl couldn't come to me any other way. These were visuals and warnings. Every aspect was an emotion or an event that was going to happen. It was symbolic. This wasn't the nightmare; the real nightmare was to come if I didn't do something.

It had also dawned on me that this was the girl that I had promised myself that I would go check up on and I had forgotten. Now I wondered if she was alright. I wondered if she had died because I didn't act and now her dead spirit had come to haunt me.

No, that wasn't right. Her words were future tense, not yet happened. She was still alive, just somehow able to reach out to me, but only in nightmares. There was still time. All I needed to do was ...

"Wake up. Wake up."

The sound of the woman's voice brought me out of my sleep. I was right, I had been dreaming. I was still on the floor of Ruth's room, on a few extra blankets. It was still 1875. This was still Virginia City. It was still freezing cold.

My drowsiness had completely worn off as soon as I realized who had spoken to wake me. It was Madam Julia Bulette, the ghost prostitute. I was beginning to feel like Ebenezer Scrooge with all of these haunting encounters.

"He's going to burn the city down." Her words were as cryptic as this whole encounter.

"Who? Who's going to burn down the city? When? How?"

I tried to rattle off as many questions as I could without waking up my daughter. If time was of the essence, I needed to know quickly, not only to prevent a disaster but because of the duration of my visitations. These ghosts had a nasty habit of disappearing before...

It was too late. The ghost of Madam Julia Bulette vanished right before my eyes and with her so did the chill. Even the smell of smoke only lingered for a little while longer before completely dissipating.

I lay there for a moment and wondered if I should try to go back to sleep or if there was something else that I should be doing. If there was a danger to this city, I didn't know where to start looking or when. I could find the correct place only to be too early and continue my search elsewhere or, worse yet, be too late.

After not being able to quiet my mind, I got up and looked out the window. It was nothing in particular, just the "off in the distance" stare that I would sometimes do when I was troubled. All was well. Nothing was out of place. A couple of drunks stumbled out of a bar further down the block and I could see two women on the corner looking for company. All was as it should be in this old western town. There was nothing of interest, until I saw it out of the corner of my eye.

Off to my right I could see a man coming from the residential area, crossing the business section and heading toward the red light district. This alone didn't strike me as odd, nor did the torch he was carrying for light and I would have passed it off as just a lonely man in search of company. That was until the light struck his face just right. It was then that I knew that this man wasn't coming here for company. It was then that I recognized this man. It was the preacher, Abraham Smith.

'He's a bad man.'

The words echoed in my mind.

'The sin in this town needs to be purged and cast into the fire so it may be cleansed.' The preachers own words came back to haunt me.

'He's going to burn the city down.'

There was no denying what I had been brought here to do and what I was going to do. I did a quick look toward my daughter and found her still sleeping. Good, let her sleep. I would take care of this and if all went well, I would be back before she awoke.

I hurriedly, and quietly, made my way out of the room, down the stairs and outside without anyone noticing me. My feet carried me with haste down the half block to the perpendicular street that I had seen the preacher man take. My eyes looked ahead as I rounded the corner and caught Abraham Smith turn the corner to his left. I had to catch up to him as quickly as possible.

I sprinted with all of my might down the street. My arms moved hard and sweat poured down my forehead. It was only a block, but it was still hot outside even if it were in the middle of the night. I found the turn off, rounded it and set off to find my target. It wasn't hard to find him.

The preacher man had made his way about halfway down the street and found a seamstress store where he stopped. At first I couldn't tell what he was doing, then I realized that he was offering his actions up to the entity that he worshipped, which despite his claims, I doubted that it was about the God that I read about in Sunday School.

It all came together right then and there. He was in fact going to set the whole area on fire. This was his personal cleansing. The clothing inside would ignite quickly. The buildings were as dry as a bone and they would all go up in flames, and not just this section. The entire city would be a raging inferno.

It was then that it had finally struck me. The one thing that had been in the back of my mind, trying to get my attention, had finally come to light. It had been like a ghost, always eluding my grasp until now. Now I remembered. I finally remembered.

Virginia City had in fact nearly been completely burned down in 1875, this very year, this very day, this very morning, October 26th. I was now in the middle of this city's biggest tragedy and I was about to watch it all unfold right before my eyes.

I simply could let this happen. I knew that this was probably going to change history, but I couldn't just let him burn down the entire city. Too many people were still sleeping. They wouldn't be able to wake up in time. They would all burn to death. I had to do something. Yet I was still too far away. I had to get him to talk to me to buy me some time. I knew that his pride would want to gloat over what he was about to do, so it was worth the effort. My words reached out to him as I continued to advance.

"Since when does a preacher, a man of the cloth, God's chosen, bring destruction. I thought you were here to bring peace, love, and understanding."

This made him stop dead cold and turn to face me.

"Think not that I am come to send peace on earth: I came not to send peace, but a sword."

I knew the scripture he was quoting. I've heard it many times by those who wanted to justify violence in the name of religion. The sword was meant to be a spiritual one, one that cuts away darkness from a person's life, from their heart like a surgeon would cut away cancer. It was never meant as a physical one, one to destroy any who didn't bow down. Perhaps there would be someone who had the authority to do such a thing in some other time, but neither this preacher nor I were that person and this wasn't that time.

"And you're going to bring this on yourself?" I had to keep him talking.

"This city is full of sin. '*Therefore shall her plagues come in one day, death, and mourning, and famine; and she shall be utterly burned with fire: for strong is the Lord God who judgeth her.*'"

"You will end up killing a lot of people, a lot of innocent people."

"*And whosoever was not found written in the book of life was cast into the lake of fire.*"

Boy he was on a roll tonight. I wondered, only briefly, if he had memorized these lines just in case he got caught doing this or did he just memorize them to justify his actions to himself.

"And what give you the right?"

"*Behold, all souls are mine' as the soul of the father, so also the soul of the son is mine: the soul that sinneth, it shall die.*"

I had closed the gap considerably yet it wasn't enough. Abraham had brought his arm back and was set to launch his torch, through the window, and into the shop that would start the blazing inferno.

Ruth woke with a start. The freezing cold temperatures inside her bedroom had brought her out of her slumber. Yet it wasn't the chill that had woken her, that had started her wakefulness, it was the dreaded feeling that something had gone wrong, had gone horrible wrong. Or perhaps it was about to go horribly wrong. It was hard to tell, but her heart was beating through her chest as though it was trying to escape.

A quick look around told her what her mind didn't want to accept, yet in her heart she knew it to be true. Her dad, her father, the one that deep down she knew she could count on, was gone. He could have easily gotten up for anything, yet she knew that there was something not right.

She quickly went toward her door, opened it and looked down into the saloon. Although it was pretty much open all night, there was no one there. She stopped and listened, yet there wasn't a sound.

Her feet carried her back to the other side of the room where she looked out her window full of bullet holes. Her eyes scanned the street below her in hopes of finding any clue or evidence to her father, or to the fear that was overwhelming her. At first she saw nothing out of the ordinary; that was until she saw him out of the corner of her eye.

There, just turning onto her block was a man carrying a lantern. His perfection in his dress seemed to be out of place for this section of town and this time of night, until she realized who it was. Her eyes went wide with anger, astonishment, and disbelief. The light had shinned just right and she was able to catch his face, it was the face of Alexander Jacobson. This was the face of the man that was trying to run everyone out of town. This was the man that had hired the thugs to stampede the city. This was the man that was responsible of her getting shot at.

At first she wondered what he might be doing back here in Virginia City, especially this time of night. Then she shook her head. It didn't matter. Whatever it was, she was sure that it wasn't any good. It was time to find out what he was up to and stop him once and for all.

Quickly she donned her clothing, pulled on her boots, grabbed her pistol and made her way downstairs. She scanned the tavern just to confirm that her dad wasn't there before heading on to the street in the middle of the night.

Her route followed the man that she had come to loath. She did her best to remain in the shadows, although she had to admit that she had no training to do so, it was more for her state of well being rather than actually hiding from her prey. Mr. Jacobson seemed very singular minded and had no intention of looking back to see if he was being followed so she wasn't too worried that she would be seen, yet she remained in the shadows as much as she could.

She continued her way through the night and followed as the business man turned down one block and then another. She let her mind wander while she kept track of him. She knew this section of town. There wasn't much out here that anyone would be interested in. There were a few warehouses and a couple of boarding houses. This rich man could easily buy everything on this block several times over. If he wanted to stay the night, then it would have been more his style to stay at the Washoe Millionaire's Club. Unless he really didn't have money and all of this was a show. Still, he was out very late.

It wasn't too long before the business man turned down an alley between two of the boarding houses and out of her sight. With as much stealth as she could muster, Ruth placed her body up against the side of the building and looked down the side road.

The backstreet only went about halfway through the distance of the block before it dead ended. This had become a place of storage for boxes, crates, barrels, old tarps, rope, and other discarded material, all of which were stacked precariously higher than they should have been.

Near the far end of the passage, Ruth could see two men talking. Thanks to the lantern that had been brought, Ruth was able to make out the details of each man quite well. The first had his back to her and yet was easily recognizable by his exquisite taste of his tailor made clothing. This was the man she had been following, Mr. Jacobson. The second man seemed more like a ruffian, less like someone that the rich business man would associate with. Unlike his personal henchmen who were well groomed and well dressed in rich fineries, the second man was dressed in grubby, dirty, clothes, something one of the miners would wear.

"I am not happy. Things are not moving according to my time table. Every day that goes by is another day that gold is being taken out of that mine. That means there is less for me and I'll make sure that there's less for you." Mr. Jacobson's voice sounded very irritated.

"It's not my fault. My men an' I 'ave done everything that you've asked. We've driven customers from the businesses and a few of the taverns like you asked. I hired the men to drive the cattle, but they failed to do enough damage. Even sabotaged most of the wood so there would be more cave-ins. The last one was supposed to set the whole operation back for weeks. Ain't my fault that the new comer would get everyone all together an' get everyone…"

"Enough. I'm tired of excuses. I want things taken care of tonight."

"But…"

"No! No excuses. Either you will take care of things tonight or I'll find someone else to take care of you."

The last statement changed the entire composure of the second man. He had gone from being intimidated, from being horrifically scarred, to a state of being irked, even irate. He seemed to grow from being shaken to a

349

more rigid form with the expression on his face as if saying "just try it."

This intense moment had drawn Ruth in. She had moved forward to get a better look. Her mind had left the thought of finding her dad and this had taken her complete attention. She simply had to watch this. Either the second man would tear Mr. Jacobson a new one and that would be the end of him, or the rich business man would mop the floor with his henchman in which case his plans would fall apart or at least be delayed. She leaned forward to get a better look, to see if she could catch the conversation better.

The sound of the falling barrel split the silence of the night and shattered the intense moment that was at the other end of the alley. Ruth almost cursed herself. She really should have been more careful.

"We've got company!" The second man had exclaimed his concern loud enough for most of the block to hear if they were awake.

Ruth had heard the henchman state the obvious. No wonder why he wasn't at the top of the criminal chain. It didn't matter. Ruth knew that she could probably outrun these two. She had always been the top runner in her cross country team, and although that was years ago, she was certain that her speed had remained. Besides, she had a considerable head start. All she had to do was…

The arms came around her and held her tight. She hadn't thought that there would be a third man present and now it was too late.

Thomas woke from his restless sleep. He couldn't imagine any other time that he couldn't sleep; he never had a problem with that before. He was a hard working man and usually pushed his body to its limits so when it came time to sleep, he fell into a deep slumber. However, that was not the case tonight. Tonight he woke with an odd feeling, a feeling that he couldn't place, a feeling that he couldn't shake.

But it was more than that. It seemed to be colder than usual. He had never felt it this cold, ever. It wasn't just a chill that came over his body to give him the shivers, this he had felt before. No, this was a cold that seemed to penetrate deep into his soul, something that gripped his heart and wouldn't let go.

And if that wasn't enough, just as he started to stir, started to wake, he could have sworn that he heard a voice. It was a woman's voice with a pleading tone.

"He's going to burn the city down."

When he had finally opened his eyes, he saw no one who could have said such words. Only he and his wife were present in this room and she lay beside him. He tried to shake the words off as something from a dream or perhaps his wife talking in her sleep again.

He rolled to his side and looked at his wife who was still fast asleep. She looked so peaceful and beautiful and he wondered how he ever managed to find someone who saw more in himself than he did. He gave her a gentle kiss on her forehead.

Since he was awake, Thomas went to check up upon his daughter. He slipped on his pants, crept through the door and made his way down the hall to his daughter's room. She was also sleeping peacefully.

Yet, despite the fact that everything seemed to be alright, there was still something nagging at his soul. Something still didn't feel right.

Cautiously Thomas crept across the rest of the house to the front door. A quick peek outside would settle his mind and his soul. He would see for himself that everything was fine. The door opened with a greater noise than he had desired and he became afraid that the sound would wake his family, yet as far as he could tell, they remained fast asleep.

Outside everything looked normal. The crisp cool morning air blew across his skin and was only a reminder of how cold he had been. The freezing temperature that he had felt hadn't come from any lack of heat from outside. Something else had chilled him to the bone. He shook his head. Perhaps he had just imagined it.

He was about to close the door and go back to bed when something caught his notice. Down the road he could hear someone singing, greatly off key. He turned his attention toward the man that was belting out some obscure song and then was about to dismiss the individual as simply being drunk. The way the man staggered and the bottle in his hand only confirmed his suspicions. Yet, despite all of this he still had a gut feeling about this man.

'He's going to burn the city down.'

The words continued to echo in his mind. He simply couldn't shake it. There was something wrong...and then he understood. First, the tone of the man's voice was unmistakable and if he had been more awake earlier, then he would have recognized it earlier. This was Luke. The bigoted, loud mouthed, rich kid was out drinking, feeling sorry for himself.

"I'll show them all. I'll show them. I'm better than me pa. Everyone will know I'm better than me pa. He can't hit me like that. No one can. I'll show them all."

Suddenly Thomas's heart sank. He had always hated the young rich kid who hid like a coward behind his father. Now he understood. His father was a tyrant and he expected his only son to follow in his footsteps.

Yet, despite Luke's broken and shattered soul, this was no place for him to be staggering about. The various individuals of ethnic diversities were scattered in their proper sectors in this area. This was not the proper place to be if one was an oppressor of said people, especially at night, alone, and drunk. Even those that had too much to drink stayed away at night. There was a racial tension that lay just below the surface of everyone living here and there was no reason to stir it up. There was no reason for him to be...and then Thomas heard it.

"I'll show them. I'll blow up the mines, I'll blow up the whole town, and I'll burn it all down, down to the ground."

'He's going to burn the city down.'

The words echoed in Thomas's mind yet again. He didn't know how he knew it had applied to Luke, or how he had even heard it the first time. Yet somehow he was now sure that Luke, no matter how much a victim he was, was also a threat to the whole city. Then it dawned on him. There was a reason why Luke would be down here. This street would take him directly to the mines. He really was going to harm the one thing that was keeping this city together. But how...?

Thomas almost gasped in horror once he saw Luke pull a long stick from his coat pocket. He had recognized the shape even in the darkness, even at this distance. The miners had used them enough times to help dig out the most stubborn of ore and he understood the potential hazards. One wrong blast from that dynamite could easily collapse the mine. But that wasn't the worst of it. Luke was drunk and if he had more, if he decided to let one of those loose in the city, particularly in this section, then the city would go up in flames.

Thomas started to make a run for Luke. He had to stop him. There was no telling...

It was too late. He could only watch on in horror as his stride carried his muscular body closer and closer to the drunken and distraught man. The scene played out before him. Luke had taken his cigarette out of his mouth and applied it to the fuse of the deadly item. He raised his arm, took aim at a random building and let his projectile fly.

Chapter: Battle for Virginia City

I poured on my speed as much as I could and launched my body sailing through the air. My flying tackle slammed into the preacher man and sent us both tumbling to the ground.

Despite my best effort, he had moved just enough so my collision with him was only a glancing blow and I took the worst of the blow. I hit the ground harder than anticipated and saw stars. My body didn't want to move and the lack of response had allowed Abraham to recover faster than I had. To my dismay, by the time I started to rise, the preacher had already stood and retrieved his torch.

"For the wages of sin is death."

The biblical quote was the only warning I was getting in regard to his attack. The torch was held high for the briefest of moments and then came crashing down upon my body. Again and again the preacher struck at me. Blow after blow came upon me. I could feel the blunt blows of the club-like torch beat against my body. Now I knew what a baseball felt like. But it was more than that. The hot, incendiary weapon scolded and burned me with each strike.

I rolled to one side as his next strike came down upon me. His rage had made him predictable and off balance. The torch came down at the spot where I used to be.

Abraham's overzealous attack had left him overreaching.

My kick out to one side was all that was needed. My leg connected with his. His knee buckled and sent him toward the ground.

We both rolled up at the same time. I was weaker from the damage and he was driven with rage and self-righteousness. I was tired, he was awake. I was older, he was younger. The best I could hope for was to stall him long enough for someone to get the sheriff.

He took a step toward me as he threw his punch. The blow connected upon my face and a second upon my already sore ribs.

I blocked the third strike and came at him with two hits of my own, both glancing blows. I had to connect if I didn't want to go down again. I had to think of something.

I waited for his next attack before I made my move. As his swing came toward me, I rushed him. My arms caught hold of him as my body drove him backwards. His body slammed against the side of the wall knocking his breath out. I grabbed him by his shirt and continued to beat his body against the wall.

His knee to my groin seemed to come out of nowhere. Pain shot through the majority of my body. A right hook across my face sent me spiraling to the ground. Before I could recover, I felt several kicks to my midsection. Consciousness started to fade.

By the time the beatings had stopped, my breathing had become shallow. Every breath was a labor and a new sensation of pain. I could barely keep my eyes open and when I could see, I couldn't see straight. But what I did see only horrified me.

I watched helplessly as Abraham made his way toward his dropped torch. I watched as he came back toward me with that wicked, sinister sneer upon his face. I watched as he brought up his torch over my body. Suddenly, His arm came down for the killing blow.

"Well, well, well. What do we have here?" Mr. Jacobson's voice was dripping with sarcasm. "If it ain't the little "Miss Heroine of Virginia City" sticking her nose into a business that is none of her concern. Your interference has cost me many setbacks. You've given strength and inspiration to many that I've been trying to squash. Did you really think that you would go unnoticed? Did you really think that this would go unpunished? You need to understand that you are inferior. I am more intelligent than you. I have more influence than you. I have more connections than you. I am richer and always will be richer than you. And to top it off, I am a man and you are only a woman. You need to learn your place in life."

The henchman that had caught Ruth by surprise had dragged her down the alley to the presence of the two other men despite Ruth's best efforts to struggle. She had even tried to call for help but the henchman had only silenced her by placing his hand over her mouth and holding on tightly.

Once she had arrived, Alexander had removed her weapon and tossed it off into the night. It landed somewhere in the darkness of the alley, lost with all of the other items that had been haphazardly stacked and piled up here. Then he had placed his lantern on top of the piles so he could get a better look at her.

Ruth understood the predicament that she was now in. She might have been able to handle two men, especially with her gun. But, now she didn't have her weapon and she was further outnumbered. No one knew that she was here and if any noise were to alert anyone nearby, it would be too late. She now understood that she should have gone for help first. This would be a lesson that she would never forget, if she lived through it, or if she wanted to live through it. She could only guess what these three men would do to her and she didn't like where those thoughts were leading.

Mr. Jacobson moved closer to Ruth and let his hand linger on her face. "My dear. What a pretty face you have. It's almost a pity…"

The scream from the henchman that was holding Ruth split the night. He immediately pulled away from her as if she had turned into some horrible, disgusting creature. His hand was dripping with blood from where she had bit him.

Before anyone could react, Ruth kicked out with her foot and slammed the heel of her boot into Mr. Jacobson's foot. He could feel something break and was certain that he wouldn't be able to walk properly for quite some time.

Ruth spun around and let her fist follow her lead. She remembered when her father had taught her how to play baseball. She applied the same technique she used to throw a ball or to swing a bat. With the pivot of her ankle she allowed her strength to build through her calf, thigh, and hip before letting her body weight be thrown into the punch. The blow struck hard and sent the henchman reeling to the ground.

By the time she had completed her attacks on the first two men, she could hear the third make his way toward her. He had hung back, behind Mr. Jacobson, and had figured that there was no need to get involved, at least not yet. But now that the young woman was proving a match for two grown men, he had decided to help, if not for his personal goals with her, than at least to redeem himself in the eyes of Mr. Jacobson.

There had been some confusion while he tried to close the gap. Alexander had hobbled backward, crashing into him. There had been a moment of confusion, but only a moment. That was all Ruth needed. She spun back around and gave Mr. Jacobson a shove. The rich businessman fell backwards and became tangled in his own henchmen. Both were taken off balance and both dropped to the ground.

Ruth then took a quick step backwards and shoved her elbow behind her. She connected with the rising henchmen. Now, if she could only get away, if she could only find her gun.

The young woman turned to sprint down the alley to escape, to find help, to do something that would allow her to survive this night. Her feet took her several steps before she realized that her elbow attack had only glanced off of her attacker.

The man's arm reached out as she tried to run past him. He snagged the hem of her pants and pulled hard. Ruth's sudden loss of momentum sent her crashing to the ground.

Thomas's body crashed into Luke's like a runaway train. The younger man's body flew through the air. The two of them slammed into the ground with Luke taking the most of the blow. Luke lay there breathing hard as he tried to figure out what had happened. In his state he could only watch as Thomas made his way toward the dynamite that he had tossed.

Thomas moved as quickly as he could. He had no idea how short the fuse was on the stick. The piece could detonate at any time and blow him apart into many small pieces as easily as it would the tons of rock and rubble that he had watched before. Yet, if he didn't at least try then the nearest building would be blown apart and every soul that was nearby could easily die in the explosion. If that wasn't bad enough, the resulting blast could start a fire that could easily spread throughout the whole city.

The huge black man continued his search in desperation. He looked behind benches, on porches, and around the side of the building. Yet despite everywhere he looked, he simply couldn't find the stick of dynamite. It was too dark and there were too many items around, it could be anywhere. His heart was starting to beat wildly, sweat was pouring off of his body. He knew that he was too close and the immediate blast would kill him instantly. He was considering running for his life when, out of the corner of his eye he saw it. The light of the burning fuse was the only indication of his impending doom.

Without hesitation, Thomas went to retrieve the explosive. If he could just put out the fuse, then he could deal with Luke. However, just as he started reaching for it, the young man's body slammed into his, knocking him to the ground, just beyond arm's reach of his goal.

My knee came up as quickly as I could muster and landed a horrible blow right on the preacher's groin. Abraham attempted to protest but the pain that was coursing through his body was far too great. All he could do was gasp in agony as he dropped his torch.

I scrambled to my feet and lead with a right hook. His defenselessness left him wide open and I connected on his jaw. A second blow struck his nose and I was sure I felt something break. Blood poured down upon his face. I thought that I had him right where I wanted him. I was wrong.

Abraham came back with a sudden jab to my already sore and aching ribs. I saw stars. My breathing became more labored and each breath was a new sensation of pain. I was sure that I had heard something snap and knew that at least one more rib had been broken.

The preacher followed up with several right hand hooks that left me reeling backwards. I was becoming dizzy and didn't know how much longer I could take this.

My right foot slipped further back than the rest of my body for support and suddenly I knew, in a flash of an instance, what I could do. I let my body weight fall back upon it for just one moment before I used my right foot to launch myself forward. My entire body weight catapulted and hit Abraham with everything that I had.

My hit connected, hard. But I didn't relent. This man was on a mission, a religious mission of self-righteousness and he wasn't going to stop until I took him down. My strikes came left and right. My awareness of my actions left me. I had no concept of space or time. I wasn't even sure if Abraham tried to counterattack or even tried to block. Yet, again, I didn't relent. My blows came hard and heavy, one right after another without stopping. This preacher only talked about hell, now he was going to feel what it felt like. I continued my attack without regard to my safety or his. I continued to pummel the man even when I was sure that he had fallen under my barrage.

I wasn't sure when it had happened, but I came out of my rage and realized where I was and what I was doing. I was straddling the preacher's fallen body; my fists were bloodied with the preacher's blood that continued to pour from his nose and lip. I could feel Abraham's body tremble under mine. His arms were doing their best to block his face and the look upon him was of shock and horror. He gave me a look that almost said "please don't beat me anymore."

Although my rage had passed, I wanted to hit him one more time. After all of this, after all of his bullying people's souls and now threatening to burn people in their sleep, he was no more than a coward that didn't want himself to be hurt. He was willing to do the deeds but not ready to pay the cost. Against my desire, I decided not to continue my pounding.

There was a higher being than myself that will take care of this man, I would let him face his own final judgment that I was sure would be far worse than anything I could deliver.

I got up from the man and walk over to his still burning torch. After a couple of quick snaps of my wrist and a few strikes on the ground, the fire was put out.

"Your self-righteous reign of terror is over," I said toward the prone preacher man. "No one is going to die this night because of you. There will be no fire, there will be no cleansing."

I had saved the town from burning down. Now my only question was, what effects did this have on history? Was I willing to pay that cost?

Thomas picked up Luke off of his body and threw him hard. The big man's muscles worked with all of his strength as he launched Luke threw the air. The younger man's body hit the side of the building hard and landed with a great thud.

The big man turned his attention back to the burning fuse. Time was running out. He didn't have time for this. He needed to...

The movement out of the corner of his eye caught his attention and was the only warning he had that had saved his life. Luke had reached behind him and pulled out an old bowie knife. The young man had taken a swing at Thomas.

Thomas had barely been able to move out of the way but wasn't fast enough for the second attack. The blade cut deep into his chest. The knife wasn't sharp enough to make a clean cut, just sharp enough to cut deep and hurt. Blood started pouring from his wound.

Luke went into a defensive position, waiting for a counterattack. He flipped his knife between his hands, twirled it around and flipped it back again. All he needed to do was to wait for Thomas to attack and he would have him.

"I've always hated you," Luke snarled. "You think you're better than me? You think you're better than us? Workin' harder? Makin' us look bad?"

"You're gonna kill us all," Thomas snapped, holding his side, trying to keep as much blood inside of his body as possible. "You don't have to be this way. Things don't have to be like this."

"You don't know nothin'," Luke yelled back. He had forgotten about the dynamite that he had just tossed and had no clue how dangerously close both he and Thomas were.

"I heard you, about your pa..."

"Leave 'im out o' this, you don't know nothin'!"

Luke's patience had grown thin waiting for the attack that never came. He took a leap forward, driving his knife towards Thomas's chest.

The attack was full of rage and reckless. Thomas moved to one side and let the knife slide harmlessly passed him. Suddenly he shot his hand towards Luke's wrist, the one with the knife, caught it and gave a twist. Pain shot through Luke's arm and he dropped his weapon. Yet Thomas knew that Luke was not about to give up. He had to end this fight soon. He picked up the younger man with both hands, held him over his head for one moment before slamming him down upon the cold hard ground.

Luke's body bounced before striking the ground a second time. His breath was completely knocked out of him. He lay there for one moment, gasping for air, before rolling over on his side. He placed his arm around his back as if to ease the pain of the several cracked ribs or perhaps to restart his breathing.

Thomas didn't even stop to notice. He immediately dove for the stick of dynamite. His hands fumbled with the explosive as the fuse continued to burn away, closer and closer to the end of the stick. Once he had a grip on it, Thomas reached with his other hand and grabbed the burning wick. The hot embers burned his hand, yet he pushed passed the pain until the fire had gone out.

The big man looked back toward Luke. He had expected him to still be recovering on the ground, but to his shock, Luke was scrambling to make his way to one of the fallen sticks that he had in his pocket. The few sticks that he had managed to procure were now scattered all over the road. Just as he reached his closest one, a boot stepped on his hand. The young man looked up to see Thomas's face staring back at him.

"No more people will be hurt by you, not anymore." Thomas's voice was flat and without emotion. He knew and understood just how close it had been to an ultimate disaster.

Ruth could feel the two henchmen hold her down on the ground while Mr. Jacobson started to close in on her.

"You have been very bad. Now you will pay for all that you have done."

Mr. Jacobson's voice had anger in its tone and Ruth could tell that she had pushed him beyond his normal limits of usual self-control. She had seen him lose that control on several other women, yet she understood that it would be far worse for her. The thought only put a chill down her spine, a coldness that she could almost physically feel all over her body and deep into her soul.

Mr. Jacobson was merely a few feet away when he stopped. He couldn't help but notice the chill that had come over the area. It seemed to grip his very being, as if he was chilled from the inside. His breathing became labored and he could see his warm breath upon the cold air.

"You won't be doing business in this town again. Leave now."

The feminine voice made everyone stop. It hadn't come from Ruth and it hadn't even come from her direction. It had come from the back of the alley where it had been a dead end. There hadn't been anyone there moments ago, but now there seemed to have been.

But it was more than that. The voice seemed to be haunting that added to the chill in the air and in the soul. Mr. Jacobson turned his attention to the woman that was behind him, the woman that had dared to interfere with "business". If she wanted to join the fate of the girl they had pinned to the ground, then so be it.

The woman seemed to be wearing an evening dress that covered most of her body. Her hair was dark and pulled back tight giving her a stern, harsh look. But none of the men seemed to be interested in what she looked like, but more of what she didn't look like. It seemed to them that they could see through her, as if she had no real physical form. Mr. Jacobson was about to protest, or at least say something, but he never had the chance.

Madam Julia Bulette struck with a right upper hook that hit the rich man straight in the jaw. The blow didn't just physically hurt, but it was like ice that penetrated deep into him. He staggered under the onslaught and remained in shock from the blow.

Ruth didn't hesitate. She took her opportunity the moment the men became paralyzed with fear. She yanked with her right hand and pulled free from the grasp of the henchman. A quick pull toward her left allowed her arm to reach over and slug the henchman on her left. As he fell off balance she reversed the process and slammed her fist into the face of the second man.

Ruth immediately rolled to one side to escape and she was about to come up to her knees and take off in a sprint when she was caught by her ankle again. As she was pulled back, she fell flat on her face. She just couldn't get a break. She felt her body start to be pulled backwards and she didn't know what to do, until her eyes caught sight of the one thing that could help her.

Her gun was lying there, not too far away, in the shadows. All she had to do was grab it. She reached and struggled and was pulled again. She fought to gain ground, kicked back and was pulled again. She threw herself forward. Her hand fumbled in the darkness. She could feel the cold metal on her hand. She was pulled back harder, this time back into the middle of the two very angry henchmen.

Ruth came up fast and unloaded all six rounds. The shots rang out into the night. Silence followed. The two men dropped dead.

Ruth heard coughing to her right, spun aimed and fired. The gun only clicked. She had lost count of the rounds she had fired.

Mr. Jacobson rose from his kneeling position. Something had choked him and nearly froze him to death. Yet, somehow he had prevailed. Whatever it was, it was no longer around. It was time to leave. His cards had been played out and it was time to retreat and draw from another deck.

The blow struck him across his jaw, another in his midsection knocking the wind out of him, and another across his eye and nose. Unlike the ethereal and freezing cold strikes from the wraith like creature that had descended upon him, these blows were solid, very solid.

Ruth didn't relent, she didn't let up. She poured her blows upon the rich business man. She let all of her frustrations, anger, and fears out as she continued to hit upon the man that was shattering everyone else's dream for the sake of his own. She hit him in the kidneys, split his lip, cracked a couple of ribs and finally raised her knee to his groin. When he bent forward, she followed through with a right upper cut.

The last blow knocked him backward, sending him crashing into the debris behind him. Boxes and barrels fell. Rope and tackle fell. The lantern, which had been left precariously on one of the crates, fell.

Chapter: Inferno

I held the preacher man up by his shirt, raising him off of the ground so he could see the look and determination in my face.

"Your time is over. There will be no fire, there will be no cleansing."

I stopped when I saw the curious look upon his face. A sinister smile had come across him that seemed to stretch from ear to ear. At first I simply wanted to slap that smile right off his face, then the strong winds, that had been known to kick up around here, had whipped up again. With them came the scent.

"Behold! For I am become Shiva, Shatterer of Worlds."

I turned toward the prone preacher man. His quote wasn't even out of the bible. Now he was just pulling quotes out of whatever reference he wanted simply to justify his actions.

But this wasn't his action. As much as he wanted to gloat and take pride over it, he had nothing to do with the scent that was on the air. There was a smell of smoke and burning wood. I had come accustomed to this smell; I had smelled it since I started my vacation. There was a fire, only this time I knew it wasn't a dream but it was a nightmare, a nightmare come true.

Now I understood the fire that I had smelled and the burns on the people that had been haunting me, but what about the prostitute? She was already dead and wouldn't be part of this fire. It didn't make sense. She would haunt her grave site even during my time. No, that made perfect sense. This was her city too. She would protect her city, even if it meant reaching from beyond the grave to get my attention. The question now was: what did these ghosts want? I didn't have to worry about saving Ms. Willows from heat stroke or stopping Mr. Jacobson from taking over the whole Washoe valley. I didn't have to worry about Luke or his pa. This fire was what I was supposed to help with. The question still was: what was I supposed to do?

There was only one thing to do. I dropped the preacher man on the ground and started to bang on doors in the hope of waking people up.

"Fire! Fire! Get everyone out of here! Now!"

People were running out of their house and businesses. I could hear screams of terror and horror. Children and babies were crying. I could hear the fire department try to coordinate their efforts. Panic was everywhere.

I continued to bang on doors and help people out of their buildings. I refused to let anyone go back inside to get valuables, I simply pushed them out into the street where they would be safe and even that was questionable. With the buildings so close together and made of wood and the winds picking up by each passing moment, the flames were jumping from one block to another. There was no way anyone could put this fire out fast enough.

My eyes went toward where the firemen were doing their best in containing the fire. I should have known. They had created a perimeter around the Washoe Millionaires Club to try to preserve it above anything else. It looked like money really could buy anything. Sad part was I knew that they would succeed at the expense of the rest of the town. If my recollection of history was correct, then thirty three blocks would burn to the ground and be completely leveled. I might not be able to stop history from happening, but I might be able to prevent many of these people from dying.

My eyes caught Sheriff Elijah moving through the crowd. It seemed to me that he was trying to find someone in charge and I seemed to be the only one trying.

"I'll send people to the mines," the sheriff yelled over the increase of volume.

The noise level had been increasing with each passing moment. With everyone yelling at each other, trying to find loved ones, calling out for their pets, demanding someone do something about the fire, screaming in terror and crying in horror on top of the roar of the blazing inferno. The flames themselves had a horrible, beastly sound as if were a living, breathing entity. It roared and hissed as it ate up one building after another. I could hear wood snapping and breaking and glass shattering under the intense heat.

"No! Don't do that!" I yelled back. "That place would be a death trap! The wooden beams would catch fire and collapse causing cave-ins! People would probably suffocate long before then once the smoke starts to build!"

"Then where should I send them? They can't stay here!"

I had to think about that. There was no place safe in town, except maybe the Washoe Building, but even then people would succumb to smoke inhalation and they would squash each other out of panic. They would trample each other just trying to enter the building. Even then that's under the assumption that history couldn't be changed. If it could, then they could still all be burned alive.

"The cemetery!" I shouted. "Take them to the cemetery."

"What in the blazes for?"

I almost laughed at his choice of words and I probably would have if it wasn't too surreal.

"There's nothing out there to burn. Plenty of room. Go! Quickly!"

The sheriff had to nod at that. It was simply best to get everyone out of town and fast. He immediately started barking orders and having his deputies lead the way as he continued to guide more and more people in the right direction.

I had wondered what had caused the fire to begin with when I remembered the preacher man that I had left prone on the ground. I turned to where he had been, but he was gone. Good bye and good riddance for all I care.

Once I was sure that the people in this area were safe, my mind went toward my daughter. Ruth was in a safer area, at least for now, but it wouldn't take long for the fire to spread in her direction. It was time for me to find her and get her to safety.

Ruth pounded on the door. The fire in the alley was already spreading faster than she had thought possible and now it threatened to catch the surrounding homes on fire. She needed to get everyone out.

"Wake up! Wake up!"

The door swung open with a vengeance. The man was ready to have a few choice words for the individual that had the nerve of waking him up this late at night, or early in the morning whichever it was. He had to get up early to get to the mines. Whoever this was …

The woman at the front door holding her gun gave him hesitation. He started to back up in panic.

"No, no. Wrong way. Get your family. Get out of here!"

The man only looked at her curiously.

"Fire! Your house is on fire! Get out!"

This, the man understood and promptly went to retrieve his family.

Ruth continued to give warnings to every household she could come across. People were coming out of their homes in droves, the question was, where she should put them.

"The church. Get everyone to the church. St. Mary's in the Mountain. Everyone, go, go."

My feet carried me up the flight of stairs to the upper level of the saloon. The raging inferno was coming up fast. It had already started to devour two buildings further down. I could already feel the heat being generated from the flames that was quickly consuming the city. Nothing was going to escape its wrath and if I didn't get out of here quickly, then that would include me. But the flames weren't the only thing I had to worry about. The smoke was becoming thick and it was becoming hard to breath, even this far away from it. On top of that, the air was becoming thin as the heat was starting to rise. I could easily die before the flames even reached me. Hopefully Ruth had thought the same and had found some place safe.

I opened the door to our room and gave a sigh of relief. She wasn't here. I could only remember how my in-laws had started a fire in our fireplace and had forgotten to close the flue. The fire burned out of control until the smoke alarm went off. It was at this point that Ruth had run up into her room and hid. Of course she was younger and didn't know better, however I was still disappointed that she had decided to run in the opposite direction of where she needed to be. Now that she was older, I was glad to see that she wasn't here in her room.

Now the question was where was she? I guess a part of me wanted to find her here so I knew where she was and I could then lead her to safety. It was so difficult being a father, proud that my daughter was making her own decisions and still worrying that she was making the right ones.

I burst back through the double swinging door and realized how quickly the fire had spread. Buildings from across the street were already aflame and the fire on my side had engulfed the building next to me and had threatened to catch the one I was exiting.

"Ruth! Ruth!"

My throat was hoarse from calling out her name, my lungs were filling with smoke and the heat of the nearby inferno was becoming very uncomfortable. People continued to run past me in panic, screaming for their lives. Moms were clinging to their children who were crying. Men were barking orders in hopes of getting everyone to safety or to help co-ordinate the firemen who were fighting a losing battle.

Smoke was billowing everywhere. A few more buildings had caught fire. I watched as the Storey County Courthouse burst into fire. I witnessed Piper's Opera House caught up in the inferno. The International Hotel was already beyond saving and most of Virginia City's businesses were already burning. Somewhere in all of this madness I had to find my daughter.

Thomas ran from one building to another in a desperate attempt to get people out of their houses and out to safety. His prominent standing in this part of the community had made him believable and he was able to get the cooperation of many that lived here.

"My baby! My baby!"

The sound pierced over the chaotic noise of total chaos. It was something that he wouldn't have heard and he was amazed that he had in fact heard it. Perhaps his senses had increased due to the dangers around him; perhaps the wind had carried her voice. Either way, he was already in motion before she had finished her sentence.

"He's still inside…"

380

Thomas blew past the woman and hit the door she was pointing at. He ignored the rest of her words, he ignored the questions of how mom and baby had gotten separated, he ignored the fact that the building was already ablaze.

His mass hit the door hard and it shattered under might and momentum. Even the frame gave way under his bulk. Immediately the smoke and the superheated air hit him hard and threatened to knock him down right then and there.

He listened and focused while trying to ignore the life threatening danger all around him. He wasn't about to give up until…

There, off in the corner, he barely saw the unmoving form. His heart wanted to break but he wouldn't give himself the time to do so. His next few moments was a decision of life or death, he had to get out of there, now.

The big man sprinted away from the door and toward the form. If there were any hope for this child, he needed to grab it. Pain wracked his body, it was becoming difficult to breathe, and he was becoming dizzy. Yet he pushed on.

He paused only long enough to reach down and grab the form with his huge paw of a hand before he turned back toward the door. He was already in motion before realizing the scene before him. What was left of the door and the frame was now a burning inferno of blazing heat.

Thomas didn't stop. He burst through the heat, feeling the fire burn his skin.

"My baby!"

The woman had run to him in hopes that he had been quick enough, but then stopped short. Her child was unresponsive. All Thomas could do was stand there, in shock, and watch the woman's heart break.

The child's cry pierced the night as it started to cough. A smile came over the big man's face. He had saved another life tonight but wondered how many he wouldn't be able to save.

"Thomas! Thomas!"

I watched as the big man turned to me as he passed off a small bundle that I could only assume was a child that he had just managed to save from the burning building behind him.

"Have you seen Ruth? You remember her, my daughter?"

"I haven't seen her, no. But many are headin' toward the church for sanctuary. You might try there."

My heart felt a pit grew deep in it and I started to panic. My head shook furiously.

"No. Don't send any more there! Send them all to cemetery!"

"Why…?"

"Because the church is going to burn down!"

My feet continued to move quickly. I had been glad for my endurance training during track and cross country when I was younger or I wouldn't have been able to continue these long runs. The rising temperature was starting to get to me. The smoke was becoming too thick and it was becoming harder to breath and hard to see. Twice I had to stop and readjust my route because of the catastrophe all around me. Yet I continued to run, with tears of panic in my eyes. I had to get to the church before Ruth did and I had to get there before the fire did, and that was under the assumption that she was on her way there. I hoped that I was right.

It was to my relief that the church was not only still standing, but the fire hadn't reached it yet. The fire that had spread all around had given an eerie look and glow surrounding the church. I could see the silhouettes of the figures of the people trying to get in through the front doors. They were like cattle being herded to the slaughter house.

"Ruth! Ruth!"

My heart skipped a beat when no one turned to my voice. Then, after what seemed to be an eternity, I saw a familiar form turn toward me.

"Daddy? Daddy!"

My daughter sprinted the distance between us and literally threw herself at me. It was reminiscent of the time when she was much younger and I picked her up from daycare. She would run like this, jump through the air, have me catch her, and scream "Daddy! My daddy's here!"

"We need to get everyone out of here." My words cut our reunion short.

"But…"

I shook my head. "No buts…it's going to burn down, with everyone inside. We need to get them out."

At first she just looked at me as if she didn't believe what I had said. Then she realized. I had read the history of the town while she was still looking at jewelry and knick knacks.

We quickly made our way to church. There, standing near the doorway, was the preacher man, Abraham Smith. I could tell that he was still bloodied and beaten from the last time we had met. Hopefully I had knocked some sense into him, and if not, then I hoped that he would realize that I would do it again if the condition warranted. It didn't take long for him to notice our arrival.

"Only the righteous can enter," Abraham said with his usual self-righteous voice.

"I'm not trying to get in; I'm trying to get everyone out. This place will burn down and everyone…"

"God will protect the innocent, he will protect his chosen. He will protect us while the wicked shall perish. They shall all burn."

"You need to stop this now. These people's lives are in danger."

"You can't stop God's will. His will shall be done. His will is being done. The vile shall burn and you shall burn with them."

"It is this building and everyone in it that will burn! Now get out of my way or so help me I'll…"

"And the beast was taken, and with him the false prophet that wrought miracles before him, with which he deceived them that had received the mark of the beast, and them that worshipped his image. These both were cast alive into a lake of fire burning with brimstone."

My fist found his face. His head hit the frame of the door. His body hit the ground.

Those that had come here to be saved all stood in awe. They were confused, like lost sheep. I had to speak plainly. I had to pull them out of their shock.

"Go to cemetery. This building is made of wood. Fire is coming. If God will protect you then he'll do it in consecrated ground of the cemetery."

They continued to stand there, frozen like deer in the headlights.

"Did God protect him?" My question was asked while pointing at the fallen preacher man. "Did God protect him from my fist? In this church? I am telling you right now that this building will burn down and if you are in it, you will die! Get to the cemetery!...NOW!"

This had finally gotten to them. At first, it was one by one, then the as the smoke from the surrounding burning buildings started to filter through the open door, the people started to be more focused about getting out of there. By the time the church had caught fire, the remainder of the individuals was in almost of a panic.

"Anna!? Anna!? Anyone seen Anna?"

No one seemed to answer Ruth's question as she continued to yell for...

"Who's Anna?"

"The little girl. Her dad asked me to take her here and keep her safe."

Anna? Where had I heard that name before? What little girl? No...I hadn't heard the name before but I knew it never the less. It was her name. It was the name of the "Little House on the Prairie" girl. It was the ghost girl who kept coming into my dreams, asking, begging me to help her. Now she was lost, somewhere in this fire, perhaps even somewhere in this building.

Ruth took off into the church that was already starting to burn. One of the side walls was already aflame and the heat was starting to build. If the little girl was still here, we needed to find her fast.

The implications of the burning flames suddenly brought a realization to mind. The first time that I was here, and now the last time I would ever be here, it had been like an oven. Also, the preacher man had preached about fire and brimstone, and now here it was. The church was becoming the very burning hell that Abraham Smith had been talking about. It was as if an omen had been trying to tell me what was about to happen and I hadn't listened.

"You'll never find her."

The voice stopped me from joining Ruth. It stopped me cold in my tracks. The voice was weak in volume, but masculine and strong in conviction and there was no denying who had said it. And it wasn't just the lack of faith that we would never find the child that was behind the voice, but a true sense of pride that he had outsmarted us. Abraham Smith had hidden Anna deliberately.

'He's a bad man.'

The words echoed in my mind as I continued to hear my daughter's cries for the little girl. Ruth was running out of time as more and more of the building was starting to burn. There were already sections that she couldn't get to and I hoped that Anna wasn't there. The roof was starting to catch fire and soon it would burn through the ceiling.

"Where is she?!" I screamed at the preacher man as both of my hands grabbed at his shirt, bringing him closer to my face. "This isn't a game!"

"She's mine!" He spat back. "God gave her to me!"

What he said made my skin crawl. It had the wrong kind of tone and implication behind it. If he was saying what I thought that he was saying then I was going to push him into the fire and watch him burn without regret. But I didn't know, not really. It could all be innocent, though one thing was certain; he wasn't going to give me any answers. Perhaps I should just push him into the fire anyway. No, he wasn't worth it; I turned to join Ruth and help her find Anna.

His wrist had shot out and grabbed hold of me before I could go any further into the church. His grip was like a vise. This man was threatening to let a little girl die and let my daughter die in the process of trying to find her. This was the last straw.

I spun in place and threw my right hand towards the preacher man's face. It was full of anger and hatred and it was clumsy. Instead of nailing him straight in the face, I only felt the block of his arm.

Abraham returned one blow after another. The air was knocked out of my ribs and a punch was delivered to my face. I felt him shove me back against the other side of the door frame and the wood jammed against my back. His fists started to strike against my body over and over.

"Daddy!"

I heard my daughter's cry of concern from across the church. It didn't matter. It didn't matter how much of a beating I was taking, I had to keep Abraham busy long enough for her to find Anna and get out of there. If I didn't keep him busy, then he would go after the both of them. I simply had to buy her the time she needed, and time was running out.

"Don't worry about me, find Anna!"

My shout was an attempt to carry my voice over the noise of the fire that was now consuming the building. The air was getting thin. Smoke was starting to build. The temperature was becoming unbearable. And all of this was just at the doorway of the church. Things were worse inside.

My adrenaline kicked in, but I knew that I would now be running on reserves that I didn't have. I pushed through the pain and threw my body at the preacher, slamming him against his door jam. It was my turn to give. My fists came on hard and strong.

Yet Abraham didn't relent. I could tell that he had reached deep as well. We traded blows as the building burned around us. A solid hit in the eye and I was sure that it had swollen twice its size. A jab from me and I could feel another of his ribs crack. No quarter was given and none was asked for. We would beat each other senseless, perhaps to the death and it would come down to the one who had the most endurance.

"I found...cough...cough...I found her."

Ruth had found a trunk, hidden under sacrament linen. Goblets and brass candle holders were on top and it had seemed to be no more than an ordinary table underneath or perhaps some storage container for sacramental supplies, perhaps extra bibles or such. However, once Ruth's calls for the little girl had reached this spot, she could hear thumping from inside. There was a faint cry for help and there was no doubt that the little girl was locked inside.

"She's mine! She's mine!"

The preacher went on a tirade. His blows became more desperate. He poured on everything he had in an attempt to get past me and to this girl that he had hidden away. However, as they were desperate and coming from a man already half beaten, I was able to avoid most of the blows and those that did connect didn't connect hard enough to put me down.

On the other hand, my fury had dramatically increased and I found the one bit of strength I didn't know I had. A knee lift hit him in the stomach, a jab found his kidney. Yet, no matter how hard I hit him, he just wouldn't go down.

Ruth did a dramatic sweep of her arm and knocked the articles off of the truck and pulled the linen off and discarded it. Immediately the linen went up in flames as it landed too close to one of the walls.

"It's locked!"

A simple padlock had been placed on the latch between the lid and the main trunk. It was obvious that Abraham wasn't just keeping her; he was keeping her for good. I wondered how often he put her in there.

"Get something to bash it open!"

My attention towards Ruth had let Abraham land two more blows on me that connected hard. Between his hits upon my body, the rising heat, the lack of air, and the smoke that was accumulating, it was getting hard to focus. It was everything I could do to remain conscious. Yet I had to hold. Ruth had to have the time she needed to get Anna out of there.

Ruth had found one of the brass candle holders and started to bash in the lock. Strike after strike came down which only resulted in an echoing clang that resonated above the roar of the burning fire. Out of the corner of my eye, while desperately try to fend off Abraham, I could tell Ruth's desperation as she gave the next few swing everything she had.

Finally, with one great, massive swing, Ruth broke open the lock. Quickly she discarded the mechanism and opened the box. I could hear Anna coughing weakly from the lack of air. I was sure that she only had moments left before she would have passed out and we would have never found her. All we needed to do now was get out of her before...

"NOOO!"

Abraham screamed in sheer desperation as he shoved my body backward, slamming me once again against the wall. It wasn't hard enough to drop me, but it was hard enough to daze me. It was the moment he needed. While I attempted to recover, he shot like a bolt toward Ruth and Anna. He wasn't about to give up his prized possession so easily.

The flaming wall buckled under its lack of integrity. The fire had degraded it far beyond its ability to stand and it came crashing down under its own weight, bringing the flaming ceiling with it. Wooden timber blazed with fire crashed to the ground. A fiery inferno engulfed the buildings.

Abraham's body was smashed to ground under the weight of the collapsed beams. I could hear his terrible screams of agony as the flames burned his body. The stench of burning flesh filled the air and mixed with smoke and burning embers.

I was cut off from Ruth. Fire and beams blocked my path. Another section of the wall started to fall. I heard a scream.

Chapter: Rest in Peace

1 woke up. My body was shaking. Sweat was pouring from my forehead. I felt like I was in shock. Everything seemed so real. Was it all a dream? I had lost track of time and space and for one moment I had forgotten where I was.

I was still here, at the graveyard, kneeling before my daughter's tombstone where I had fallen. It had truly seemed like I had lived all that time in the late 1800's but by looking at my watch only a few minutes had gone by. It was the same day, nothing had changed, not even the grave that I was kneeling beside. I reread the marker and finished what I hadn't before:

In memory of Ruth

Died   1915

Loving wife, dedicated mother

Here lies an honored woman who helped save the citizens of this town Virginia City during its great calamity fire of 1875. May she know the peace that she has brought for so many.

Somehow she must have escaped the fire, probably when the walls had collapsed she had seen an opening and ran. She had lived, had loved, and had raised a family all without me. She was an inspiration and a town hero. I didn't know if I should be proud of her for her success or broken hearted for my loss.

Tears rolled down my cheeks. The realization that I would never see my daughter again had hit me hard. She was gone. She was dead. She had been dead for over a hundred years now. There was no getting her back. I would never hold her in my arms again. I would never hear the words "I love you daddy" again. I would never...

The welled up emotional dam broke and I started to cry aloud. My heart was broken and I knew it would never mend.

When my tears finally stopped, I realized the grave next to hers. It was Anna. This was the little girl that had haunted me on the road, at the hotel, and in the Washoe Millionaire's Building. This was the little girl that Ruth had run into the church to save. She had also grown, had a family and had a full life. If it wasn't for Ruth, the girl would have died in the fire, burned alive in the church.

That's what the haunting encounters were about. The ghosts were the souls that had died prematurely. They weren't haunting me; they were trying to talk to me, trying to bring me back to save them. They were supposed to live and we had to go back and save them. We couldn't stop the fire, but we had directed so many people out of the city and out of the church. All of them would have died. Instead they had lived, like my daughter, like Anna. Now their lost souls could rest. There would be no more haunting nightmares.

I came up from my kneeling position to head back to my car. It was time to tell my wife what I had found. I didn't know how I would be able to do that. I knew how bizarre it would sound, I barely believed it myself. I would have to bring her back here, to this grave and show her.

The lone figure in the black car gave a twist of her wrist and looked at her watch. It was time. She had watched as the couple had pulled into the parking lot with bated breath. It seemed like an eternity waiting for what she knew would come, and yet when it did, it still broke her heart. The couple had lost their child somewhere in the graveyard. Each call of the young girl's name only twisted her gut like a knife cutting deep into her soul, and yet she waited.

However, now was the time. She made her way out of the car and started to proceed up the slight incline toward the heart of the Masonic section of the graveyard. There she would find the person she was looking for. Yes, it was now time.

The lonely feminine figure started walking toward me. She had purpose of direction. There was resolve in her eyes and she never wavered from her step. She never paused at any grave or tombstone, like some curious tourist would have. She never wavered or turned. Her path continued in a straight line, a line toward me.

Yet, for all of the strength that I could see in her, I could tell that it wasn't out of complete resolve. It was as if she were dreading this walk. She was unsure, reluctant, yet she pushed on using every ounce of her will to cover the distance between us.

She wore casual clothing of blue jeans and a light green blouse. Her light brown, worn-in ankle high hiking boots were ideal for the terrain in this area. My guess was that she was in her very early twenties, if that. She had shoulder length light brown curly hair.

When she finally arrived I could tell that there was something vaguely and strangely familiar about her. There was something in her eyes, her chin, and her hair. Then I noticed her earrings. They were the same kind we had bought Ruth back in the tourist trap shop. They were the same kind Ruth had been wearing back in 1875.

She avoided my eyes for just a moment before gathering her resolve once again. When she did, she spoke, but only hesitantly.

"Are you....?" She stopped, unsure what to say next. "She had mentioned that you would be here."

I gasped. My mind had speculated what my heart didn't want to accept. Somehow I knew what she meant. My eyes drifted down towards my daughter's grave once again.

"Grandma Ruth, that's what she was called you know. She had left word and it was to be passed from generation to generation that you would be here, at her grave. She said that I had to come today, at this time and that you would be here."

"Somehow Ruth had saved a great majority of this town. She had even put her life on the line to help a young girl named Anna from a burning building. From the stories, Anna had lost her father during the fire and Ruth had adopted her. She gave her a good home. There are so many stories about Ruth. Once she…"

She stopped as if she suddenly realized how bizarre the whole thing sounded, how unbelievable this really was.

I looked deep into her eyes and recognized the familiarity that I couldn't place earlier. They were her eyes, her chin, her hair, and her features. For one moment I thought I was looking into the eyes of my daughter even if I knew that she was a descendant of the child that I would never see again.

She gave a little blush once she saw the recognition in my eyes.

"I wish I had been alive to meet her. I would have loved to have gotten to know her." She said.

I took her hands in mine. There was a lot to talk about. I would tell her about the young girl that I had raised and she would tell me about the young woman that I had only barely had time to come to know.

Notes from the Author

This story is based on a series of true events. My wife had planned a trip down to Lake Tahoe and over to Virginia City. It would take place over the course of about a week. We left the Seattle area and traveled to Yreka where we stayed at her aunt's place and had gone to visit the ranch where she worked. Our travel then took us to Lake Tahoe through some great scenic routes. From there we kayaked on the lake, rafted on the Truckee River, traveled to Donner's Pass, and had gone over to Virginia City.

While at Virginia City, we did tour the haunted Washoe Millionaire's Club and the haunted graveyard. While we were there, Ruth had, in fact, disappeared. The scene of me running around the graveyard was real. What we found out later was that she had decided to follow a family, who had a daughter her age, down into a different section of the graveyard.

During the time that I had spent looking for her, I couldn't help but think "This sounds like a Stephen King novel. I wonder what he would write." My first assumption was that the dead had risen up and had caught hold of her. I don't know why I thought that, but I had. When I had combined this with all the other adventures we had earlier and the history of Virginia City, this novel fell into place.

Currently Ruth is doing well, playing her flute in concerts and acting like a typical teenager.

We are planning another trip to California soon and from the sounds of things there may be another inspiration to continue this story. Only the future events and the ghosts of past will tell what will transpire next. Until then, I hope that you've had a good read.

76157988R00246